# Sacred Ground

*A novel by*

## Linda Lazore

iUniverse, Inc.
Bloomington

**Sacred Ground**
**A Novel**
*Copyright © 2011 by Linda Lazore*

*iUniverse books may be ordered through booksellers or by contacting:*

*iUniverse*
*1663 Liberty Drive*
*Bloomington, IN 47403*
*www.iuniverse.com*
*1-800-Authors (1-800-288-4677)*

*Because of the dynamic nature of the Internet, any web addresses or links contained in this book may have changed since publication and may no longer be valid. The views expressed in this work are solely those of the author and do not necessarily reflect the views of the publisher, and the publisher hereby disclaims any responsibility for them.*

*Any people depicted in stock imagery provided by Thinkstock are models, and such images are being used for illustrative purposes only.*

*Certain stock imagery © Thinkstock.*

*ISBN: 978-1-4620-0962-6 (sc)*
*ISBN: 978-1-4620-0964-0 (e)*
*ISBN: 978-1-4620-0963-3 (hc)*

*Library of Congress Control Number: 2011904965*

*Printed in the United States of America*

*iUniverse rev. date: 10/3/2011*

# Contents

## Sacred Ground

There is a place called paradise
Where everyone is considered wise
The wind always gentle and mild
And beautiful flowers grow wild
You shouldn't intrude upon this land
Unless the Great Spirit takes your hand
The grass soft as feathery pillows
And yonder waves the pussy willows
It's forbidden for all to set foot on
The Sacred Ground is the world beyond
This is the place where dreams are made
From a natural spring flows a cascade
High above, the eagle soars around
Keeping an eye on the Sacred Ground

**This Book is dedicated**
To my Mom Minnie who always enjoyed everything I wrote
Also
To Virginia, Heather and Crystal for
helping me to wander back into the light
and making life worth living.

Also

To Anna, Andrea, Brenda, Becky, Bula, Candy, Debbie, Debra,
Darcy, Freda, Janet, Marlyn, Roberta, Sher, Teresa, Wanda &
Victoria for your loving support and friendship

# *Foreword*

It is with pride that I introduce the publication of this book. The author, Linda Lazore, has adequately captured many of the issues medicine people and their ceremonial helpers have faced over many generations.

Long before movies such as The Exorcists, Twilight and Harry Potter, the battle against evil has long been fought with the light workers. We call these people shape shifters because they can come in all forms and shapes, carrying bad medicines and dark dreams.

Many of our all night ceremonies are done to block or destroy these evil beings that have been sent against our people to hunt or seek one's powers. These strange forces of evil are all around us. This book contains an element of truth that many are blindly unaware of.

This writer has taken the reader into a world more different and more intense than the average person will ever experience during their lifetime. Hopefully you will never enter this world of the continuous battle between darkness and light.

Ted Silverhand
Native Seer

# *Guiding Path*

The alarm clock wakes me at 6:30 sharp. I turn and hit the snooze button. Except for the light from my alarm clock, my room is still dark. I want to turn on my side and go back to sleep, but I promised Alexis I'd go with her to pick up her dad Alex and her mother Misty at the airport. They flew to Buffalo, New York shortly after receiving word that her Uncle Jack had suffered a minor heart attack the day before Christmas.

Alexis and her family always spend Christmas vacation on the Tonawanda Reservation, but her parents decided not to make the trip this year because they wanted to save for her graduation and college fund.

Alexis is one of my best friends. She is Native American with straight black hair that flows down to her waist. Her stunning tan skin gives her that added beauty. Her Mother is from the Hopland Band of Pomo Indians and her father is a Mohawk who came from a reserve in western New York. Both of her parents work at the National Indian Justice office here in Santa Rosa. Alexis knows a lot about her culture and traditions. Her background and teachings both tie neatly into the supernatural world. She told her dad she saw her Uncle Jack gasping for air, in a vision, just two days before his heart attack. Alexis always knows when something is going to happen. My friends and I call her our personal physic seer. If you believe in the occult, you would be amazed by her predictions. She can read people like an open book. There are times when she answers our questions before we even ask them, but she only did stuff like that within our small group of friends.

Alexis had been our guest since Christmas Eve. Our home had never been this busy over the holidays.

On New Years', our other best friend, Aimee came over to watch movies and sing karaoke. Aimee is the tallest of my friends. She likes to wear her layered reddish hair just below her shoulders. She has the most attractive eyes. Some days her eyes look light gray, while other times they look light green. Throughout high school, she talked about being an actress or model. Her life-long dream was to move to Los Angeles or New York after graduation to pursue her goals.

So when we turned on the karaoke, it was Aimee who took the microphone before any of us could decide on a song.

"I'm going to act out someone's lines from a movie and you have to name the movie and actor or actress," said Aimee, clearing her throat and making her way to the middle of the room.

She acted out her chosen scene with perfect delivery. Even her facial expression matched the attitude of her character. When she completed the scene, she giggled, took a bow and took in our applause.

"Wow," I thought to myself.

"Okay, who knows the movie and the actor or actress?" She asked.

I looked over at Alexis and saw that she was just as amazed as I was. We knew that Aimee was active in the theater for the past two years, but we had never seen her perform like this.

My brother Jamie raised his hand.

"Is it from a new movie?" he asked.

"No, the movie came out in 1993," Aimee responded.

My mom Angie, who had been in the kitchen, came and

stood in the doorway with her cup of tea. She smiled and nodded at Aimee and said "That was amazing. You did that really well."

"Thanks Mrs. Niles." Aimee said.

"Aimee, please call me Angie," mom said.

"Mom, did you recognized the actor?" I asked.

"Yes, it's Demi Moore in A Few Good Men."

"Do another one," Alexis requested, as she moved to the recliner.

Aimee got into entertaining us. She did role after role. I guess you could say mom was the movie expert. Mom let the rest of us guess until we gave the right answers. Aimee's dad, Larry, came to pick her up at ten o'clock. My mom couldn't wait to tell Larry about Aimee's talents. He beamed with pride hearing of his daughter's talent. As Larry and mom talked in the foyer, we helped Aimee gather her stuff.

"Hey, have a safe trip to San Francisco," Aimee whispered in my ear as we hugged.

"Alexis is driving, so we'll be safe," I whispered back and we chuckled at that remark.

As soon as Aimee left, Alexis and I went to my room. I grabbed my pajamas and went to take a shower so we could leave before 7. When I came back to my room, Alexis was on the phone with her boyfriend Hunter. She was telling him about her uncle's progress.

"Yeah, they'll be flying back in the morning," she said, before placing her hand over the phone. "Hunter wants to say hi." And she handed me the phone.

I had spoken to Hunter over the phone many times since he and Alexis started dating but I haven't met him in person.

"Hi Hunter, how was your Christmas?" I asked.

"Hey, Emma, we had a great Christmas. It was a bit lonely, but we had a good time."

"Ah, you could've stopped over. When Alexis came to stay with us, I thought we'll finally get to meet you."

"Yeah, I wanted to, but we were busy doing ceremonies. We'll meet someday."

"Cool, I can't wait."

"Can you put Alexis back on, and um, have pleasant dreams tonight."

"Okay, I'll talk to you later," I said as I shook my head and handed the phone to Alexis. She noticed the look on my face but turned away. I began to wonder why Hunter would say such a thing. I leaned around to get Alexis attention, but she turned away and walked to the window. As Alexis continued her conversation with Hunter, I turned my iPod on and put the ear pieces in my ears and relaxed on my side on the bed. I didn't hear when Alexis hung up the phone or turned off the light. Nor did I notice when she moved the pillow to the opposite side of the bed.

When the alarm went off, I reached over to wake Alexis, but she wasn't there. There was a strange smell in my room. I threw the blankets off me, turned off the alarm clock and switched on the radio. When I turned the light on, I saw the small abalone shell sitting on my desk. I examined the shell with its burnt contents and realized that it was part of Alexis' ritual. I put the shell back on the desk and I leaned my head against the wall. There was no sound coming from the bathroom. All I could hear was the rain hitting our tin roof.

"Uh, another gloomy wet day," I thought to myself.

I quietly opened the bedroom door and walked down the hallway. As I stood at the bathroom door, I heard voices coming from the kitchen. I took a few more steps and - to my surprised - saw that mom was already up. So I went back to my room and got dressed.

I was brushing my teeth, when my mom knocked on the bathroom door. "Emma, are you almost ready?"

I rinsed my mouth quickly and yelled "Yeah, I'll be right down."

I rushed back into my room to fix my bed and grabbed a clip

for my hair. In the kitchen, Mom was fixing breakfast sandwiches for us. She was buttering the English muffins.

"Emma can you turn the eggs over and put cheese on it?"

"Alexis do you want cheese on yours?" I asked.

"Sure."

"Two cheese coming up."

Mom put the English muffins on napkins and placed them closer to the stove. I put the cheese on the muffins and mom put the eggs on top. Then she handed one to Alexis.

"You two better get going. Emma, make sure you take the umbrella. It's raining out," mom said.

"I've got it. Thanks for breakfast, mom."

I put my jacket on, gave my mom a hug. Alexis was coming down the stairs with her small luggage and umbrella.

"Thanks for the breakfast sandwich, Angie."

"No problem. Say hi to your mom and dad for me."

"Oh, I will and thanks for letting me stay here."

"You're always welcome here," mom said as she hugged Alexis.

We opened our umbrellas and ran out to her car. Alexis and I didn't say a word to each other until we reached the main highway. It wasn't because we were upset with each other; we were just too busy enjoying our breakfast muffins. When I took my last bite, I handed Alexis a bottle of orange juice.

"Alexis, what time did you get up?"

"At six o'clock," she said and she gave me this look like I should have known.

"I didn't hear you get up. I didn't hear you move to the other end of the bed either. What time did you go to bed?"

Alexis just smiled and shook her head. "It was late. Hunter finally said good night around midnight. Do you know that you have violent dreams?"

"What? I don't have bad dreams. I don't dream at all. Wait, I do remember this one dream. It was about you and Hunter gabbing on the phone all night," I said jokingly and we both laughed.

"I'm serious, I moved to the other end of the bed, because you were kicking me and screaming my name."

I took a drink of my juice and thought about my night. My mind was totally blank. I shook my head and glanced over at Alexis.

"Sorry, but I don't remember dreaming."

"I knew you would say that."

Alexis reached into her pocket and handed me a small bottle. It was a bottle of sandalwood.

"What's this?"

"It's an essential oil that will help with emotions and memory."

I took the oil and giggled a little as I read the bottle. Alexis didn't think anything was funny. She just wanted to help me.

"It doesn't work if you just hold it.

I wanted to burst out laughing at her remark. As funny as it was, I remained calm. Was there something about her supernatural world that I was afraid of? I thought about it for a minute then realized that I wasn't afraid. Alexis had been a friend for almost 10 years, since her family moved here from New York. I knew all about her special gift of seeing into the future and her ability to whisper to those no longer apart of our world. I open the bottle and smelled its pleasant aroma.

"All you need is one drop in the middle of your palm. Rub the oil between your palms and then rub some on your temples and chest. When you're done, put your hand over your nose and inhale"

I followed her instructions and when I finished, I gave her magical oil back to her.

"I didn't know you were into aromatherapy."

"How can you say that? You once told me you liked the fragrance I was wearing and I told you that it was a combination of oils."

I nodded my head. The memory of that day came back to me. I couldn't be suffering some form of dementia; after all I had just turned 18 on October 1. I turned to Alexis and said "I'm sorry. I don't understand how I forgot that."

"It's okay. You have been under a lot a stress because of your parents' separation and divorce."

We were approaching the bay area, so I reached to lower the volume on the radio. Right at that moment, a memory flashed in my mind. I stared at the radio with my finger still pointing at the volume button.

"Emma, what's wrong?"

I slowly sat up straight and looked forward.

"Emma, are you remembering something?"

"Yes, it's about our graduation."

"Your dream was about our graduation?" she asked, a bit surprised.

"Yeah, that's what I was dreaming about when the alarm went off."

For the first time in years, I was remembering a dream. I was so excited.

"Okay, what was I wearing at our graduation."

"You wore your cap and gown."

"No, I mean what kind of outfits did we have on?"

"I didn't notice what we were wearing."

"It's really important. You are dreaming of the future. You're having premonitions."

"No, it was just a nice dream."

I turned and looked out the window, thinking about my dream. As I took a few deep breaths, more memories of the dream flashed in my mind. I turned and looked at Alexis and she was smiling.

"This is crazy, but I just remembered that I was wearing a white denim type skirt with a blue sleeveless blouse, and you were wearing a khaki skirt with a green top." And Alexis smile got bigger.

"Oh my God, Alexis, why did Hunter tell me to have a pleasant dream?"

"Don't get upset with me, but I told Hunter that you have nightmares every night. You talk, scream and yell out names and it's very clear."

"Why don't I remember them?"

"Well, I think that you put them in that same box you put the pain of your parents divorce in. Does that make sense?"

I nodded my head and looked away from her, so she wouldn't see the tears welling up in my eyes. Alexis was right. My parents' divorce was painful on all of us. My mom did a great job hiding it from Alexis these pass eight days. Normally, I had to wake her up in the morning and help Jamie and Ashley get ready for school. We always had our house decorated the first week in December. This year it was Alexis who helped me decorate, on Christmas Eve.

"Alexis, what exactly did you tell Hunter?"

"I just told him that I didn't get much sleep since my parents flew to New York, and he thought it was because of my uncle. I told him it was because of your nightmares. You move your legs like you're trying to run from someone or something."

"And, what did he say?"

"We both agree that these dreams are premonitions and we want you to keep a journal of them. I promise I won't tell Hunter anymore of your dream, especially the one you had this morning."

I gave Alexis this surprised look and shook my head. "There was nothing violent about our graduation."

"I wasn't talking about that one. I'm talking about the one that got me and your mother up at six o'clock this morning."

We were close to the airport and had to focus on the directions. At the airport, Alexis drove until she found the spot where her dad had told her to park. Alexis checked her watch as we ran toward the building. We checked the incoming flight schedule and Alexis' parents were to arrive in half an hour. The lobby area was quite busy. People at the check-in counter and others were saying good-bye. A group of arriving passengers were waiting for their luggage. I saw the sign for the ladies room and went walking in that direction. When I came out of the washroom, I saw Alexis coming out of the gift shop. She sat on the bench near the exit sign and waved at me.

"I bought you a journal to record your dreams," she said as she gave me the book.

"Thanks."

"Emma, the reason I need you to remember this dream is because you whispered someone's' name that you haven't met yet."

"If I'm dreaming of someone, shouldn't I know that person?" I said as I laughed.

Alexis shook her head. She opened the journal and counted eight pages.

"Okay, listen, on this page write down every detail of the graduation dream. When you finished, we'll move back a few pages and I'll help you remember that other dream."

I took the journal from Alexis and wrote "*Graduation Dream*" on the top of the page. "*The crowd's hooting and cheering made me feel like I had just achieved a major goal like finishing the Boston Marathon. Aimee was wearing a soft pink floral dress. Cindy was wearing a long black skirt with a slit up the side. She also wore a white short sleeve jacket type top with a black belt. Carol wore a black sleeveless mini dress. I even remembered the last sentence of Carol's speech, she delivered to the graduates. 'By believing in ourselves, we can reach the summit of any mountain and turn any dream into reality.'*"

At the bottom of the journal, I wrote "*this was a wonderful dream. I wanted this dream to continue because I was so happy*".

I gave Alexis the journal to read. We kept no secrets from each other. She read over the graduation dream and smiled. Then she went back a few pages and said "That was really good. Now, you need to remember the nightmare."

"What if I can't remember?"

"I'll help you. I woke up when you called my name. I sat up and looked at you. Your eyes were closed, but you said 'which one do you want to do volcanoes or tornados?' Then you stopped talking and I tried to go back to sleep. You started talking again about two minutes later. This time you said, 'well, let's get the books.'"

As Alexis was talking about the things she heard me say, I started to remember that dream. I took the journal from her hand and began writing.

I wrote *"A Nightmare"* at the top of the journal. *"We were at school and you (Alexis) told me to meet you at the library. At the library, you showed me a paper with four topics. You already had hurricanes' and earthquakes crossed off. Volcanoes and tornados were the two topics remaining on your list. I asked you (Alexis) which one do you want to do volcanoes or tornados. We decided on tornados and went to the card catalog to select books on the topic. You (Alexis) went down one aisle and I went down another. I had two books in my arms and was reaching for another."*

Then I stopped writing, took a deep breathe and looked at Alexis.

"What's wrong?" asked Alexis as she took my journal and read over what I had written. I took another deep breathe.

Now I knew why I was trying to run.

"When I took the third book from the shelf, there was a guy on the other side looking at me. He startled me and I ran from the library. So what is the guy's name that I yelled out?"

"The guy that I know wouldn't scare or startle you enough to run away. You need to describe the guy who startled you."

"He was tall and he looked like he needed a shave. Although he wore a black hood, I could see his dark wavy hair. He had the most evil looking eyes," I said as I took a deep breathe.

Alexis told me to write down the description of this unknown guy. As, I was writing, I heard Alex and Misty call out to Alexis.

I finished my last sentence, closed my journal and went to greet her parents.

On the ride back to Santa Rosa, I tried to write as much as I could. I wrote: "*I saw myself standing in a beautiful meadow. This strange guy from the library was also there. He was dressed in black and he was very angry with me. For some reason, I knew we weren't alone. I whispered, Sky, why can't I see you? As soon as I asked that question, a guy appeared a short distance behind the one all dressed in black. He was wearing a pair of shorts and nothing more. His long braided hair hung over his right shoulder. When the guy dressed in black moving in my direction, the guy named Sky told me to move. I ran as fast as I could.*"

I didn't feel like I was done writing, but we were pulling into my driveway. Alexis reached for my journal but I held it to my chest.

"I'm not finished," I whispered.

"Okay, I'll call you later," she whispered.

As soon as Alex put the car in park, I noticed mom's car was gone. Misty turned and handed me a bag.

"This is a thank you gift for your mom. Please tell her I'll call her later."

"I'll tell her," I said. Then I turned to Alexis and whispered "call me later."

I got out of the car and ran to the house. There was no need to use the umbrella because the rain had stopped. I put mom's gift on the coffee table and went to my room. It was important to finish writing the last details of my dream. I opened my journal and wrote: "*When I heard footsteps behind me, I turned and raised my arms to block my head. That's when I yelled, help me, he wants to hurt me. The last thing I remembered was seeing the guy dressed in black reaching for my arm. My eyes were closed but I could hear a ferocious growl close by. This was a very scary dream.*"

"Hey Emma, are you home?" yelled Mom.

"Yeah, we got back a few minutes ago," I yelled from my room.

"Come down, we have pizza."

I put my journal on the side on my bed and went down stairs for pizza. The aroma was making my mouth water. We hadn't had pizza since Jamie's birthday last summer. When we finished eating, I told mom about Misty's thank you gift and went back to my room. About an hour later, Alexis came over. She read over my journal as I listened to my iPod. When she closed the journal, I turned my iPod off. We stared at each other until I couldn't stand it anymore.

"Well, the suspense is killing me," I said.

"I'm not sure if the guy with the braid is Sky. It could be anyone."

"Does someone by the name of Sky exist?"

"Yeah, I have a cousin named Sky. This dream is definitely a premonition."

"Please don't tell your cousin or Hunter about this dream."

"I won't tell a soul," she promised as she handed me the journal.

Alexis went home shortly after that. The next day was our first day back to school. I sorted through my clothes and put them in a neat pile on top of my journal. Then I went on facebook, just to see if any of my friends were online. As soon as my home page opened, a small window popped open.

"Hey, how was your Christmas?"

It was from Carol, another one of my friends. She was the shortest of our group of friends. Her small stature didn't hold her back from being athletic. She was one of the top figure skaters in the state of California. Depression nearly took her from us, when she missed the Olympic try-outs due to a sprained ankle and then because of the flu. She is the only person I know who says exactly what's on her mind. When Carol is around, all we do is laugh.

"It was great. How was your vacation?"

Carol and her mom Sue went to Acapulco for the holidays.

"It was fabulous. The weather was nice the whole time. Mom

and I both got sunburn the first day. I wore my thong and forgot to turn and burnt my buns. Bahahahahah."

"OMG, LOL, I missed you so much."

"Oh, I missed you too. So how is Alexis' uncle?

"He's doing great. Alexis said that he has to change his diet and exercise more."

"It's too bad that some people have to get kicked in the pants before they listen."

"LOL, yea, I know what you mean."

"Well, I need to unpack, do laundry and put aloe on my burnt buns. I'm just kidding about the last part. See you at school."

"Yeah, see you tomorrow."

None of my other close friends were online. I was just about to log off when another small window popped open.

"Hey, Emma, did you have a great Christmas."

It was from my friend Joel Turner.

"Hi Joel, yes, it was really nice. What about you?"

"Yes, Lana and I stayed in LA this year and our parents came to visit for a few days. So what did you get for Christmas?"

"Well, lets see, I got an iTunes gift card, new clothes and a lap top. What did you get?"

"That's cool. My parents gave me some cash, new clothes and a lap top. So, did you pass all your classes?"

"Yes, I passed all my classes. I can't wait to graduate."

"So, have you decided which college you'll be going to?"

"No, I haven't looked at any colleges yet."

"Well, you have to apply early. Don't wait until it's too late. Oh, by the way, my mom or dad will be stopping by with an application from UCLA. They left here this morning."

"Gee, thanks a lot."

"You're very welcome. I'll talk to you soon. Someone is at the door."

"Talk to you later and say hi to Lana for me."

"Bye Emma."

I met Joel two years ago when we accidently ran into each other at school. He spilled his hot coffee on me and still blames himself for burning me. Joel and Lana are high school sweethearts. They graduated together and are both second year students at UCLA. A couple of weeks after our little accident, Joel and Lana gave me a friendship ring. I didn't want to accept it but Lana insisted. We've been friends ever since.

So I turned off the computer and went to get a glass of water. Ashley was already taking a bath and Jamie was on the karaoke. Mom was on the phone with Misty. I blew her a kiss and went to bed.

# *Priorities*

I woke up when my journal and clothing hit the floor. It was just seconds before my annoying alarm when off. I hit the snooze button and turned onto my side and tried to stay comfortable. Beep. Beep. Beep. Now it was 6:39. This time I turned the alarm off and sat up. I started to think about school. We had five months until June. I could count the weeks, days and hours left before graduation. My tiredness was replaced with excitement.

I couldn't wait to get to school and hang out with my friends. At my locker, I hung my jacket and made sure I had everything I needed in my book bag. I saw Cindy waving from the end of the hall. You could see her tan, when she smiled. Cindy and her parents vacationed in the Bahamas. We all assumed that she was keeping herself busy when she didn't post any of her daily activities on facebook. She had told us that her parents had made a list of activities to do: deep sea fishing, snorkeling, jet skiing, wind surfing and her favorite- spending a day at the spa.

I closed my locker and met Cindy by Alexis' locker.

"Oh my God, I love your tan," I said.

"Thanks, I was hoping I would tan like Alexis," she said and we laughed.

"So how was the Bahamas?" Alexis asked.

"It was unbelievable. We went on a bike tour and the guide showed us the President's Pink Place, their casino, Eddie Murphy's cabana and the whole countryside. Oh, I caught a tuna when we went deep sea fishing. It beat the crap out of me. My dad had to reel it in for me. We should all go there when we're in college. Spring break in Florida is not my cup of tea," Cindy said as we went to our English class.

Carol was already in class, when we walked in. She was talking to Jeff Morales, who sits behind her. They had seen each other in Acapulco. As soon as Carol saw Cindy she yelled "Oh my God, Mama Mia you look great."

Everyone in class had a good laugh, until our teacher Mrs. Harvey told us to pay attention. She gave us an outline with a list of required readings along with essays and book reports to do before our final exams.

It was great to be back in school. We looked at the photos our friends took of their vacation and enjoyed the stories that went along with them. Both Cindy and Carol were grateful that their parents were young and healthy enough to have fun with them. Carol felt bad for Jeff Morales. According to her, his parents watched him snorkel with Carol and Sue from the beach. He spent most of his vacation with Carol and Sue. We understood the bond they had was merely friendship and gratitude. None of us ever teased Carol about Jeff. He was like the brother she never had.

After dinner, I started to read "The Great Gatsby" for our English class. It was one of the books we had to do a book report on. From the corner of my eye, I saw Alexis as she walked through my bedroom door.

"Hey, doing homework?"

I showed her the cover of my book and said "It's my mom's book. I saw it on the list. I might as well get it out of the way. Oh, did you see the outline for earth science?"

"Yeah, that's why I went to the library," she said and she pulled two books from her book bag on tornadoes.

"Cool, but that's not due until April."

"Well, 'The Great Gatsby' isn't due until March." And we both laughed.

"Mom said she read 'The Great Gatsby' in college. She wouldn't tell me anything about the book."

"How far are you?"

"I just started."

Alexis adjusted the pillows next to me and I let her start from the beginning. F. Scott Fitzgerald is considered one of the top American writers. There were many moments, as I read, that I wanted to slap up his characters and tell them to smarten up. I could tell by Alexis breathing that she was probably feeling the same way. The narrator was told by his father not to judge people. I wondered, was that the reason he never confessed that Daisy was the one who murdered the mistress and not Jay Gatsby. It was full of lavish parties every weekend. Gatsby lived in the past, clinging to a love that had given up on him, and then there was all that cheating. It was kind of upsetting, making me think about my parents. I mean they weren't that bad, but I still was able a make the connection. By the time we finished reading the book, I had a headache. I closed the book threw it at the end of my bed.

"I'm so not looking forward to Shakespeare."

"Oh, I know. I better get home and do my report while I still remember it."

"Hey thanks for coming over."

"No problem, I'll see you tomorrow."

A couple of weeks later our guidance counselor advised us to start applying to colleges. When Joel and Lana got accepted at UCLA, I wanted to go there too. A lot of things had changed since then, and I was hesitant about leaving Santa Rosa. It was Cindy who wanted us to apply to colleges with the best athletic programs. We were all top basketball and volleyball athletes, and together our team had placed second in the CCS Division III Tournament. Our team defeated the #1 seeded Los Altos' High School in the semifinals to qualify for the northern California

17

championships. It made perfect sense to apply for athletic or scholastic scholarships.

For the next few weeks of January, we looked over Cindy's list and the brochure of colleges. As I looked over her list, I felt a little sick about leaving California. My mom was still having a hard time with her divorce and I felt that I should study close by just for her. When I saw Stanford University on the list, I did every thing I could to get the girls to apply to it.

"Alright, I'll apply to Stanford but you need to apply to Tennessee," said Cindy.

"Tennessee, that's half way around the world!" I said, and all the girls started laughing.

"Cindy is looking at Tennessee because it's best known for country music," said Aimee.

"Cindy, don't you want to study at UCLA with JJ?" I asked.

"That's not going to be a problem. JJ said that he would transfer to what ever college we decide to go to."

"Hey how about Duke University, they have a pretty good team," said Carol.

"I was looking at this university in Canton, New York. Let me find the brochure, oh here it is. St. Lawrence University, It's located in a small community in upstate New York. They're programs are excellent," said Aimee.

"Yeah, let's apply to that one," said Alexis with more enthusiasm that ever.

The more they talked about these far away places the more my stomach turned.

"Emma, what the heck is wrong with you? Where the hell are you? All through high school this is all we talked about. Don't you remember?" asked Carol.

I looked at the girls and they were trying really hard not to laugh at either me or Carol.

"Well?," said Carol.

I took a deep breath and said "I'm really having a hard time trying to think about going half way across the country, when my mom is having such a hard time."

"You need to stop using your parents' divorce as your sorry-ass excuse. If you go to some local college, your mom will never move on. Quit being a crutch for her. Some day when we all graduate, you're going to wish you had come with us," said Carol.

"You're right," I said with big tears filling my eyes and I remembered "The Great Gatsby" and how I had wished someone could've told Gatsby to smarten up.

"Ah, I'm sorry for being such a bitch, but you know we really need to get our priorities in order," said Carol as she came over and gave me a hug. And once again everyone started laughing.

I wiped the tears off my face and tried to laugh with them. So we filled out several applications and we agreed that we would check out other top colleges as well. After the girls had all gone home, I sat in my room and decided to write about how I felt. I opened up my diary and started writing.

*Today my best friends came over so we could apply to colleges. I was feeling sorry for myself only because I knew that my mom was suffering. Carol made me realize that I'm the child and as a child I need to learn something from my parents and my friends' mistake and move on. My mom on the other hand is the parent who needs to start pulling herself back together. I can't continue to wake her up and tell her to get ready for work, especially on the days when she just wants to sleep until noon. My mom needs to get back to the way she was before the separation and divorce. So, if I do stay here just to be her crutch, as Carol had said, she'll never recover from the wounds of her divorce. Tonight, right now, I promise that I will start thinking about myself and make sure that my priorities come first.*

As soon as I finished writing, I put my diary away and went down stairs to sit with my family. September would roll around before long, and I'd be leaving for college, so I wanted to share time with them. My mom was sitting on the far side of the sofa staring at a magazine. My brother Jamie and sister Ashley were lying on the floor watching "The Grinch who stole Christmas."

Those two have watched this same movie almost every night this week.

"Mom, what are you reading?"

"Ah, oh, nothing really, I was just thinking," she said.

"Mom, why don't we do something together?"

"Like what," she said.

"Let's do something together. Let's make cookies, pies or something," I said.

"Yeah, let's makes cookies," said Jamie and Ashley as they turned away from their favorite movie.

"Oh, okay, let's make cookies?" she said.

We all rushed into our bright yellow kitchen. Mom put a bowl on the counter and we grabbed flour, milk, butter and other stuff from the refrigerator and cupboards. I stood back and watched how much fun my siblings were having as they helped mom mix and stir the batter.

I think this is all mom needed to make her feel like we needed her. Mom, Jamie and Ashley scooped the batter on the cookie sheet and mom put the cookies into the oven. With in a few minutes, you could smell the peanut butter cookies. Just before the cookies were done, I whispered to my brother Jamie to get the small plates out. Then my sister Ashley took four small glasses out of the cupboard, and the two of them set the table. I filled each glass with milk and placed them on the table. My mom put the cookies on the small plates and we all sat around the table enjoying each other's company.

As soon I finished my first cookie, I looked at my mom and in a low whisper said "Thanks Mom."

My mom looked at me and said "No, thank you. This was fun, right guys?"

Both Ashley and Jamie agreed.

I told my mom the girls and I were applying to colleges all over the country. She needed to know that I wouldn't be around to help her out forever and that I needed to start planning for my future.

"Emma, I'm so glad you have good friends and that you have a good head on your shoulders," she said.

"Thanks mom," I said as I gave her a hug.

"So tell me, have you made up your mind what your major will be?" she asked.

"No, I was thinking of Liberal Arts just for the first semester or year and then if I find something that's interesting, then I'll declare my major," I said.

"Well, that's a good start. Most students change their majors after the first or second year. I did," she said.

"Mom, I'm going to remember nights like this when I'm gone," I told her.

"Well, you know what, we'll have more nights like this," she promised.

"Cool," I said.

I cleaned the mess we made and put everything away. Then I went into the living room and gave my mom a hug and told her that I was going to finish my homework.

I was glad that Carol was bold enough to say the things she did. It snapped me out of what I was doing to myself. Without realizing it, Carol's words helped me. In return, I was able to help my mom. While I was finishing my essay, my cell phone rang.

"Hello," I said.

"Hey, what are you doing?" asked Carol.

"I just finished my essay on 'Hamlet,' I said.

"Oh, crap," said Carol.

"Did you forget? It's due tomorrow," I said.

"I'll get to it later. Hey don't get mad at me, but I told my mom about your mom, and my mom is going to ask her to go out with a couple of her friends," said Carol.

"Why would I get mad? That is so thoughtful. Carol you're awesome. Thanks so much," I said.

"Well, the girls said I was a bit nasty to you earlier, so I thought I better make it up to you," she said.

"Carol, listen, I needed someone to tell me that. You were

21

absolutely right. I would have regretted not going to college with you guys. I believe I owe you," I told her.

"I'll remember that. Someday I'm gonna say Emma you owe me a favor, a big one," said Carol laughing.

Carol had a dirty mind; I knew exactly what she meant when she emphasized "a big one."

"You're such a pervert," I said.

"Yeah, I know. I'll see you tomorrow at school," she said.

"Yeah, see you later," I said.

As soon as I put my cell phone on the night stand, my mom knocked on my door.

"Emma, you still awake?" she asked in a low voice.

"Yeah, I just finished my essay," I said.

"Carol's mom Sue just called me. She invited me to out with her friends tomorrow. You don't have any plans do you?" she asked.

"Mom that's great. You need to get out. I'll watch Ashley and Jamie," I told her.

It was nearly 10:30, when I finally turned the lights off and went to bed. I never have a hard time falling asleep, but that night, I tossed and turned. I looked up at the clock and it was 11:45. My body was exhausted, but I couldn't fall asleep. I tried counting sheep, but, that didn't work. Finally I threw my pillow to the other end of the bed. The last time I looked at the clock, it was 2:50. It seemed like I had just closed my eyes when I heard my name.

"Emma!" yelled my mom as she opened my bedroom door. "We're late!"

The power went off some time this morning. I could see the lights on my alarm clock flashing. I rushed as quickly as I could to take a shower, threw on whatever clothes I could find and ran downstairs. My mom was already in the kitchen. She handed me a granola bar and an apple and I went on my way. The day flew by very quickly, probably because it was Friday and the weekend was upon us.

I knew that my mom would be going out tonight. So,

I invited the girls to come over. The plan was to watch movies while I kept an eye on Jamie and Ashley.

"What kind of movies do you have?" asked Cindy.

"My mom just bought 'Maid in Manhattan' and 'Sweet Home Alabama,'" I said.

"Cool, I haven't seen those yet," said Carol.

"Yeah, I like those," said Cindy.

"I'll bring '50 First Dates,'" said Alexis.

Jamie and Ashley were going to watch their favorite movie first. They promised mom they'd go right to bed after that. Aimee said she would be over as soon as she could. Carol and Cindy, on the other hand promised to stop over by 7:30.

As soon as our last class ended, we all went our separate ways. Alexis offered me a ride home. On the way to my house, her cell phone rang. It didn't take me long to figure out that it was Hunter.

"I'll spend the rest of the weekend with you, I promise. My friend Emma invited the girls over to watch movies with her. Her mom is finally going out," she said and handed me the phone.

"Hey, Hunter, you have any plans tonight?" I asked.

"Hi, Emma, yea, I'm on a mission. So what kind of movies do you like?" he said.

"Oh, let's see, comedy, drama and true stories. You're welcome to stop over if you miss Alexis," I said.

"Wow, for real? Can I bring a friend?" he asked, jokingly.

"Sure, why not?" I said and he laughs.

"Hey, thanks for the offer, maybe next time."

"Why do you have plans?"

"Yeah, I'm picking up a gift. Can you put Alexis back on please?" he said.

"Are you guys coming over? Alright, I'll see you tomorrow, you big chicken," she said and we both started laughing.

"They're not coming over?" I asked.

"No, he's at the Redwood Shopping Plaza picking up a gift. His mom's birthday is tomorrow," she said.

23

"Let's go over and you can surprise him. I need to pick up some drinks anyway," I said.

When we got to the shopping plaza, Alexis drove around until she found an open spot. I didn't realize she was looking for Hunter's car; I just assumed that she was looking for a parking spot. As soon as she parked her car, I ran over to Longs Drug Store to buy some drinks. As I walked toward the drug store, I met two Native guys walking near Big Lots. I looked over at them but, they were busy talking and didn't notice me. I figured one of them had to be Hunter.

As soon as I came out of the store I noticed that Alexis was standing by her car. There was a guy standing next to her. I couldn't tell if it was one of the two guys I met. I put the drinks in the back seat of her car. Then I walked around to where Alexis was standing.

"Emma this is Hunter, Hunter this is Emma," said Alexis. I reached across to shake his hand.

"Hi Emma," said Hunter.

"Hi Hunter, wow, it's the guy at the other end of the phone. We finally meet face to face. So, um, this little bird told us you're afraid to come watch movies with a bunch of girls?" I said.

"Nah, I'm not afraid, but my friend is," he whispered and laughed. I looked in his car at his passenger and waved and his passenger waved back.

Neither Alexis nor Hunter introduced their friend to me.

"It was nice to meet you, Hunter," I said and then I turned and walked around to Alexis' car. I opened the front door and looked back at Alexis before I got into the car. Alexis opened her door and said bye to Hunter.

"Why didn't you ever mention how handsome Hunter is?"

"Well, he was kinda goofy looking when we first met, besides, I didn't think it was important."

We were about two blocks from the shopping plaza when Alexis started laughing.

"What's so funny?"

"They're following us."

"Who's your other friend?" I asked.

"Oh, that's my cousin. I'm sorry I didn't introduce you. He's 20 years old and single. Both he and Hunter are studying computer science here at the college."

"Is that why you sometimes leave school in a hurry, so you can go meet Hunter?" I asked.

"They only have class on Tuesdays and Thursdays."

"When did you meet Hunter?" I asked.

"We met four years ago, but we didn't start dating until last summer," she said.

"He sounds like a nice guy," I said.

"Oh, he's just so awesome," she said.

"Well, I'm really happy for you," I said.

We pulled into the driveway at my house, and Alexis turned off the car. Hunter pulled in right behind us. Alexis and I got out of the car at the same time. I opened the back door and reached for the bag of drinks. Then I went walking toward the house. When I got to the porch, Alexis called out to me.

"Hey, Emma, come here a minute."

I put the bag of drinks down by the door and walked over toward Alexis. Hunter and his friend got out and stood in front of the car.

"So, Hunter, did you change your mind?" I asked and we started laughing.

"No, Alexis said it was girl's night out. I just wanted you to meet my friend. Emma this is my buddy, Sky. Sky, this Emma," said Hunter.

We shook hands and said hi to each other. If my hand was butter it would have melted in his very warm hand.

That was the first time we looked into each other's eyes. His eyes were the darkest brown I'd ever seen. From a distance, they could've passed for black. He was just as tan as Alexis and Hunter.

"Wow," I thought to my self. "This guy is so handsome."

My mind started to race through my memory. I know I met Sky before, I just couldn't remember when or where. It was his voice and those eyes that were so familiar.

"So I hear you're into movies. What are you watching later?" he asked.

"I do like movies," I said. "Oh let's see, we have 'Sweet Home Alabama,' 'Anger Management,' 'Maid in Manhattan' and '50 First Dates.'"

"You're going to watch all that tonight?" he asked.

"Yeah, but, I think I might've forgotten a few titles. It's my mom's first night out in years, so the girls and I decided to hang out," I said.

"What, no boyfriend?" he asked.

"Um, no, I don't have a boyfriend," I said.

"Oh," said Sky, seeming a bit shocked.

Before I could ask Sky if he had a girlfriend, Hunter reminds Alexis about his mother's birthday party and he asked Alexis to bring me along.

"Oh, I'd love to go, but I have plans," I said

"Who's the chicken now?" asked Hunter as they laughed. I tucked my arm up and did my imitation of a walking chicken.

"I really do have plans, but I'll take a rain check."

"Okay, mark you calendar. We're having a birthday dinner for my dad on June 24th," Hunter said as he jumped in his car and started it.

"June 24th, we'll be there."

I reached my hand back toward Sky.

"It was nice to meet you."

Sky held my hand.

"Likewise," he said, smiling.

That smile was enough to make my heart skip a couple of beats. Hunter pulled out of my drive way and we all waved at each other.

I walked over to Alexis.

"You're leaving?" I asked her. "We need to talk about your cousin. I think I've met him before."

"I promise I'll be back soon. We'll talk later," said Alexis and she got into her car and drove away.

I walked back to the house, grabbed the bag of drinks and placed them in the refrigerator. I was going to do my homework when I realized I had left my book bag in Alexis' car. I called and left a message to remind her that my bag was in the back seat and asked her to bring it with her later.

# Big Changes

It's been almost a month since Sue, her friends and my mom first went out. Their Friday night outings were now a part of mom's regular routine. You could see the changes in her attitude. She was so much happier than before. We could hear her singing or humming while we were having breakfast or dinner. She started wearing makeup and spending money on herself. I would even help her apply eye shadow to match her outfits. On Sundays mom would take us to the mall. She'd give Ashley and Jamie money to spend at the arcade, while she and I sat in the food court. She would sip on café latte and I would have a fruit smoothie. Saturdays and Thursdays, we would hang out in the kitchen and help her bake. This became our family's weekly event. Ashley and Jamie looked forward to helping mom bake treats. We were all glad to have mom back to her old self.

Last December mom wouldn't even decorate the house or help with the Christmas tree. Now she had our house decorated for Valentines Day.

"Wow, Mom, this is so cool," I told her.

"Yeah, I decided to have a little party for us," she said.

"Cool, I can't wait," I said.

"You have mail; it's on the table by the stairs."

I grabbed the envelope and headed down the hallway.

"I'll be in my room doing homework," I yelled, almost to my room.

"Alright, I'll call you when dinner is ready."

I went into my room, put my book bag on the chair and put the hot pink envelope on my desk. When I bumped the mouse on my desk, I noticed the instant messenger was letting me know I had mail.

The instant message, along with the hot pink envelope, would have to wait. I always liked to change into relaxing clothes before I did homework, chat on facebook or talk on the phone.

I put on a light blue t-shirt and black sweat pants. Once I was changed, I took my dirty clothes to the laundry room. Outside my room, I caught the scents wafting from the kitchen. Whatever mom was cooking sure smelled good.

I considered going downstairs to give her a hand, but then I decided mom needed to do her own thing. So I went back into my room and checked my instant message. While I was waiting for it to pop open, I grabbed the hot pink envelope and held it to my chest, wondering who it was from. It was obviously a Valentine's card from one of my best friends, or maybe they all had signed it. I'd had known Joel for over two years now, and he had never sent me anything on Valentine's Day. And I knew Joel was committed to his girlfriend Lana, so it had to be my best friends. I pulled the card out and - skipping the entire note - looked at the signature. I was shocked. It was from my dad.

*Emma my love, I am sending you this message for many reasons. The first one is to let you know how much I love you and that I will always be a part of your life. The second reason is to let you know that Shelby and I have decided to get married at the end of the month. We would like very much if you would be in our wedding. Please say yes. PS. I never meant to hurt you, your brother or sister. The problems your mom and I had were not your problems. Please remember that. Love you always, your dad.*

I closed the letter as tears welled up in my eyes. And I wasn't crying because I was angry at my dad for wanting to marry his girlfriend. I was crying because my dad stopped saying he loved us almost five years ago. That was when the problems between my parents became noticeable. I put the letter on my desk and opened the waiting message.

*Hey baby girl, I hope you read the letter/card I sent to you. If you didn't, please stop reading this and open the card first. If you've already read it, then scroll down this page. Shelby and I want you to be in our wedding. Baby girl, if your answer is no, then there is no need to reply to this email. But, if you are willing to do that for us, just reply to this email. I will need your size so that Shelby can purchase the dress. She wants to make sure she picks out the right color and style. I will talk to you soon.*

I sat back on my chair and wondered what I should do. If I agree to my dad's request, what will it do to my mom? Will it make her upset when she finds out dad will be remarrying so soon after the divorce? Will it make her upset if I agree to do this? This was a very hard decision for me to make on my own.

I got on the phone and called Alexis and explained everything. She told me I should call my dad and ask him to tell my mom that he has decided to remarry. To my surprise, Alexis told me to consider my dad's offer.

"Emma, how many times in our life time do our parents present us with such a request?" she asked.

"So you think I should say yes?" I asked.

"Well I love both my parents that much that I would say yes," she said.

"Alexis, you're the best," I said.

"Don't forget to tell your dad that he should be the one to tell your mom. He owes her that much. After everything he's put her through," said Alexis.

"You're right," I said. "I'll e-mail my dad and I'll let him know. Thanks for your help. I'll talk to you later."

I started to write my dad an e-mail. Half way down the page I stopped writing and highlighted the entire page and hit the delete

Spanish

button. After sitting there for a few minutes, I picked up my cell phone and called my dad.

"Hello."

"Hi, Dad, it's Emma."

"Is something wrong Emma?" he asked in his concerned voice.

I took a deep breath.

"Dad, I got your letter today and I also read your email," I said.

"I'm listening," he said his voice still very concerned.

"Well, I wanted you to hear my answer, not read it in an email," I said.

"I'm listening," he said, with the concern less noticeable in his voice.

"I'd love to be a part of your wedding."

"You had me worried," he said.

"There's just one thing," I said.

"Can you call mom right now and tell her about the wedding?" I asked and made a face like he might say no.

"Emma, I told your mom a few days ago," he said. "She's okay with everything."

"Mom knew for the past few days?" I asked, shocked.

"Yeah, we had a long talk and everything is cool."

"Why didn't you let me know that mom knows?" I asked.

"She thought it was best if we surprised you and it seems that we did."

"Size 6, I wear a size 6."

"Great the dress should arrive in a few days."

"Okay. So you'll let me know when, where and the time?" I asked.

"I sure will," he said.

"Alright, so I'll talk to you later. Love you, dad."

"Bye, baby girl," he responded. "Talk to you later. Love you, too."

After I composed myself, I went downstairs to find my mom. She was in the kitchen tasting whatever she was cooking.

"You're just in time," she said with a big smile on her face.

I helped her place the food on the plates and set them on the table. We all enjoyed mom's surprise dinner: chicken and biscuits. She had gotten the recipe from Sue and decided to try it for us. It was so delicious we could have asked for seconds.

After Jamie and Ashley were tucked in bed, I called out to my mom and asked why she didn't tell me that she and dad had talked about his upcoming marriage.

"Emma, dear, I told your dad that it was his responsibility to let you know," she said.

"So you're alright with it?" I asked.

"Yes, I am. I think that maybe a month ago I would have been really upset, but since I have Sue and my other friends, they've really helped me out with it," she said.

We hugged each other for the longest time. I didn't want to let her go.

"Don't worry about anything. Everything's going to work out just fine," she said as she let go of me.

"Mom, I'm so glad that you and dad can finally put all that bad stuff behind you and just be friends," I said.

"Yeah, it was hard at first, but he knows that he broke my heart and that he caused me a lot of pain," said mom.

I reached over and gave my mom another hug.

"I'm so glad that you found your way back. I missed you so much," I said.

"You have no idea how much you helped me to find my way," she said.

"I better get my homework done. Goodnight, Mom," I said.

"Goodnight, Emma," she said as she kissed my forehead.

She had the most beautiful smile I'd ever seen on her face, and even her eyes had a sparkle in them. I was so glad that my parents were able to be friends after all the bitter fights they had during the custody and divorce hearings.

It was a little hard to concentrate on some of my classes with this wedding on my mind. My friends were all excited, when I made my dad invite them to the wedding. The wedding was to take place in San Francisco at the Hilton Grand Ball Room. My dad and most of his family lived in and around the bay area.

Just like dad promised, a garment bag and box was delivered to the house within the week. Inside the garment bag was a beautiful pale blue gown. Inside the box was a pair of pale blue high heels, a pearl necklace, matching earrings and a gift certificate to get my hair, nails and makeup done. My mom was sitting on the couch with a huge smile on her face.

"Go try it on, Emma," she said.

I put everything back in the box, grabbed the garment bag and ran upstairs. About ten minutes later I came walking down the hallway. When I reached the top of the stairs, I saw my mom standing at the bottom step. She immediately put her hands over her mouth and shook her head.

"Oh, Emma," she said. "You're so beautiful. You look really great in that color. It's perfect. I just love it."

"Mom, are you sure your okay with this?" I asked. My mom just smiled and nodded her head. She placed her hand on my cheek.

"Emma, you're doing the right thing," mom said. "Sue really helped me to understand."

The look on my face must have let my mother see I was confused. How she could change her outlook in just over a month?

"Sue told me to reverse the roles," mom explained. "She said to pretend I was the one cheating; I was the one who wanted a divorce; and I was the one who wanted to marry someone else. So I thought about it. And you know what? She's right. If I were in his position, I would want your dad to be happy for me. I guess I finally realized I was just feeling sorry for myself and blaming others for nothing."

"Mom, you're the best," I said as I hugged her. She smiled at me and told me to go change before I tore the dress or stained it.

After I had the dress back in the garment bag and all the accessories back in the box. I made a conference call to my friends.

"Hey guys, I just got my bridesmaid's dress delivered today. My mom made me try it on. It's so awesome."

"What color is it?" asked Cindy.

"It's blue, pale blue."

"Is it sleeveless?" asked Carol.

"It has one sleeve and the other arm and shoulder are bare. It's just like the dresses that Princess Diana liked to wear," I said.

"I can't wait to see you in it. So, did it make you feel like a princess?" asked Aimee.

"Yes," I said.

"Come on Emma, tell us more," said Alexis.

"He sent me matching high heels, a white pearl necklace and a gift certificate to get my hair and nails done," I said.

"Cool," said Alexis.

"So when can we come over and see you in it?" asked Cindy.

"You have to wait until the wedding," I said.

"Ah, come on, we're your friends," said Carol.

"My mom doesn't want me to ruin it," I said.

"Yeah, knowing you, you'll probably stain it," said Carol, eliciting laughter from everyone on the line.

"Gee, thanks, Carol," I said.

"Oh chill, girlfriend, you know we're just kidding," said Carol.

"Oh, I know that. Well, I'm going to let you guys go. I need to get my homework done," I said,

"Okay, see you tomorrow," said Cindy

"Later, gator," said Carol.

"Bye, Emma," said Aimee.

"See you tomorrow, Emma," said Alexis.

"Bye," I said as I hung up the phone.

I had just finished my math homework, when I heard the doorbell ring. I walked out to the staircase and saw mom open the door. It was one of my mom's new friends, and she looked like she'd been crying. I went down stairs to get a glass of water and to see if mom needed my help in the kitchen.

"Emma, is that you?" asked mom.

"Yes," I said.

"I have lasagna in the oven. It should be done. There's salad in the fridge. Tell Jamie and Ashley dinner's ready, " she said.

I set the table and went upstairs and told my siblings that dinner was ready. We ate while mom and her friend sat in the living room and talked. As soon as we finished, we cleaned up the mess and put everything but my mom's plate away. I went into the living room and asked mom and her friend if they wanted some tea.

"No, thank you, I was just leaving," said mom's friend.

"No, honey, I'm okay," said mom.

"Okay," I said.

I went back upstairs, but I kept my bedroom door open, just so I would know when mom's friend left. As soon as I heard the front door close, I went down stairs to see if mom was okay. I found her sitting at the kitchen table having her dinner. She told me her friend, Jodi, was having marital problems and wanted advice.

"Did she think that you were able to help her?" I asked.

"Well, she believed it just started a couple of months ago. And I told her that she needs to do something now and not four years from now," said mom.

"That's really good advice: it's bad when kids have to witness all the atrocious abuse for years," I said.

"I'm so sorry we put you guys through all that nonsense," said mom.

"At least you're trying to help someone else to do the right thing sooner rather than later," I said.

"Emma, just because you witnessed the horrible side of

marriage, it doesn't mean it will happen to you. You may be the lucky one who finds someone who knows exactly what it takes to be a man. So don't let marriage frighten you," said mom.

I smiled at my mom and gave her a hug. I told her I wasn't interested in boys just yet. Then I went to bed. Busy days like today drain me of my good energy and leave me very tired. I turned on my music, put the ear pieces in my ears, turned the lights off and took several deep breaths to relax, and then I made myself comfortable.

# The Big Day

On the last Saturday in February, I got up real early and took a shower. My hair was still wet as I drove over to Sue's beauty shop. Sue was standing outside her shop having a cigarette when I pulled up.

"Good morning Emma, you look rested."

"Good morning, Sue, I don't feel rested. I had one of those nights. It seems like I just closed my eyes and a minute later it was already time to get up."

"Oh, don't worry, these fingers can do wonders. You'll be so beautiful, the bride will be jealous!" said Sue as we laughed.

Sue started blow drying my hair. I put in my ear pieces and listened to music to drown out the noise. Sue did an excellent job on my hair. She braided the sides of my hair upward and then pinned the back of my hair up so curls hung down the back. It took her almost an hour just to do my hair.

"So what do you think?" she asked, as she turned me to face the mirror and held another mirror to the back of my hair.

"Wow, I like it. It looks really cool," I said.

"You look awesome. Like I said, that bride will be so envious," said Sue.

"Thanks, Sue," I said.

"I'm going to put a lot of hair spray in your hair. It's going to rain or drizzle in San Francisco," said Sue.

Then she put my fingers in a small dish to soak. She filed my nails and oiled my cuticles. Then she asked me the color of my dress.

"I'll do a French manicure, it will look good," she said. "Lucky for you, we don't have to use fake nails."

Just doing my nails took another half hour. Finally, Sue turned my chair around and started doing my makeup. She applied the foundation, followed it up with eye liner and eye shadow, and then finished with mascara.

"You're so lucky we don't have to touch your eye brows," she said.

Then she took a brush, dabbed it in powder and brushed it over my face.

"Oh, you're so beautiful. Are you ready for a look?" asked Sue.

"I'm ready," I said.

Sue turned the chair around, and I looked at the girl in the mirror. I was stunned to see this gorgeous girl looking back at me.

"Well what do you think?" asked Sue.

"I look so different. I look like I could pass for a twenty-year-old," I said.

"That's what makeup does. So what do you think?" she asked again.

"Wow, you don't think it's too much?" I asked.

"Hey, trust me; I know what I'm doing. So what do think?" said Sue.

"I like it," I said.

"Listen, step into your dress so you don't get the makeup on it, okay?" said Sue.

"Okay," I said.

Sue handed me a small container of lip-gloss.

"Don't put this on until just before the wedding."

"Okay," I said.

"You girls have fun. And Emma, tell your dad I wish him all the best," said Sue then she made a face like she didn't really mean it.

"What?" I asked.

"Emma, do you know what karma is?" asked Sue.

"I heard something about it," I said.

"Okay, listen, your dad flirted with a lot of women while he was with your mom," Sue explained. "Then he had affairs with other women and he made your mom so miserable only because he wanted her to throw him out. Your dad broke your mom's heart. You don't do things to another human being and think that someone won't do it back to you. That's karma - what goes around comes around. The hurt he caused your mom will come back to him, and he will hurt worse than your mom did."

"Thanks for explaining it that way," I said.

"So, just tell your dad I wish him well," said Sue.

"I will, and thank you so much," I said.

After I left Sue's Beauty shop, I went home and gathered my dress, shoes and accessories. I gave my mom a hug and told her I would meet her and Sue later at the Hilton. I placed everything neatly into the trunk and drove to pick up Alexis and Aimee. Carol and Cindy were driving down later with my mom and Sue. My brother and sister were already with my dad for the weekend, and my uncle Bill would be driving them home Sunday night.

On the way to San Francisco we sang songs that were blasting from the radio. We all laughed at each other when we sang the words wrong. When we got tired of the radio, we started playing "I spy with my little eye."

Then, all of a sudden, Aimee saw the big billboard about Abortion Kills and said "Oh my god, I just remembered Robin Miller is getting married by the justice of the peace today."

"Who's Robin Miller?" I asked.

"She's one of the cheerleaders," said Aimee.

"No shit, oops sorry," I said.

"Wow. Are her parents upset with her?" asked Alexis.

"Yeah, shot gun wedding," said Aimee.

No one uttered a word as we crossed the Golden Gate Bridge. Aimee looked over the map and gave me directions to the Hilton. When we parked in front of the hotel, the doorman opened the car doors for us, unloaded my stuff from the car and handed it to Alexis. I drove to the parking lot and went to meet Alexis and Aimee by the front door.

"Wow, check out those chandeliers, they're the size of my bathroom," said Aimee.

We all busted out laughing. Leave it to Aimee to come up with something like that.

We walked up to the check-in counter and asked where the Niles' wedding would be held. The girl behind the counter pointed down the hallway.

"At the end of the hallway turn left," the girl said. "The wedding will be in the Grand Ballroom. There's a dressing room in there."

"Thank you," we all said.

When we got to the Grand Ballroom, I opened the door and saw several men decorating the room with floral arrangements. We found the small changing room at the end of the ballroom. Shelby had just gotten there a few minutes before us. I introduced Aimee and Alexis to Shelby, and she introduced us to her two sisters. The tall one is Tina and the other one is Shelly. We couldn't help but notice that Shelly and Shelby really looked alike.

"Are you two twins?" asked Aimee.

"Yes," said Shelby.

From the dressing room, we could hear a lot of noise. Aimee opened the door to see what they were doing.

"What's going on out there?" asked Shelby.

"There's a crew setting the chairs up at the other end of the hall and two guys are laying out a pale blue carpet," said Aimee.

"Oh, no!" said Shelby, as she went out to the hall.

We all followed her, of course.

"Excuse me, that carpet is suppose to be dark blue," said Shelby.

"Oh sorry, we'll change that right away," said one of the guys.

We all walked back into the room and started changing into our dresses. When we were all dressed, I noticed that my dress was a little different than the one the two sisters were wearing.

"Our dresses don't match," I said to Shelby.

"That's because you're my maid of honor," said Shelby.

"Oh, my dad never told me that. He just said that he wanted me in the wedding," I said to Shelby.

"Is that okay with you?" asked Shelby.

"Wow, I just assumed that one of your sisters would be, but I'm honored to be your maid of honor," I said, and then I walked over and gave her a hug.

For the first time since we got into that room, I saw Tina and Shelly smile at me. We all helped Shelby get into her dress and high heels, and I grabbed her bouquet for her.

Then her sister Tina, who is older than Shelly and Shelby, told Shelby to stand at the end of the room, so we could have a look at her.

"Wow," said Shelly

"You look fabulous," said Aimee.

"You're one gorgeous bride," said Alexis.

"You're so beautiful," I said.

"Shelby you're stunning," said Tina.

"Thanks, you girls are making me nervous," said Shelby.

"Breathe," said Tina.

"Emma do you want to put some lip stick on?" asked Shelby.

"Oh, I have some. Alexis can you put it on me. My hands are shaking so much I'll probably put it all over my face," I said, then everyone in the room starting laughing.

As we were laughing, someone knocked on the door. Aimee

went over and cracked the door very slightly. The person behind the door said, "Ladies, you have five more minutes."

I went over to the table and picked up my bouquet and took a deep breath.

As soon as the music started playing, our faces all lit up. Alexis and Aimee walked out to take their seats. Tina, Shelly and I got in line in front of Shelby. As soon as the Wedding March started, we walked toward the door. One after another, we filed out of the dressing room. I was so glad Tina was taller than the rest of us. Because of her height, we were able to hide almost completely behind her.

There, in the back row, stood my mom, Sue, Carol, Alexis, Aimee and Cindy. They pulled up their cameras and started taking pictures as soon as they saw me.

As we slowly walked down the aisle toward where my father waited, I couldn't help notice all the smiles. I felt like the room was filled with a positive energy. I guess you have to make a few mistakes before you finally get it right. I felt like dad's friends and family believed that – or at least hoped that – in that moment. Sure, he had a habit of jumping into things without thinking, like he did when he married my mom at an early age, but he never considered his children a mistake. To him, we were his greatest accomplishments.

I didn't want to think about what Sue had said about karma, but deep inside I knew that some day, dad would get back that bad feeling he dished on mom. But it wouldn't be today, because today was going to be another happy moment in his life.

As we met my dad at the front, he smiled and winked at me. I turned and waited for my dad's beautiful bride to walk past me. Shelby's dad placed her hand in my dad's hand and they both smiled at each other. The minister gave his traditional speech, but whatever he said went in one of my ears and slipped out the other. The whole time I stood there, it took everything in my power not to cry. I just kept telling myself, "This is a beautiful wedding. There's no need to cry."

Finally, I heard my dad and Shelby say "I Do." When it was finally over, I felt tears run down my cheeks. I lifted my head just as the minister pronounced them husband and wife. After my dad kissed his new bride, he motioned me over and gave me a hug. He kissed my forehead.

"Thank you for being here and for understanding," he said, just above a whisper.

"Dad, Shelby, I wish you both the best," I said. "And, Shelby I hope we can be friends, not just for today."

"Emma, you're crying," dad said.

"Yeah, it's only because I'm happy for you both," I said.

As guests lined up to congratulate dad and Shelby, a group of men came in to rearrange the room. Uncle Bill, dad's best man, gave me a hug and told me I was beautiful. He couldn't believe how much I had grown since that last time he had seen me. I didn't want to remind him that it was almost six years ago, since we last seen each other. My dad's family stopped visiting when they realized that my parent's marriage was in trouble.

Uncle Bill is a handsome man who never married. In fact, in all my years, I never saw him with a woman. I learned that day why he was still single. When he introduced me to his friend John, I understood his reason and choice. While I was talking to Uncle Bill and John, I felt a tap on my shoulder. It was Grandma and Grandpa Niles. We hugged each other.

Seeing them, I began to feel more emotional that I did during the ceremony. They were both apologetic for being strangers and they promised to keep in touch. I was so grateful that Sue had put waterproof mascara on me.

Jamie and Ashley were spending the weekend with our grandparents, and they were excited about getting to know them. They had finally come to accept Uncle Bill's lifestyle and knew we were the only grandchildren they would ever have. Well, unless dad and Shelby decide to start their own family.

The work crew pulled tables off a rack and placed them in various spots around the room and chairs were set around them in an orderly fashion. When the tables were all set with white and dark blue tablecloths, we took our seats. Servers entered through the side door with our dinner. When the last plate was taken away, dad and Shelby moved to the far table and began to cut their wedding cake. Once again the servers came in and passed the cake around.

As the guests enjoyed the cake, a small group assembled in the space in front of the dressing room. These four guys and one woman set up their band instruments to entertain my dad and Shelby for their first dance. Uncle Bill waited until the crowd stopped taking pictures, and he took me to the dance floor.

"Uncle Bill I really can't dance."

"Just follow me Emma."

We danced the entire song together, while everyone cut in on dad and Shelby. As the band played the second song, Uncle Bill whispered "go ask Grandpa to dance and I'll dance with Grandma."

We walked hand in hand to their table. Uncle Bill reached out his hand and said "Mom may I have this dance?"

Then he looked at me and winked.

I looked at Grandpa.

"Grandpa would you like to dance with me?" Grandpa held my hand and walked me to the dance floor. He held me tight as we danced. Before the song ended, I looked at Grandpa and whispered, "I missed you and Grandma so much."

He held me tighter.

"I'm so sorry about that Emma. I promise I'll make it up to you."

He kissed my forehead.

Finally I went over and tapped on Tina's shoulder, so I could dance with my dad.

"Finally, we get a minute alone," I said.

"Yes, I just hope it lasts longer that a minute. By the way you look gorgeous, Emma," said dad.

"Thanks, Dad, so do you."

"So tell me, have you decided what college you're going to?"

"No. My friends and I applied to a few. I guess we'll decide once the acceptance letters come in."

"You keep me posted. I've put some money away to help you out."

"Gee, thanks Dad."

That was it for our dance. Shelby's mom was tapping on my shoulder.

"Thanks for the dance, dad," I said as we kissed each other on the cheek.

"No, Emma, thank you," said Dad.

My Mom and Sue were the only ones who didn't dance with my dad. Sue later said they didn't want Shelby to feel awkward, or to have her family talk because my Mom was there. When Carol, Alexis, Cindy and Aimee all had their dance, we went and sat with my mom and Sue. Just before 9 p.m., I went over and thanked my dad and Shelby for the dress and everything else, and told them we were heading home. I gave my dad and Shelby a hug and then I went into the dressing room to change. I met my dad in the lobby and waved goodbye to him and blew him a kiss. He reached for the kiss and put it into his pocket. Then he blew me a kiss and I pretended that it almost knocked me over. He laughed loudly and waved goodbye to me.

As we drove home, Alexis and Aimee talked about how beautiful everything was. They also told me that they were proud of the way I handled the situation. I told them I owed my friends a lot for that. All the talks that we had shared throughout our lives are what truly helped me to be the person I turned out to be. I just hoped that we would continue to learn positive thing that would keep us on this right path. Our little group of friends relied on each more than we knew. Sometimes we were a crutch for each other.

# The Mystery Guy

At the end of February, this new kid, Bobbie Watson, walked into our geography class. He and his mother had moved here from some place in Louisiana. He made heads turn.

Bobbie was six feet tall with shoulder-length, wavy, dark brown hair, and his face had an unshaven look to it. He could pass for a rock star. As he walked over to take a seat at an empty desk, he looked at every girl in the room, pausing long and hard on Cindy and me. I turned my head before he could look me in the eye. I looked to my right at Lacey Smith, but Lacey was checking out Bobbie. As soon as he was in his seat, Carol looked at me.

"Oh my," she said, in a low voice. "There is a God after all."

I hit Carol in the arm.

"Oh God, Carol you're so embarrassing," I said. "Don't forget you have a boyfriend, Toby. Remember him?"

"Oh, chill out, Emma" Carol said. "I have eyes and I'll look at what ever the good Lord puts in my view."

And we both started laughing real low. She was always so quick with her responses.

"Besides, who knows what Toby's up to at Montgomery," she said, again in a whisper.

There wasn't a girl in the room who wasn't glancing over to give Big Bobbie a look over.

Carol's attitude and her ability to say what was on her mind were probably the main reasons we were good friends. We all needed someone like her in our circle of friends to make us laugh. Carol knew that by making us laugh, she could distract us from any problems or issues we were dealing with. Carol's motto: "Never leave any stone unturned; there just might be something funny behind it."

Carol took a piece a paper out from her notebook and began writing. When she was done she handed the paper to me.

*"Emma, I was just about to yell over to the hunky new guy in class and ask him if I could call him Bubba Watson, but then I saw Alexis looking over at us shaking her head no. So, I think I need to talk with Alexis before I say anything to the new guy."*

I took Carol's note and began to write.

*"Yeah, I'm interested as to what Alexis has to say about the new guy."*

Then I gave Carol the note. Carol looked at it and placed it in her notebook.

Like everyone in class, I, too, was thinking about the new guy. Unlike my friends, though, I wasn't lusting over him. My mind was trying to remember that hair, that face and those eyes. Perhaps we had passed each other at the mall, the movies or at my fathers wedding. I finally gave up trying to remember where I had seen him.

When the bell rang, Carol and I stood up and walked over to Alexis. The three of us headed over to our gym class without saying a word. On the way to the gym, we saw Bobbie talking to a couple of girls. He was asking them how to get to his history class. Sharon Wilson looked at his schedule to find the room number.

"Hey! We're in the same history class, just follow us," she said.

The two girls, Rhonda Wilson and Sherri Bailey, had a reputation for being the wild girls of our school. Every guy in high school talked about Rhonda and Sherri, except for the geeks and the nerds. As we walked behind Bobbie, Rhonda and Sherri, we notice the plays they were making on Bobbie. Everyone turned their heads when they saw the two girls with the new guy.

"Hey, Rhonda, do fries come with that shake?" yelled Bill Mason, and the rest of the guys he was walking with cracked up laughing,

"Hey new guy watch out for the mutts," said Jake McCormick.

"Yeah, sleazy," said Travis Jones.

"Gee, I thought I was bad with the words," yelled Carol.

"Hey, they have no shame or respect for themselves, so why should we respect them," said Bill Mason.

As soon as we got to the gym, Carol grabbed Alexis by the arm and went running into the locker room.

"Hey, girlfriend, what's going on?" asked Carol in a low but demanding voice.

All five of us stood around her waiting for her to answer. Alexis put her finger to her lips and whispered

"Just wait one minute; I need the rest of the girls to leave the locker room."

We stood there perfectly silent, for what seemed like forever. As soon as the last of the girls left the locker room, Alexis looked at us.

"There' something bad about that guy. I can feel it in my gut."

"Ah. No way. How can you say that about him? You don't even know anything about him," said Carol.

"Yeah," said Cindy "How can someone with that body and that face be evil?"

"Listen to me," said Alexis "I can see his aura and there is something really wrong with him. You guys are going to have to trust me on this one. Please stay away from him."

"What?" we all responded.

"Well, okay," said Alexis. "You guys can talk to him only if he asks you a question first. You know, just act normal."

There was a pause.

"Alright listen," Alexis continued. "Tonight, I will ask my mom to help with a small fire ceremony, and if we happen to come up with anything, I'll e-mail all of you as to what mystery lurks within him."

"Okay," said Carol.

"Alright," said Cindy.

"Sure," said Aimee

And all I could say was, "sounds good."

As we stood in the locker room staring at each other, Alexis and I both got cold chills and goose bumps on our arms.

"Okay," said Carol "So what do we do? Do you want us to just ignore him?"

"No." Alexis said. "You can talk to him if he talks to you first. Just do your very best not to make eye contact. Just be yourself and don't try to piss him off. I don't know what else I can tell you guys until we do a fire ceremony."

After a few seconds Alexis took a deep breath and said in a low whisper, "You guys really need to trust me on this: but I can truly feel that there is something very wrong with this guy. Do you guys know the saying: looks can be deceiving? Well this is what I'm talking about."

While we were standing there talking, Mrs. McGee walked into the locker room and said "Come on, girls, get into the gym and do your laps." We all went running into the gym and started our laps. There wasn't one girl in the gym who wasn't talking about Bobbie Watson. All the chatter about his stunning dark eyes, his rock hard body and gorgeous rock star features was now starting to get on my nerves.

Knowing Alexis for as long as I have, I knew that if she saw or felt something, I was going to listen. My thoughts drifted back to a time when we were all going to the beach for a bonfire and to have a few drinks with our friends. Alexis knew two days before we left that something was going to happen there. She even gave us the exact time. I couldn't help myself as I drifted back to that night at the beach. We had this huge bonfire running wild. The music was echoing loudly over the beach. Everyone was getting a little drunk, and it was really loud. I started to get this awful chill as I remembered seeing the four college-age guys coming into view from the western side of the beach area. I remembered Alexis' warning and looked at my watch, it was the exact time that she had predicted that the guys would be coming to the beach. I couldn't help but notice that these guys were carrying weapons like a whip or a rope and a shiny object that I couldn't make out. I never felt the kind of fear I was feeling at that moment. I took off running before the guys got any closer. Later, I regretted that I didn't stay and help those who were badly injured.

In the gym, we did our laps and warm-up before our volleyball scrimmage. It was hard to concentrate on the game. I kept remembering the beach party and the two freshman girls who were skinny dipping with their boyfriends and were badly beaten and raped by those party crashers. The guys and girls who tried to stop then were also cut and bruised up. It was a terrifying moment for me to realize that her prediction had come true. After that party, whenever Alexis warned us about anything, we paid attention.

Mrs. McGee yelled out my name several times when I missed the ball and twice when I was hit with it.

"Pay attention, Miss Niles!"

Our school had one of the top volleyball teams; I couldn't afford to be pulled off the team because I was distracted. I got myself back into my athletic form. My team beat the other side by two points.

Once gym was over and we all went back to the locker room, Alexis told us that she didn't feel comfortable sitting in the cafeteria if Bobbie Watson was going to be in there.

"Alexis, where are you going to have lunch if not in the cafeteria?" asked Cindy.

"I think I'll just go to the Molly's café for something," said Alexis. We all agreed to jump in her car with her and go to Molly's café for lunch.

At the café, we each ordered the house salad with a large glass of iced tea. You would think by the way we dressed, spoke, and our choice of food, that we were all joined at the hip.

"Ah, you know what?" asked Cindy, "I'm glad we decided to have lunch here."

We all agreed with Cindy.

"Yeah," said Carol. "It's so relaxing here."

As we were munching on our salads and sipping on our iced teas, an unfamiliar middle-aged woman walked into the café. She walked over to the far end of the café and sat at a small table.

When I looked back at our table, I noticed Alexis had pushed her half eaten salad in front of her and was staring at the table. When I looked over at her, she was sitting very still with her eyes closed and taking in very shallow breaths. We all began looking at each other wondering, "What could she be thinking now."

She started to make a face and raised her hand to her forehead like she had a headache or something.

"Alexis are you alright?" asked Cindy in a concerned voice.

Alexis slowly opened her eyes.

"I don't feel well."

"Let's just finish up here and get back to school," said Carol.

We put money for our bill on the table and helped Alexis to her car. Carol offered to drive us back to school but Alexis insisted that she was okay. I didn't have as much psychic awareness as Alexis, but I could tell by her voice and by the way she looked that it had something to do with the woman who entered the café.

By the time we drove into the school parking lot, Alexis looked better.

"This is so strange," she said, sounding almost surprised. "I don't feel sick to my stomach and I'm not feeling tired anymore. I felt so awful earlier that I felt like I might have to go home."

We went through the rest of the day watching Rhonda and Sherri doing their best to win Bobbie Watson's affections. You could tell by the way Bobbie was acting that he really enjoyed the attention he was getting from the two girls known as the junkyard dogs. He had to have known what these two girls were up to.

Two days later, Aimee brought a newspaper clipping with her. It was an obituary of the woman we had seen at the café. It stated that Mrs. Hernandez lost her battle with stomach cancer. This made Carol and Cindy believe that Alexis was able to feel how sick Mrs. Hernandez was. Alexis read the obituary.

"I knew that woman was terminally ill. I was afraid to say anything because I didn't want you guys to think I was a freak."

After that Cindy and Carol avoided Bobbie like the plague and trusted Alexis more that ever. We would wait for Alexis to do her ceremony.

# A Dance Announcement

A week after Bobbie arrived; Rhonda and Sherri wore sexy tops and mini skirts. Both girls were still hanging all over Bobbie Watson. Rhonda and Sherri tried to share more than just English and history class with Bobbie. Both girls had some of their classes changed, just so they could share the same lunch break with him. In the cafeteria, we sat in the far corner. It was really amusing to watch Rhonda and Sherri with Bobbie.

"Hey, look, Rhonda is hand feeding Bobbie," said Carol.

"For his sake, I hope she washed her hands," said Cindy.

"You guys are disgusting," said Aimee.

"Oh my God! This is like watching a raunchy movie," said Carol and we all started laughing.

"Yuck! Did he just lick her finger?" Cindy asked, scrunching up her face in disgust.

To me, it was almost sickening.

"Will you guys quit watching them?"

The five minute warning bell rang and we got up to go to class. Just as we walked into chemistry, the principal's voice came over the PA:

"Attention, senior students. Mrs. Dorian would like all seniors to report to the cafeteria at 2:30 this afternoon. She would like to make a small presentation concerning your prom. That's

2:30 for all senior students in the cafeteria. Thank you for your cooperation."

At the designated time, the seniors marched into the cafeteria. The chatter and laughter was a little louder than usual. We were animated, probably because we all knew prom meant the end of our time in this building. You could feel the sudden gust of excitement in many of the students.

Some - maybe even most - of the students applauded as Mrs. Dorian walked into the cafeteria. Mrs. Dorian put up her hand, and we understood it was time to be quiet.

"Okay, guys… I mean… Okay, ladies and gentlemen," Mrs. Dorian started. "We have a couple things to go over. First, a student from Montgomery High School went missing two days ago. We have a request from the school. They're hoping our students will help with the search. If anyone would like to help, please sign up at the office."

She didn't even pause before moving right on to the next topic.

"Second, we desperately need to get a prom committee formed today. I know it's your first full day back after exams, but - believe me - the remainder of the school year is going to go by rather quickly. Generally, the committee is chosen by vote, and that seems to have worked well in the past. So do we have anyone who would like to start the nominations?"

Before anyone could raise their hand to make a nomination, Cindy stood up on a chair and cleared her throat.

"Alright, listen, attention everyone. I just want everyone to remember that this prom is for all of us. This is our time to celebrate what we've accomplished in the past four years. This should mean something to each one of us. I would like it better – no, I think it would be better if everyone in this cafeteria contributed."

The entire room began clapping and cheering loudly.

Mrs. Dorian suggested the committee start by holding an event to raise money for the prom, a dance, maybe.

"Okay, Cindy," Mrs. Dorian said. "Take the reins. Do you have any ideas as to how we should plan this dance?"

"Yes," said Cindy. "We have so many students here who are musically inclined. Why should we hire a band when these students can show off their talents?"

The room filled with clapping and cheers again.

"That sounds really good," said Mrs. Dorian, "So how many students here want to form our Spring Dance Band?"

Several students raised their hands and Mrs. Dorian took out her pen and began writing.

"Okay, Jose Lopez what instrument do you play?"

"The drums," said Jose.

"Marty Flesher, what instrument do you play?"

"Guitar," said Marty.

"Lacey Smith, what instrument do you play?'

"Tambourine and vocals."

"Brit Walker, what instrument do you play?"

"Guitar."

"Sam Taylor, what instrument do you play?"

"Keyboard," said Sam.

"Jessie Lewis, what instrument do you play?"

"Saxophone," the response came, from the back of the room.

"Kirby Jones, what instrument do you play?"

"I don't play, but I'm good on vocals," said Kirby

"Bridgette Wilson, what instrument do you play?"

"Just vocals," said Bridgette

"I'm sorry; I don't know your name," Mrs. Dorian said to someone up front, who we could not see.

"Bobbie Watson," said the guy with the soft spoken voice.

"Okay, Bobbie Watson, what instrument do you play?"
"Guitar," said Bobbie.

"Okay so this is going to be our Spring Dance Band," Mrs. Dorian said, glancing around the room to make sure she didn't miss any raised hands. "And Cindy, I hope you'll sing some Cindy Lauper for us!"

"Well of course!" Cindy answered, smiling. "I wouldn't want to disappoint anyone."

And the clapping and cheering and hooting were heard out in the hallways.

"Okay," said Mrs. Dorian "Everyone I just listed as our band members, you guys are dismissed from the rest of this meeting. Go see Ms. Hall in the music room and give her this note. She'll give you instruments if you don't have your own. The auditorium will be open in 20 minutes for you guys to start practicing. All music choices must be cleared with Ms. Hall and me, and she'll be your supervisor in the auditorium."

As the band members gathered their belongings and headed for the door, Mrs. Dorian told them they would be allowed to practice in the auditorium during lunch break and after school.

Mrs. Dorian then began to address the rest of us.

"I think, like Cindy said the rest of you should get together and discuss what the theme for this dance should be. Then come up with decorating ideas, posters, invitations, food, drinks and whatever else you would like to have. Once you have every thing down on paper, please come see me for approval. One more thing, you have 20 minutes so get started. Oh, one more important note, this dance should be open to all high school students, okay, not just the senior class. Thank you for your time and let's strive for an excellent dance."

As Mrs. Dorian walked out of the cafeteria, Cindy stood up on a chair.

"Alright, let's hear some theme ideas."

"Red carpet gala," said Toni.

"Hollywood nights," said Carrie.

"Casino Royale," said Todd.

"Reach for the stars," said Beth.

"Blast from the past," said Larry.

"Does anyone else have any other suggestions? Going once, twice, three times... Alright," yelled Cindy.

Cindy got five sheets of paper from her notebook and wrote down one theme on each sheet. She put the five papers on a table, and asked everyone to vote for one by writing their name on its page. A few minutes later, Cindy collected the papers and started counting.

"Okay, listen, our Spring Dance theme will be Hollywood Nights. I want everyone to bring baked goods in on Friday for a bake sale. All the money raised will be used to purchase props."

As soon as Cindy was done with her speech, just about everyone in the cafeteria stood up and cheered for Cindy. Cindy was in her glory, she just loves being in charge of events. This afternoon's announcement put a spark into every senior student. It didn't seem like there was a student in the cafeteria that wasn't smiling or beaming with excitement.

# *Event Planning*

For the next few days, we couldn't find Cindy at home. She spent her evenings at the library or on her home computer doing research on other school dances and themes. Whenever one of us called her at home, she had her mom tell us she was busy and that she'd call us when she was free.

On Thursday morning, Cindy came to school with a small binder full of papers. She seemed to be in a hurry to meet with Mrs. Dorian, probably to give her an update or get her work approved.

We watched Cindy as she went dashing to Mrs. Dorian's office.

"I'll see you guys in class," Cindy blurted out as she rushed by us.

Alexis, Aimee and I went over to Carol's locker.

Jeff Morales was talking to her, and it looked like he was showing her a document of some sort.

"Hi Jeff, Hi Carol," I said.

"Hi, Emma you look awesome today," Jeff said rather nervously. "Oh, thanks Jeff."

"Holy shit man. Can I tell them the news?" Carol asked.

"Tell us what?" Aimee asked and Jeff nodded.

"Jeff just got accepted to MIT."

"I'm so happy for you," I said as I gave him a hug.

"Congratulation, that's great news," Alexis said as she hugged him.

"Wow, that's awesome news! When did you get your acceptance letter?" Aimee asked, and she also hugged him.

"My mom gave me it yesterday after school."

The five minute bell rang, and we went walking into our English class. We could hear Cindy's platform heels out in the hall.

"Hey, girlfriends, Mrs. Dorian said she would look over my dance portfolio and that she would make an announcement some time this morning or maybe right after lunch," said Cindy gasping for air.

A few minutes after our pledge and morning prayers were done; Mrs. Dorian announced that a senior meeting would take place at 2:30 in the cafeteria for all seniors except band members. We all looked at Cindy with shock and surprise that Cindy's portfolio was already approved.

"What did you have in your portfolio, the Presidential inaugural ball event?" asked Carol and we all laughed.

"You'll have to wait for Mrs. Dorian's announcement," said Cindy.

"Ah, come on, just give us a little hint," said Carol.

"Not a chance," Cindy replied, grinning.

When Bobbie Watson walked into class, he was escorted by Rhonda and Sherri. They hovered around his desk until the teacher told them to take their seats. It's been almost a week since Bobbie came to our school and both Rhonda and Sherri were still trying to win Bobbie's affections. Maybe he was holding out on the both of them because he knew what kind of girls they were. Usually, those two would stop hanging around with a guy once they got what they wanted. After that, they'd have no use for them, except maybe when they couldn't find a date. That's the only time they'll hit on the same guy twice. Most of the guys at our school dislike what they put them through.

At 2:30, we gathered in the cafeteria and Mrs. Dorian updated everyone about Cindy's research and portfolio.

"To make this much easier, the papers will be in the following order. The first sheet of paper will be for the food and drinks. If you think that you can contribute some type of food item and drinks then put your name on this paper. Also list the food or drink that you will be bringing. For example, write large bag of plain chips. This way we won't have ten bags of plain chips. The next sheet is for posters, flyers and class invitation. The next paper is for props. This sheet already has a list of props that will be needed so just put your name next to what ever item you have or might be able to find. The last paper is for decorating. We will need those individuals to organize all the props and be creative in decorating," said Mrs. Dorian.

She asked all students to look over the papers and write down their names where they felt they could help.

"When you are done, you are free to leave for the day. Oh, where is Cindy?" said Mrs. Dorian.

"I'm right here," said Cindy.

"You did an excellent job gathering all this information," said Mrs. Dorian

"Thanks," said Cindy.

"The new band members have been practicing for a week now. Don't you think you should go practice with them?"

"Sure," said Cindy.

We walked over to the auditorium giggling and complimenting Cindy for her work on the dance. As we neared the auditorium, we could hear the melodies coming from the auditorium. The thumping put a big smile on our faces.

"Wow they sound pretty good," said Carol.

"Yeah, I'm really getting into the mood," said Cindy.

"This is so exciting," I said with my hands over my lips.

Alexis didn't say a word. She just followed behind us as we walked into the back of the auditorium. We all sat in the last row of seats by the door and watched as Cindy went walking up to the front.

We all started clapping and cheering when the song ended.

"You guys are awesome!" yelled Cindy.

"So, Cindy, are you ready to join us?" asked Ms. Hall

"Well…" said Cindy

"Ah, come on, Cindy," Mrs. Hall said. "Just one song. I'm not taking no for an answer."

"I just stopped by to see how everything was going. I think you guy should get all your songs down and maybe in a couple of weeks I can stop by to practice," said Cindy.

"So which songs do you want us to practice?" asked Ms. Hall.

"I'll leave that up to you, Ms. Hall. Just make sure it's the upbeat ones," laughed Cindy.

"Sure we can do that, but I want you to come up here right now and sing a song for us," said Ms. Hall.

"Oh, alright then," said Cindy, walking toward the stairs up to the stage.

We all knew Cindy didn't need practice. Ms. Hall told the band to follow her and they began playing a tune of Cindy's favorite artist. We all watched as Cindy held the microphone with both hands and sang her heart out. Within seconds she was moving her body to the rhythm of the song. Carol and Aimee stood up and began singing along with Cindy. Alexis and I just sat there clapping along with the beat. When the song ended, we all stood up and cheered. Even the band members were clapping and hooting.

"Well done. Well done," said Ms. Hall.

"Thank you, Ms. Hall and you guys too," said Cindy as she pointed to the band.

"So we'll see you in a couple of weeks," said Ms. Hall.

"Yeah, I'll see you guys," said Cindy as she walked off the stage.

As Cindy approached us, she had this huge smile on her face.

"Wow, when I sing, it makes me want to go dancing," she said.

We all took turns giving her hugs and telling her how great she was. It's not that we had to tell her that, she already knew she could impersonate Cindy Lauper. She didn't have to go to college to find an excellent job. All she would have to do is go to Las Vegas and perform.

As we went down the hall Carol said, "Oh my god, did you see how hot Ms. Hall is?"

"Yeah, Ms. Hall is gorgeous," said Aimee.

"Did you see the tattoos on her arms?" asked Cindy.

"Yeah, she could pass for a Native American," said Carol.

"She is a Native American. I talked to her last year when she started teaching here and she told me she's from the Wounded Knee area. No the Pine Ridge reservation," said Alexis.

"Yeah, I remember her telling us in music class how hard her life had been on the reservation," said Cindy.

"She is probably one of the best music teachers this school's ever had," said Carol.

"Yeah, Ms. Hall's music students are going to China to perform this spring," said Aimee.

"Oh, wow, that's great," said Cindy.

"Well, it sounds like we are going to have some rocking dance party," said Aimee.

"Hey, Alexis did you do that fire thing that you said you were going to do?" asked Cindy.

"No. Not yet," Alexis answered. "My mom said we have to wait for the right moon before we can start the fire ceremony."

"So when do you think that will happen?" asked Cindy.

"Next Wednesday night," Alexis said. "My parents and I are going to the reservation. Sometimes it'll take just a few hours and other times it could take all night to get the answers."

"So if you're not here on Thursday, you'll let us know by e-mail?" said Cindy.

"You know I will."

"I heard he's already dating a girl in my math class," said Aimee.

"I thought he was seeing Rhonda or Sherri" I said.

"I think he's just hanging out with them. I think he overheard the guys talk about how easy they are," said Alexis.

"Yeah, I heard he's dating Missy," said Cindy.

"Her name is Missy Hart," said Aimee.

"What is she, hard up?" said Carol.

We all burst out laughing and pushing Carol around.

"Gees, Carol that was nice!" said Cindy.

"It just popped into my head," said Carol.

"Missy's really pretty," said Aimee.

"Ah, I shouldn't have said that, I couldn't help myself, it just popped out," said Carol.

In the parking lot, Aimee told us she had received two acceptance letters. One was from UCLA and the other from St. Lawrence University in New York. She told us the letters arrived sometime before lunch and her mom had sent her a text with the news. We were all excited and happy for her. We all said our usual goodbyes and Alexis offered me a ride home. When I got home, I found two acceptance letters. One was from Brown University and the other from St. Lawrence University. I was so excited, I ran up to my room to call Alexis. Just as I got to my room, the house phone rang. It was Alexis.

"I've got my acceptance letters. One's from UCLA, the other is from Brown University and the last one is from St. Lawrence University."

"I've got my letters as well. It's the same as yours except for UCLA."

"I'll call you right back," Alexis said.

She got a hold of Cindy and Carol and we had a conference call. Aimee did not answer the phone. We all shared the news. We decided to wait at least a month or so before we made our final decision.

# *Bad Feelings*

The day before the fire ceremony, Alexis sent me an e-mail asking if she could stop over to talk around 6 p.m. I told her it was okay for her to stop over.

I did all my homework and after dinner I cleaned up the kitchen. Then I told my mom that Alexis was coming over for a visit.

"Just send her to my room when she gets here," I said.

"Alright," said Mom.

At 6 o'clock I heard the doorbell ring. I listened as Alexis and my mom greeted each other and Mom told her that I was in my room. Alexis came to my room and we gave each other our normal hug. Then I asked her what was going on.

She told me that she saw something unusual. I couldn't understand what Alexis was talking about. Her cultural beliefs were way out there. It was like listening to a scary story. Certain things she talked about couldn't happen in the real world. It sounded more like make believe.

She explained that Ms. Hall had asked her to go to the music room to get some music notes she had left on her desk. When she took the music notes to Ms. Hall, she witnessed Bobbie Watson's guitar pull on Ms. Hall's hair. Once she got home, she explains what she had witnessed to her parents and they called Ms. Hall.

Alexis and her parents agreed that Bobbie purposely pulled on her hair. They also believe that his true intention behind his action would be confirmed soon. I lived in a different world from Alexis and Bobbie. They both seem like they belong in my world but their world included premonitions, illusions, ceremonies for the life and the darker one that destroys.

"I'm a little lost. I don't understand any of this."

"Well, it's just a hunch, but we think that he might be into some sort of craft."

"What?" I said.

"It's just a hunch," said Alexis.

"What do you mean by craft, is that bad?" I asked.

"Yes, I know this sounds strange, but this kind of stuff is real," said Alexis.

"Wow," was all I could get out?

We were both silent for a while. Then Alexis told me everything Ms. Hall had told her. Going back to the day when the Spring Dance Band was formed, Bobbie had been stalking Ms. Hall. He'd wander into the music room when he knew she was alone. According to Ms. Hall, one time at lunch break she was playing the piano and he walked in, sat next to her, and started playing along with her. She didn't like it that he always tried to get to close to her.

"Oh my God! That's creepy," I said.

"Yeah, I guess a couple of days ago he found her in the music room and asked her to go on a date with him. She told him it's against policy for a teacher to date a student," said Alexis.

"I can't believe he's that bold," I said.

"Ms. Hall said ever since they started practicing together, he's been trying to get close to her. She said when they're on stage, he's always trying to touch her arms, her back and her hair," said Alexis.

"I thought Bobbie was dating Missy and having a blast with Rhonda and Sherri," I said.

"Well, all I can say is this guy is strange. Today, Ms. Hall told me that while she was in the music room, Bobbie walked in and went over the piano where Ms. Hall was and he stood behind her and told her that he loved her music. Then when she got up, he pushed her against the piano and tried to kiss her," said Alexis.

"Oh my god, he's deranged," I said.

"Yeah, Ms. Hall said she tries real hard not to let him see that she's afraid of him," said Alexis.

"So this Fire Ceremony will tell us what kind of person he is?" I asked.

"Yeah, Ms. Hall and I can't wait for the Fire Ceremony to be over. Anyway, I better get home," said Alexis.

I walked Alexis to her car and gave her a hug and told her I would see her at school tomorrow. Then I watched as Alexis pulled out of my driveway and we waved to each other.

Later that night, I told my mother I didn't feel well and went to bed early. I think I was just upset about everything Alexis had told me. Soft relaxing music is what I needed to relax. I reached for my iPod and knocked it off the nightstand. Fumbling, I turn on my light and looked behind my nightstand. My iPod had fallen on top of my journal. There was a layer of dust on it. The last time I had written or touched the journal was the day after New Years. I searched through my iPod, and put in the ear pieces. I thought about reading my journal, but the soft music took my thoughts back to my Dad's wedding. Instead of reading the journal, I put it back on the nightstand and turned off the lights. I tried to picture myself slow dancing.

That night, I had a vivid dream. I was riding in a car with Cindy and Carol, or people I thought were Cindy and Carol. It was a bright sunny day and we were talking about the upcoming dance. Cindy was talking about having her hair bleached lighter just for this dance. I remember looking out the window and noticing we were heading toward San Francisco, or a place that looked like it. Then all of a sudden the sun disappeared behind clouds. The clouds got darker and darker. Big rain drops started falling. I could hear tires squealing and the car started spinning out of control. Suddenly there was a huge bang, and the car was heading down a small hill. At the bottom of the hill, I could hear a loud splash, as the car dropped into a river below. I could feel something warm running down my face and water seeping into the car. I tried to scream Cindy and Carol's names, but no sound would come out of my mouth. I tried to scream again. This time, it felt like there was tape across my lips preventing me from screaming out. I could hear myself moaning and I started to tell myself that I was dreaming. Finally, I was able to open my eyes. Immediately, I began gasping for air, like I had been holding my breath under water.

When I finally realized that it was just a dream, I began to cry. I looked over at my clock radio and it was just 10 o'clock. I finally got control of myself and walked into the bathroom to wash my face. I came out of the bathroom just as my mom was walking by the doorway. Startled, I screamed.

"I thought you were in bed?" my mom said.

"I was asleep. I had a bad dream and just got up to wash my face," I told her.

"Ah, Emma, do you want something to help you sleep?" asked my concerned mom.

"No, that's okay, I'll be alright. I think I'll read a book until I get tired," I said.

"Goodnight, Emma. I'll see you in the morning," said mom as she gave me a hug and kissed my forehead.

"Night, Mom. I'll see you in the morning," I said.

When I went back into my room, I went over to my bookshelf and read over the titles. Then I decided to write down my dream while I still remembered it.

After I wrote about my dream, I read over my journal entry about the dream I had back in January. Certain parts of that dream were jumping out at me. It was then that I realized who the guy in my dream was. It was Bobbie Watson I saw in the library, and it was him standing in the meadow. The other guy with the braid hanging over his shoulder was Alexis' cousin Sky.

Now I knew why Sky looked so familiar to me that first time we met. I started remembering the day I met Sky. I remembered telling Alexis that we had to talk about her cousin. She purposely avoided that conversation by arriving 20 minutes after Aimee. She knew if we didn't talk about it that I would forget, and I did. Now, I needed some answers. I called Alexis on her cell phone. Her phone was busy. I tried again and it was still busy. I took a sheet of paper from my notebook and wrote myself a note to call Alexis in the morning.

It was almost 1 o'clock and Alexis' cell phone was still busy. I fixed my pillow, turned off the lights and covered myself.

In the morning, my mom called my name several times before I woke up. I sat up in bed real slow and looked at my mom.

"Emma, are you alright?" she asked.

"Mom, I don't feel so well," I told her as I dropped my head back on the pillow.

I lied; I was too tired to get up.

"Do you want me to call the school and have you excused for today?" she asked.

"No, Mom that's okay, I'll just get bored if I'm home alone. I'll be fine," I told her.

"Well, as soon as you're ready come downstairs, I'll have breakfast ready," said my concerned mom.

"I'll be down in a little bit," I told her.

It took every ounce of energy I had to get myself dressed. I grabbed my toast and put jam on one piece of it and started chewing it slowly and I took small sips of my orange juice. In an instant, the orange juice was turning in my stomach. I jumped up and went running into the bathroom. I never should've lied to my Mom about being sick. Now I was really sick.

"Emma, you're staying home today. I'll call the school and let them know you're not feeling well." yelled my mom from the kitchen.

I just couldn't say anything to her as I struggled to bring up the last bit of my toast.

"It's all taken care of, I called the school and I let them know you won't be in. Go back to bed Emma, we're leaving. I'll see you after work," said mom.

As soon as my mom, Jamie and Ashley left, I went back to my room. I got back in bed and turned on the TV. I flipped through the channels until I found the Discovery Channel. It was a show on tornados. How lucky can one get? Our report will be due in a few weeks, so I took notes. When the show was over, I decided to watch a movie. I looked through the stack of movies I had and pulled "The General's Daughter" from the stack. The movie was just starting when the phone rang. I got up and turned off the TV and went to answer the phone.

"Hello," I said.

"Emma, are you alright?" asked Alexis.

"Yeah, I got sick to my stomach this morning and my mom told me to stay home. Hey, I had a nightmare last night and I remembered every last detail of it," I told her.

She knew I didn't often remember dream details, so she shared my surprise.

"Did it have anything to do with a car going into the river?" she asked jokingly.

Then there was a bit on silence.

"Why did you say that? I said in a very surprised voice. "Alexis, what is going on? How do you know about my dream?" I asked in an overly surprised voice.

"Emma, I was just joking. I had no idea that we might've had the same dream," she said.

"That can't be possible, right!" I said.

"I'm on my way to see my mom at work and then I'll stop over right after," she said.

"Okay, I'll see you in a little bit," said Alexis.

I sat back on my bed and put both hands on top of my head wondering how two people could have the exact same dream. My mind was shifting back to the dream and to the moment when I was unable to scream. This was a frightening feeling not be able to yell and to think that Alexis and I both had this horrible dream at the same time. I took my journal and the movie "The General's Daughter." and I decided to watch the movie in the living room, that way I would hear when Alexis arrived. I got all the way to the part where the murderer lured the female investigator to a field buried with black Betties, when I heard the door bell ring. I pushed the pause button and walked over to open the door. As I opened the door, I saw Alexis leaning against the house. She turned to me with a small smile on her face.

"Hi Emma… Wow, you really look sick," she said.

"Quit teasing. I really was sick. Are you going to come in or are you going to just stand and poke fun at me?" I said and we laughed. Alexis and I talked about our dream. We both realized that we had the exact dream at the exact time.

"Can I use your computer?" she asked.

We went into the den and I turned the computer on.

Alexis clicked on the Internet Explorer and the Google screen popped up. Then Alexis typed in "mutual dreaming." A page popped up and Alexis clicked on mutual dreams. Two people can have the exact dream, at the exact same time by some form a telepathic activity. Then Alexis typed in certain parts of our dream. Each one of the interpretation was positive. For example dreaming of an accident means anxieties and fears. To dream of the river symbolizes peace and prosperity and to dream of friends' means that good news is coming.

"So, as scary as the dream was it all means that good things will happen," I said.

"Yes," said Alexis.

"Do you think we had this dream because of what we were talking about last night?" I asked.

"I don't know."

"I tried calling you last night after I recorded that dream. It was the first time I had a dream since you gave me that journal. I wanted to tell you that I realized that Bobbie was that guy in the library, and he was the one in the meadow, where Sky and I were.

"I think you should come to the fire with us."

"Alexis, I don't understand anything about that. Isn't your tribe's culture sacred?"

"It is sacred. Besides, you're more involved than you realize. You're the one who had the premonition of Bobbie long before I knew something wasn't right with him. Come with us."

"I don't know. I would go if I understood more about sacred fires and how these things worked," I told her.

"Okay, I'll explain it as we go," said Alexis. "If you have any questions, just ask."

From what Alexis told me, there are vision fires, healing fires, letting go fires, and fires for the dead. She also explained that before a sacred fire can begin, the ground must be blessed. The spirits from the four directions – fire, water, air and earth - would be called to protect the ground and those who set foot on it. She told me Sky had an important role. He's in charge of the young men's society.

Though she didn't say much about the society, she said all the young men respected Sky and followed his orders. When we entered the camp fire area, we would have to smudge ourselves with sage. The smudging helps to release bad energies from the body, mind and soul.

All I really needed to do was smudge, listen and not refuse any food or drink, Alexis said.

"Can you explain how they bless the ground?" I asked.

"Do you remember Sky?" asked Alexis as she looked at the floor.

"I don't know if I'll recognize him, I only saw him for a few minutes, and it was over a month ago. We were supposed to talk about him, remember?" I said.

"Yeah, I'm sorry about that. When we met at the shopping plaza, I didn't want you two to meet. I didn't want your premonition

71

to happen. He's the one who asked Hunter to introduce him to you."

Alexis continue to explain how they blessed the ground. Sky would put tobacco in one of the four directions. Then he would put sage in the opposite direction. Cedar would be placed between the tobacco and sage. Finally he would put sweet grass across from the cedar and then he would call out to our spirit protectors to watch over the sacred fire. The sacred fire is always in the center.

"So Sky and Hunter will be at the fire later?" I asked.

"Yeah, they'll be watching the fire when we go up the hill, to what we call sacred ground," she said.

"So what time is this Fire Ceremony taking place?" I asked.

"My mom and I are heading to the rez at 4 o'clock. My dad and the guys are already getting the fire started. The ceremony itself will start around five," said Alexis.

"Oh," I said.

"Emma, come with us," said Alexis.

Then after a few moments of silence, she spoke again.

"What is it? Are you afraid?" asked Alexis.

"Well, yeah, it's a whole different world to me."

"Yeah, but you know what? You'll have a better understanding of everything if you're there and you see things first hand," said Alexis very calmly.

"I don't think that my mom will let me go since I missed school today," I told her.

"I can talk to your mom if you want," said Alexis.

"I'll call her. What should I tell her?" I asked.

"Just tell her we're doing a Fire Ceremony and would like you to participate. There's no need to lie," said Alexis.

"Gosh, I wish I had as much confidence as you have," I said.

"Is that supposed to be a compliment or are you selling yourself short again?" Alexis asked.

I grabbed the cordless phone and dialed my mom's work phone number. Once the phone started ringing, I walked into the kitchen. When Mom got on the phone, I told her that Alexis and her family were doing a Fire Ceremony and they wanted me to attend. I never realized how cool and understanding my mom really was. She really liked Alexis and thought that it would be great for me to learn something about the Native American heritage. When I first became friends with Alexis, my mom told me I would learn a lot from her. She told me to thank Alexis for the invitation.

Wow, I was just amazed by my mother. I always knew she was outspoken when it came to protecting or defending Native American culture or its people.

I walked back into the den and told Alexis I had permission to go and everything was cool with my mom.

"Alright, you need to put your sweats and sneakers on, and bring a sweatshirt or a warm jacket, just in case it gets chilly on the hill," Alexis said.

At first, I just stared at Alexis. I couldn't believe my mother allowed me to participate in something very few get to experience.

Finally, I went running up to my room to change into my sweats and sneakers. I grabbed a sweatshirt and took my windbreaker out of the closet. The whole time, I kept telling myself I had nothing to worry about. I knew that as long as I was around Alexis, I would be safe.

# The Ceremony

When we got to the reservation, we drove past the Nokomis Road and parked along the side of the road, behind several other cars. We walked a short distance to where a group of young men had gathered. They all were very handsome. They had long straight black hair. Only a few of them had their hair in pony tails.

"Hey there!" yelled out one of the guys.

I looked over but I didn't recognize any of them.

"Hi, Hunter," said Alexis.

"Hey, Alexis, nice to see you again," yelled one of the guys by the fire.

"Hey, Justin, nice to see you too," said Alexis.

"Hey, Sky, do you remember my friend Emma?" asked Alexis, as we walked over to the camp fire.

"Ah, sort of," said Sky.

"Alright, pay attention this time. Emma, this is my cousin Sky, and this handsome one over here is Hunter, and that guy with the firewood is Justin," said Alexis.

"Hi, ah, Emma," said Justin.

"Hey, Emma," said Sky.

"Hey, Emma," said Hunter.

"Hi Justin, Hi Hunter, Hi Sky. See if you would have come to watch movies with us, we probably would have remembered each other," I said as we all shook hands and Alexis and I laughed.

"Well, we could go to the movies tomorrow if you want," said Sky teasing back.

"Are you hitting on Emma?" asked Alexis and everyone started laughing again.

"I'm trying to make up for missing her first movie offer," said Sky.

"Yeah, he's hitting on you," said Alexis.

"So you guys better get going up the hill," said Sky.

"You guys aren't coming with us?" I asked.

"Oh, no, we're the Fire Keepers. We need to make sure that no one tries to disrupt the Fire Ceremony," said Sky.

"Yeah, we have to stay here until the ceremony is done. That's how it works," said Hunter.

"Oh, wait a minute. You guys need to smudge before you go any further," said Sky.

"Hey Sky! What happen? Did the pretty girl make you absent minded?" yelled Justin.

The rest of the guys sitting around the small fire began laughing and teasing Sky. I followed Alexis and her mom, Misty, as they walked toward the small fire. Alexis bent her head toward a small burning shell and started moving the smoke over her face and then over her head. I watched closely as she moved the smoke around her arms and around her legs. Then Misty did the same thing with the smoke. While Misty was doing her smudge, Alexis began explaining the process to me. I pulled the smoke toward my face and followed the steps that Alexis and Misty did.

"You two can go up the hill. I'll wait for Summer," said Misty.

Alexis put her arm through mine and we went walking up the hill.

As soon as we entered the clearing, I noticed a pole with a red strip of fabric hanging from it. I nudged Alexis.

"What's that?" I asked, gesturing to the fabric.

"Look straight ahead," she said, quietly. "There's a pole with a black strip of fabric on it, and over there is a yellow strip of fabric. There is a white strip on that pole. Those colors were put on those poles when Sky blessed the ground for the ceremony. He also placed sage, cedar, sweet grass and sacred tobacco on the ground by the poles. You are now walking on sacred ground," said Alexis.

"Wow, this is so educational," I told her.

Alexis laughed and grabbed me by the arm and walked me toward the fire.

Around the fire were several old wooden benches. There was an elderly man and an elderly woman sitting on the bench. There were two other men standing by a small pile of wood. One of them was Alexis' dad, Alex.

"Hey, dad," called out Alexis.

"Hey, baby girl," said Alex.

"Hi, Emma, how you doing?" asked Alex.

"I'm doing okay," I said, as we gave each other a hug.

"Come sit over here," said Alex as he led me and Alexis to the bench. This is Chip Otter; he is a very well respected medicine man. Chip walked over and reached for my hand.

"Hello, Emma, it's good to meet you," said Chip.

"Hi, Chip, it's a pleasure to meet you," I said to Chip as I shook his hand lightly. Chip pulled me toward him and gave me a hug. Then Chip pointed to the woman sitting across from him and said "This is my wife, Sara." Sara was wearing a long skirt, boots and a homemade wool sweater. She stood up and walked around the fire.

"Hi, Emma," said Sara, hugging me. "We have heard a lot about you from Alexis. I'm glad to finally meet you."

"I'm pleased to meet you, too," I said.

As soon as I let go of Sara, I heard voices. I turned toward the edge of the woods. It was Ms. Hall and Misty coming over toward the fire.

"Hey, Summer, you made it," said Alex, as he hugged Ms. Hall.

I looked at Alexis and said, "I didn't know that was her name."

Alexis bumped me in the arm.

"You're so cute."

I watched as Ms. Hall greeted everyone there and gave them hugs. When she finally got to me she said, "So you're Emma Niles."

"Yes," I said.

"It's really nice to meet you. Away from school you can call me Summer," she said.

"I'll try to remember that," I said.

"Okay, it's almost 5 o'clock. Shall we get started?" said Chip.

We all took a seat around the fire. Chip stood up and opened a leather pouch. He began with this loud yell that sounded like "ho." His yell echoed of the hill top. Then he put his hand into the leather pouch and took out something and slowly put it into the fire. As he was doing this he began speaking in his own language. Every time he put this stuff into the fire, the flames grew in a quick burst.

As I was staring at the fire, I thought I saw a wolf and a bear deep within the burning wood. I had to blink my eyes a couple of times. I thought I was hallucinating. When Chip finished speaking to the fire, his wife, Sara, got up and picked up a cooler and started passing out some tea for us to drink. It had a really bitter taste to it. I didn't want to be disrespectful, so I drank it.

Whatever was in this tea was making my heart race. Each time I blinked my eyes, I saw Bobbie Watson's face flash across the burning fire. I looked at Alexis.

"Just go with it," she said, smiling calmly. "Don't panic and everything we need to know about Bobbie Watson will be revealed."

Once everyone was done drinking their tea, Sara stood up and cleared her voice to speak.

"Emma, I know you are new to this Fire Ceremony, so I will explain some of it. This tea is a very powerful medicine. It will help you and the rest of us to see what kind a bad energy this young man at your school has with him. So, don't panic when you see this young man's face. We will all see the exact visions. Okay?" said Sara.

"Yes," I said.

"If at anytime you start feeling anxious, just lay down next to the fire, alright?" said Sara.

"Okay," I said.

Within a few minutes, my head started spinning. I felt light headed. My body felt like it had the weight of a ton going down toward my legs. It almost felt like I was going paralyzed. I tried my hardest to keep my eyes focused on the fire. From the corner of my eye, I saw Ms. Hall hang her head down. Everything, including the fire, looked like it was moving in slow motion. Even the sound of my heart beat pounded in my chest was scary.

I slid off the bench and my body crashed to the ground below. I could see I was about a foot away from the fire, far enough away to keep me from getting burned. As I laid there with my eyes open, I saw Bobbie Watson standing in the hallway at school. He was talking to a girl who looked like she was a junior or sophomore. Standing just inches from the girl, I saw him put his hand on her left shoulder and he asked her, in a soft, sweet voice, to go to the movies. The girl seemed to be in some kind of trance as she stared into his eyes.

It seemed to me that this scene I was witnessing had not yet happened, but that it would in the near future.

Suddenly, the image changed.

I was standing in Ms. Hall's music room. I saw Ms. Hall standing by her desk holding a stack of papers. The door opened and Bobbie Watson walked in. He greeted Ms. Hall and walked over to her. They talked a little about the songs she had selected for the dance. He moved closer and closer to her until she was backed up against the wall. Bobbie put his hands on both sides of her shoulders. He asked Ms. Hall to go to the movies with him as he slowly pushed his body against hers.

Ms. Hall slipped under his arms and moved away from him.

"It's against policy for a teacher to date a student," Ms. Hall said.

Bobbie Watson stomped out of the room, slamming the door behind him.

As quickly as Bobbie Watson had walked out of the room, I was seeing another vision.

Cindy and Bobby were standing at the back of the auditorium looking through a stack of sheet music. Cindy had her back to Bobbie and was reading the papers. Bobbie started moving closer to Cindy.

Just as he got close enough to touch her, Cindy yells over to the band members and asks if they could play "Twilight Zone." Some of the band members yelled back that they could.

When Cindy went back to look through the stack of music, Bobbie walked over to Cindy again. This time he got real close to Cindy and asked her to go to out to dinner with him.

Cindy flashed her ring.

"If I wasn't engaged, I would definitely say yes." Again you could see the anger in Bobbie's eyes as he turned away from Cindy.

Another vision creeps in.

This time it's a dimly lit street. As I looked toward the darkness, I could see Bobbie Watson holding hands with a girl who couldn't be more than 16. I had never seen this girl's face anywhere at school before. I watched as he walked her to the front door. They stood there for a moment talking about the movie and their late dinner. This girl looked so young and innocent. While they were talking to each other, the front door opened and the girl's mother or babysitter opened the door. Bobbie gave the girl a kiss on the forehead, said goodnight and walked away.

As I watched him walk into the darkness, everything around me went black. I couldn't even see the fire, though I thought I was staring at it. I was trying to find the courage to scream at the top of my lungs, when I heard a girl's voice shriek and gasp for air. There were sounds like banging and thumping and the sounds of glass breaking. Something was going on with some girl but I couldn't tell what it was. I tried taking deep breaths, just to calm myself down. Then I saw the girl. She was lying on the hardwood floor, her face badly beaten with cuts on her forehead and across her nose. I could see the blood dripping down her nose, and her lips were puffed and cracked. Her right arm was twisted in an odd way, like it had been broken and her left arm lay above her head. I could see her night gown pulled up toward her chest with blood stains on it. I could also see that the girl's bed room window was still opened, like someone had come in or used it as an escape exit.

Once again the fire came into view, first it looked like a flicker from a lighter. Then it got brighter and bigger. Suddenly the fire was out and I heard a heavy downpour of rain. I waited for my body to start feeling the rain but not a drop was falling on me.

Then I heard a phone ring and Ms. Hall's voice so clearly said "hello."

She was telling the caller that she was just leaving the school dance and that she was on her way home.

"Everyone had a very good time. The students did an excellent job decorating, and you should have heard the band."

There was a bit of silence and then Ms. Hall continued. She named the caller and I knew she was talking to Misty. Ms. Hall lived outside of Santa Rosa in a small town near Bay View. She said she would probably make it home by midnight. Suddenly she gasped and swerved her Jeep to avoid a pedestrian in the middle of the road. That person on foot looked every bit like Bobbie Watson standing on the roadway. You could hear the tires squealing against the wet pavement as she braked and swerved from left to right and then went rolling end over end. Her Jeep landed heavily near another road. I could not see Ms. Hall in the vehicle. She must have been thrown out. Then I heard the moaning sounds. She was trapped under the Jeep. Blood was gushing out of her mouth. Again, I tried desperately to scream out loud, but my lips felt like they had been sealed shut. Every thing around me went black again, as the burning fire seemed to extinguish.

My body ached from the cold ground I was laying on. It seemed like hours had already passed, but in fact it was just minutes. I closed my eyes and tried to convince myself that I wasn't feeling any pain.

When I opened my eyes, there in front of the school, I saw my friends Cindy and Carol, along with their boyfriends. They were dressed in beautiful gowns and both Toby and JJ were wearing black tuxedoes. This couldn't be the spring dance because they weren't wearing a coat or a sweater. Then I saw Cindy, Carol, Toby and JJ getting into Cindy's Ford Taurus. They were all talking about the prom and what a great time they were having. Toby mentioned that he had brought some towels with him so that they could go skinny dipping at Bodega Harbor by the Doran City Park. I saw the road sign very clearly as they approached it. The arrow on the sign pointed to Doran City Park, 15 miles away. Cindy began driving a little bit faster once she started heading toward the park. Once again, just past the sign, there appeared a dark figure standing in the roadway. Cindy was driving a bit too fast and she wasn't paying attention to the road. Someone in the car, maybe JJ, yelled for her to slow down and watch out for the guy in the road. By the time Cindy noticed, it was too late. She turned the car hard into the opposite lane and struck the other car head on. The impact of the two cars sounded like an explosion. I couldn't see any movement from either of the two cars. Then suddenly, Cindy's car caught fire. Within minutes, both cars were engulfed in flames. The stench was horrendous. I could have sworn that I heard screams coming from one or both of the cars.

But the witnesses standing around were saying that everyone died on impact and the sounds were coming from the metal of the cars as they were being heated beyond extreme.

This was one of the most emotional visions I had seen. The tears were streaming down my cheeks as I lay on the ground. Still frozen in this state of illusion, I prayed for it to stop and for everything to end. I knew that my praying would not be answered just yet. The fire shot higher and burned brighter.

Suddenly it was complete darkness again, and I could hear someone crying. It sounded like it was coming from a distant tunnel. Slowly, the crying got louder and louder. I couldn't tell who it was, for it was too dark. When I finally heard the crying at its loudest, I was able to see the place where the girl was sitting. The weeping girl was sitting in my living room. I could hear my heart beating louder and my head throbbing in pain. Then suddenly I felt the need to turn and look at the girl who was in dire need of a hug. I wanted so much to turn and look at who was in my home and grieving out of control. It took me a while, to finally get the courage to turn and look. I felt my body drop to the floor in disbelief when I saw myself on the sofa. My head on my mothers lap. The look on my face was total shock. Why was this happening to me? For what - or for whom - am I grieving? Again, I wanted nothing more than to be at home in my bed, safely away from the bad things I knew I couldn't handle.

"Enough," I wanted to say. "Make this stop now, please."

All my inner pleading fell upon deaf ears.

Finally, I was looking directly into the burning fire. There stood Bobbie Watson. All dressed in black from head to toe. Why is he here in my visions, I thought. Then I watched as he pulled various shades of hair from his pockets. It seemed like he was standing outside somewhere. As soon as I was able to focus, I noticed he was standing in someone's backyard. He also had a small fire going. I watched him walk over toward a small stand with a large bowl on it. He placed the hair into the bowl and mixed whatever was in the bowl together with the hair. Suddenly he began chanting over and over and raising the bowl into the air. Throughout his chanting he mentions several names. Cindy and Ms. Hall's names were very recognizable. He then took a match, lit it, and held it to whatever was in the bowl. I also saw him as he spit on the ground after saying each name, including Cindy's and Ms. Hall's. With every spit he'd look up at the dark sky and laugh in a grotesque way. What kind of monster is this guy, I thought to my self.

"Enough! I've had enough," I kept telling myself.

Just as I was convincing myself, that all of this needed to stop. I began to choke on the smoke from the fire. Finally I was able to move my stiff body.

"Ah," I said, as I tried desperately to move my half frozen body to an upright position.

"Oh God, I had the most disturbing dreams," I said.

Sam and Alex stood up and came over to help me get back up on the bench.

"Okay, so now we know what we are dealing with," said Chip.

I looked over at everyone sitting around the fire. Truly confused by what Chip had just said.

"I don't understand. What are you talking about? I asked.

"Emma, the tea that we all shared gave us the ability to see the same visions, or dreams if you want to call it that," said Sara.

"Do you mean . . . you saw what I was seeing?" I asked.

"Yes," said Sara.

"You saw that girl?" I said.

"Yes," said Chip.

"Ms. Hall," I said in a shocked whisper.

"Yes, we saw that," said Sara.

I looked toward Ms. Hall to see if she needed comforting. But, Ms. Hall was staring at Misty. After a brief moment of silence, Chip got up and grabbed a book bag. He reached in and pulled out a bottle of water and asked if anyone wanted a drink.

Some nodded and others reached for the water without speaking. After Chip had passed the water around, he looked at Sara.

"So what are we going to do about this guy?"

I watched as Sara got up and went to sit next to Chip. They began to talk very quietly to each other. I couldn't understand a word they were saying. I had never been so freaked out in my entire 18 years of existence. I began trembling so hysterically that those sitting near me could hear my teeth chattering. Misty grabbed the blanket she was sitting on and wrapped it around me. Then she sat next to me and hugged me very tightly.

"It's going to be okay. Try to calm down. Take slow deep breaths," said Misty.

"I've never been to anything like this in my life. It's just so new to me. Can he be stopped?" I asked her in a low whisper.

"Yes," said Misty.

Then Alex kneeled down in front of me and said, "Don't worry, the good forces always overpower the evil forces."

"I hope so. I've never felt this much fear in my life," I said.

After I warmed up, I looked toward Ms. Hall. She had her arms resting on her legs and her hands reaching toward the fire.

"Ms. Hall, I mean Summer, are you alright?" I asked her.

Ms. Hall sat up straight and looked toward me.

"I'm fine. I just can't believe that this guy is capable of something like this. But, you know what? I'm not going to let this son of . . ."

"Ah, NO, don't say anything bad. Remember this is a sacred fire we're sitting at," said Chip.

"Sorry," said Ms. Hall.

"That's okay. I would feel the same way if someone wanted to harm me that way," said Chip.

"I just can't believe this, he comes into my room and he talks so sweet and innocent like a real gentleman," said Ms. Hall.

"You've been alone with him in your room?" asked Chip.

"Yeah, we just talk about music. He's really creative and could be a great musician," said Ms. Hall.

"Wow, I didn't know that," I said.

Chip and Sara continued to talk to each other. Finally Chip and Sara finished talking and Sara went back to the bench.

"Okay," said Chip. "We are going to pick some medicinal plants tomorrow and we'll gather here again, say about 5 o'clock and we'll bless the medicine pouches so you'll all be protected.

"Um, what time is it?" I asked.

"Well, let see, its 5:30," said Alex.

"Five thirty? It felt like we were here for hours," I said. And everyone started to laugh.

"Fire Ceremonies can throw you off a little if you're not used to them," said Chip.

"Do I have to be here?" I asked.

"It's best if you finish what you started. If you don't want to come all the way up here, at least be present at the entrance camp fire," said Sara.

"Yeah, that way you're fully protected," said Chip.

"Okay I'll be here," I said.

"So, does anyone have any questions before I close out the ceremony?" asked Chip.

We all sat there for a brief moment then Alexis raised her hand.

"Yes, Alexis, what is it?" asked Chip.

"Why did Bobbie and his mother move here and does his mother, um, is his mother just like him?" she asked.

Chip reached into his leather pouch again and took out a handful of tobacco and spoke in a whisper into the fire. Then he sat down on his bench and gazed into the fire. Finally after a few minutes he stood back up and said:

"I see his mother and it seems that she took a job here because she was most qualified to start up some program. No, I don't see her doing or having any of the bad qualities that her son has. This is what the fire is showing me. Any other questions?"

"If we have this medicine on us for protection, it will prevent the bad things from happening?" I asked.

85

"No. The things that are going to happen can't be stopped. The medicine we make for you will protect you from getting hurt. The only way someone will get hurt is if they lose, misplace or forget to wear their protection," said Chip.

"Oh," I asked.

"That's right," said Sara.

"I have one more question. Alexis and I both have a similar dream that we were riding in a car that went off the road and the car went into the river. What does this mean?" I asked.

Again Chip stood by the fire and spoke a few words and put his tobacco into the fire. A few minutes later he sat down.

"It doesn't mean you or Alexis will be involved in an accident. It just means that you will be going through a new change. That kind of dream has a lot of good meanings behind it," said Chip.

For the first time since I had gotten to the campfire and to Fire Ceremony on the hill, I felt relieved. I was even amazed at how Chip knew about the meaning of our dream and about Bobbies' mother.

"So any more questions?" asked Chip.

No one had anymore question for Chip, so he stood by the fire and gave thanks that we were able to have the same visions. He also asked the fire spirit to keep the vision in the fire so that it does not interfere with our sleep. Everyone stood up, and Chip went around and hugged everyone. Then Sara did the same and so on down the line. We all walked together down the hill to the camp fire. When we got back to the campfire, the boys were all messing around with each other.

"Hey you guys, this is Emma Niles, Emma this is Sky, this guy over her is Hunter, Justin is on the other side of Sky, Montana is the one putting wood in the fire, and this one is Doug," said Chip.

"Hi Emma" said each one of the guys. Then they all started laughing and poking at each other.

"Alexis already introduce us," I said.

"Hey, Uncle Chip, how'd it go up there?" asked Sky.

"Well, we got the answers we were looking for. Hey, I need a couple of guys to watch this fire all night, and we need the one on the hill started again tomorrow for 5 o'clock, Okay?" said Chip.

"Yeah, I'll make sure someone stays all night. Is it that bad?" asked Sky.

"Yeah, it seems that this man is pretty evil," said Chip.

"Hey, Emma, are you coming back tomorrow?" asked Sky.

"Ah, yeah, I am," I said.

"She's not sure yet, if she'll be going up the hill." Chip said.

"Cool, we'll keep you company if you decide not to go up the hill," said Sky in a voice that sounded almost excited.

I turned and gave Sky a quick look and he smiled. Alexis came to me and wrapped her arms around me.

"You're a guest here so come and have a seat over here."

She pushed me lightly down on the bench next to Sky.

"Come on you guys pass the fried bread and water around," said Chip.

"Its coming," said Misty.

"So you got freaked out?" asked Sky.

"I've never been through anything like that in my life" I said.

"So, do you know this guy?" asked Sky.

"He's in our English class. I've never talked to him so I don't know anything about him except what I saw in the fire," I said.

"Are you afraid of him?" asked Sky.

"I was a little before but now I'm terrified of him," I said.

"Don't be afraid of him. If you let him know how he makes you feel, he'll take away your inner power. Besides I won't allow anything to happen to you," Sky said, his voice trailing off into almost a whisper.

"You believe you can protect me from him?" I whispered back.

"That's part of my job, to lead and protect. We're nothing like that guy," whispered Sky.

"What are you two talking about?" asked Chip.

"I was just telling her that we're nothing like that guy from their school," said Sky.

Chip looked at me and said "these guys are really decent boys."

"Hey, Uncle, we're not boys, we're young men," said Sky.

The rest of the guys at the fire agreed that they were young men. While everyone ate their fried bread, Chip started to explain that the medicine they would pick would act like a magic shield. Tomorrow I would learn all about this different kind of magical medicine and get to spend more time with Sky.

We all sat around the campfire and listened to Chip tell stories about the medicine. As I sat there, I could feel the heat coming off Sky's body. I wanted so much to move closer to him. Then Ms. Hall and Misty asked if I could move over. I moved right up against Sky until the entire sides of our bodies were touching each other. Sky didn't move.

As Ms. Hall was eating her fried bread, she looked at me and said, "Are you still cold?"

I turned toward her and whispered, "not any more." Then I turned and looked toward Sky and saw him smile. I placed my bottled water between my feet and then I placed one hand between my knees to warm it. Slowly I slid the other hand between mine and Sky's leg. Then Sky turned to me and whispered, "Your hand is freezing."

"I know. You should have heard my teeth chattering up on the hill," I whispered back.

Sky grabbed my hand and held in between his. His hands were so warm! It didn't take long to warm up my hand.

"Hey, Emma, are you still freezing?" asked Chip.

"Not any more," I said, and everyone started laughing.

I pulled my other hand out from between my knees and looked at Sky.

"Here you might as well warm this one too."

Once again everyone but me and Sky started laughing. Sky reached for my cold hand while he held on to my warm hand. His warm hands were making my entire inside tingle with warmth. I didn't want this moment to end.

"So are you warmed up yet?" asked Sky as he smiled at me.

"If I say yes are you going to let my hands go?" I whispered.

"Do you want me to let them go?" whispered Sky.

"No I kind of like how it makes me feel inside," I whispered and Sky turned and looked me in the eyes.

"Me too." he whispered and we smiled at each other.

My heart was thumping so fast it was warming the rest of my body.

"Hey, Emma, are you ready to go?" asked Alexis.

"Say no," whispered Sky.

"I really don't want to go," I whispered to him as we both hung our heads toward each other and laughed.

"Yeah, I'm ready if you are," I said to Alexis.

Alexis and Hunter got up and started walking toward her car. Sky pulled me up and walked me to the car. He finally let go of one of my hands and opened the door for me. As I got into the car he kissed the hand he was still holding.

"I'll see you tomorrow," he said, looking into my eyes.

"Yeah, I'll see you tomorrow," I said.

"Remember don't ever show fear around that guy," said Sky.

"I'm not afraid of him any more," I said.

Then Alexis started the car, and Sky closed my door and waved. I waved back to him and watched him as we pulled away. Misty and Alex were riding back with Ms. Hall.

## *Magic Against Magic*

I could see the sun setting as I looked out the window. The various shades of pink and lavender swirled across the sky. The warmth and beauty filled every part of me. My entire body, mind and soul was filled with an enormous sense of well-being. There were no dark images in my mind that would haunt my dreams tonight or any other night. I could see short glimpses of the future, and no matter how terrible some might be, there would always be a way to overcome. Knowing this is what gave me the courage to not fear whatever lurked deep within the dark side.

I had never felt this way in my entire life. I knew I was falling in love with Sky. And somehow I knew he was falling in love with me, too.

When I walked into my house, my mom was sitting in the living room watching her favorite show, "General Hospital," she gestured to me, beckoning me over to sit on the couch next to her.

"So what did you guys do at the rez?" she asked.

"Gee Mom, you talk just like the people on the reservation," I said.

"What do you mean?" asked Mom.

"Well, it seems like everyone I hang around with, except for

Alexis, says 'reservation.' Alexis, her family and her people say 'the rez,' just like you did," I said.

"Okay. . . Emma there is something I should have told you years ago. Your grandma Jane, my mom, was a native from the reserve," she began saying.

"What?" I said, shocked.

"When I was growing up, mom would take us to the reservation to visit our relatives every weekend," she said.

"I can't believe this," I said, still very shocked.

"I stopped going to the rez after I met your dad. A few years after we were married, I told him I was Native American. Whenever he was angry about anything, he would call me "squaw." That's the real reason I didn't want you to know," she said, with tears in her eyes.

"Mom, I am so sorry," I said as I hugged her.

"When you started hanging out with Alexis, I couldn't have been happier. I knew that someday, I would be able to tell you the truth," she said.

"Wow. Well, I'm glad you finally told me. I met some guys from the reservation this evening and most likely I'll see them again tomorrow. You know some of those guys at the fire are really good looking. What if I'm related to some of them?" I said stunned.

"I'm sorry, Emma, I was just trying to protect you. You can ask if anyone is related to Jane Simon, that way you will know if you're related to any of them," she said teasingly.

I began to tell my mom what was going on and what had happened earlier this evening. My mom was not shocked at all. She was calm. She may have known that people on the reservation do different kinds of ceremonies. There was so much I wanted to know about my mom's family but I needed to take a shower and relax. So as soon as "General Hospital" was over, I gave my mom a kiss and went up to my room. I fell into a deep sleep away from the dreams and dark images that I had seen earlier that evening.

The next day was just like any other normal day. All of my

classes seemed to fly right by. I was really glad - and a bit excited - that I would be going back to the reservation. When the final bell rang, I grabbed my books and rushed out to meet Alexis.

"Hey Alexis, are you going to pick me up at my house or do you want my mom to drop me off at your house?" I asked.

"We'll stop by in a little while to pick you up," she said.

She looked like she was wondering why I was so eager to be on our way. But she never said a teasing word to me.

"Okay, I'll be waiting," I said.

About 20 minutes after I got home, the doorbell rang. My mom yelled to me that Alexis and her parents were there. I grabbed my blue jacket and went running down the stairs.

"I'll see you later," I yelled as I went walking toward the door.

Mom didn't answer. As I walked out the door; I saw her standing by the car talking to Alex and Misty. I closed the door quickly behind me, ran to the car and jumped in the seat next to Alexis in the back.

"I'll see you later, Mom," I said.

"Yeah, see you guys later," said mom.

Mom stood there in the driveway waving to us as we pulled away.

On the drive to the reservation, Alexis handed me a note. She wrote: *So what did you think about the Fire Ceremony?*

I took her pen and paper from her hand.

*At first I was scared to death; I had no idea that we were all seeing the same thing.*

I handed the note back to her. Alexis started writing something else and handed me the note.

*So your mom finally told you that you're part native?*

I looked at Alexis and whispered, "You knew?"

Alexis just smiled at me and looked out the window.

So I wrote on the note.

*How long have you known about it?*

I handed the note back to her. Alexis read the note and then looked at me and whispered "For a while. I'm glad she finally told you," I just shook my head and rolled my eyes.

When we got to the reservation, the same guys were waiting at what Alexis called the base camp. They had their small fire burning strong. We all walked over and started smudging ourselves with sage. I grabbed Alexis by the arm and walked a short distance away and told her that I was going to stay at the base camp. Just as we were walking back to the campfire, Ms. Hall drove up in her Jeep. As soon as Ms. Hall had finished smudging, Alex announced that we should go up the hill.

"Hey you guys, Emma is not going up the hill so keep her company," yelled out Alexis.

Sky stood up and said, "come sit over here Emma."

As I walking over to the campfire, I turned and waved to Alexis, her parents. Then I went to sit on one of the old benches.

"Hey Emma, Alexis said that your grandmother came from our rez. Is that true?" he asked.

"When did she tell you that?" I asked.

"About a month ago," said Hunter.

"Um, yea, her name was Jane Simon," I said.

"No way," said one of the boys.

"I'm sorry, what's your name?" I asked the guy.

"His name is Doug Simon," said Sky.

"My grandfather's sister was Jane Simon," said Doug.

"Okay, so that makes us cousins, right?" I said.

"Yea," he said in a disappointed voice

The other guys sitting around began chuckling.

"Last night he said you were hot," said Hunter.

"Shut up," said Doug.

After that it got pretty quiet around the fire, I looked around at the guys sitting there and that's when I noticed their tattoos.

"What kind of tattoo is that?" I asked Sky.

"Oh, this is a tattoo of a wolf," said Sky as he looked at the other guys.

"Why would anyone get a tattoo of a wolf?" I asked.

"Wow. You don't know much about our culture," said Doug.

"I belong to the wolf clan, that's why I have a wolf tattoo," said Sky

"So do you all have wolf tattoos?" I asked.

"No I belong to the bear clan, so I have a bear tattoo," said Hunter.

"Hey Doug do you have a tattoo?" I asked.

"Yeah, bear. I belong to the bear clan," said Doug.

"So Justin what kind of tattoo do you have?" I asked.

"A wolf," he said.

I started to get a flashback to the Fire Ceremony last evening and I remembered that I saw a bear and a wolf in the fire. I began wondering what the significance was between the guys' clans and what I had seen in the fire.

"What are you thinking about? Is it that lunatic at your school?" asked Sky.

"I saw a bear and a wolf in the fire last evening, what does that mean?" I asked.

"Oh those are your protectors," said Sky.

"Protectors?" I said.

"Yeah," said Doug, like I should have known that.

Once again it got quiet around the fire. Then Hunter got up and grabbed a couple of logs and placed then into the fire. I felt bad that I didn't fully understand the culture and truly wanted to learn.

"So did you sleep alright last night? Did you see that lunatic at your school?" asked Sky.

"I slept really well, and no that lunatic wasn't at school today," I said.

"I heard about that lunatic, are you afraid of him?" asked Doug.

"If you hang out with us you won't have to be afraid of anything," said Hunter.

"Yeah, I told you yesterday we wouldn't let anyone bother you," said Sky.

I suddenly felt like I had a group of guys who would protect me from anything. I felt like I had gained an enormous amount of confidence in myself. If Bobbie Watson were here, I would be able to dance around him and look into his dark eyes and not feel fear.

I smiled at the guys as I looked at the fire. Sitting here with them made me feel at ease. I felt that I belonged here.

"So, I see you have a ring on your finger, I thought you said you didn't have a boyfriend?" asked Hunter.

I looked down at my hands and started moving the ring with my other hand.

"No, I don't have a boyfriend. It's a friendship ring," I said.

"What does that mean?" said Hunter.

"It means that we're just friends, nothing more," I said.

"So if he were sitting here, would you still say you're just friends?" asked Hunter.

"Yes I would. We met by accident. I got burned by his coffee and he couldn't forgive himself. The ring is from him and his girlfriend. He's been at UCLA for the past two years. He lives with his girlfriend who's also his high school sweetheart. They both know that once I graduate, I plan to go away to college or university somewhere," I said.

"So, are you planning to go to UCLA, as well?" asked Sky.

"The girls and I haven't made our mind up yet. We're looking at colleges with good volleyball teams," I said.

"What about you? Are you going to college?" I asked Sky.

"Yeah, Hunter and I are studying computer science in Santa Rosa. We're thinking about going to college or university in New York, somewhere with Alexis," said Sky.

"Oh, so all three of you are going to New York," I said.

"That's the plan," said Sky.

"Now it makes sense why Alexis was so eager to apply to this one college in New York," I said.

"Yeah, well she has family who live in New York," said Hunter.

Suddenly I began to wonder why Hunter asked if I had a boyfriend. Was he asking that question for Sky? Just as I looked over at Sky he took his eyes away from the fire and gave me a glance. When he smiled at me, I felt my heart skip a beat. I smiled back at him and quickly looked down at my hiking boots.

"How long do you think they'll be up there?" I asked

"Not very long," said Sky.

"So what are they doing up there?" I asked.

"They're giving power to the medicine so that it can protect them and you," said Sky.

As soon as he was done explaining it to me, we could hear voices coming down the hill. It wouldn't be long before everyone would be gathering around the campfire. I wanted so much to keep talking to Sky. There was so much about the culture I wanted to learn, and I didn't want to hear it from anyone but him. But before I could ask him how the medicine gets its power, I could hear Alexis, her parents, Ms. Hall, Sara and Chip approaching. Everyone around the fire stood up and took several steps back. They smudged themselves again with the sage. Once everyone was done smudging, Sky grabbed the tray and began smudging me. Chip and Sara walked over to me and handed me a small leather bundle. It had a long string of leather attached to it.

"Hang this around your neck and have it on you at all times. When you take a shower in the morning, take it off, and then once you're dressed put it back on," said Sara.

"The medicine will provide an invisible shield around you. If someone tries to harm you, their negative powers will not pass the shield," said Chip.

"It's like magic fighting magic. Everything in these bundles is good medicine, and once it has the power to protect, it becomes magical. This is really powerful," said Sara.

As I looked at the guys sitting around the fire, every one of them was nodding in agreement. But there weren't just the six guys from earlier and last night. There were about 20 other guys standing around. I was stunned. I had no idea where they had come from or what they were doing there.

Chip and one of the young men were talking. I couldn't understand a word that was being said, but I knew it had to be in their language. What ever was being said, Chip was agreeing with the young man, and he did not seem upset, so I assumed that everything was cool. Chip sat back in his seat for a few seconds, looked at Alex and they both smiled at each other. I was so new to all of this but deep inside I knew that something more was going on.

"Chip can I ask you a question?"

"Yes, Emma." he said.

"What about my friends?" I asked.

"Well, you will have to try to convince them to wear these leather ties that we've made for them," said Chip.

"If they refuse or don't believe in the power, then it's out of your hands," Sara added. "You can't force them or anyone to believe in anything."

I took my medicine bundle and looped the string around my neck. I clasped the bundle tightly in my hands for a little bit and then I placed it inside my shirt. I grabbed the extra leather ties and put them in my pocket for my friends.

Alexis and I would have to try to convince our friends that they would have to wear the ties to protect themselves.

That's when I noticed Alexis and her father whispering to each other. Something was going on, but no one was saying anything out loud. The suspense was starting to take control of me. I looked over at Chip to see if I could get a reaction from his face. But Sky and his friends just stared at each other.

"So, Alex, what have you decided? You know that our power is stronger only if we keep the fire going," said Chip.

"Keep the fires going, Chip, and we'll continue to come here until it's over," said Alex.

Okay, I thought to myself, I could tell that something was

going on and the need to know was causing my legs to shake. I knew that I shouldn't be afraid - I was told that by several of the young men here. So why did I have this urge to scream like a crazy woman.

"What's going on?" I asked.

I didn't care who would answer me, I just needed to get beyond the mystery.

Chip stood up.

"These guys have been watching the entire perimeter of the hill," he said. "Yesterday and just earlier, someone tried to enter the perimeter. So this person is probably very angry that he or she couldn't find out what we were doing up on the hill. So in order to keep our medicine strong, we need to keep the fire going."

I was puzzled and a bit confused as to whom this person would be, and then it hit me.

"Chip, do you mean?" I tried to ask, but Chip put his hand up to silence me.

"No. Don't say his name. You can no longer say his name out loud, especially around this fire."

Sara and Misty started handing out fried bread and water to everyone. I took a bottle of water and asked Sky if I could talk to him. Sky got up and walked toward me and we went walking over to the car. I put the water on top of the car and turned to face Sky.

"Did you see this person who tried to enter the perimeter last night?" I asked.

"No, I didn't know anything about it until after you and Alexis left," Sky said.

"What about earlier?" I asked.

"When the guys came out of the woods, I looked over to them and they confirmed by nodding their heads that someone was out there," Sky said

"So can this person wander up to the fire?" I asked.

"No, Uncle Chip moved the perimeter farther back last night," Sky said.

"Why did Hunter ask me if I had a boyfriend?" I asked.

"I asked him to ask for me," he said, grinning.

"So, do you have a girlfriend?" I asked.

"No," said Sky.

Then before he could say another word I asked, "Okay. So are we related?"

"No," he said, almost laughing.

"Well that's a relief. I was a bit upset with my mom last night when she told me I have relatives here. I mean I'm not upset to have relatives or that they're from here. It's just that it could be my cousin I'm falling in love with. Oh, crap, I meant to say.... Oh, crap, I'm so embarrassed," I said lowering my head to avoid his eyes.

Sky reached and pulled my head up.

"Don't be embarrassed. I feel the same way about you."

"You do," I asked.

"I thought my heart was going to jump out of my chest last night when I held your hand," he said.

"I thought it was just me," I said.

"I want to kiss you so badly, but I know the guys are watching us. It'll probably make them howl all night," said Sky.

I looked over toward the fire and, sure enough, most of the guys were looking at us.

"I suppose I can wait until later for that kiss," I said.

"Deal," he said.

"Emma is it a problem for you to come here every day?" asked Alex.

"No. I'll be here," I said.

As our gathering had come to an end, everyone got up and started hugging each other.

We left the reservation at 6:50 that evening and headed back to Santa Rosa.

Now, more than ever, I felt that I could face up to any challenge, no matter what tomorrow may bring.

# *Disturbing News*

The following day, Alexis and I talked with our friends about the leather ties that we wanted them to wear for their protection. It wasn't as hard as I thought it would be to convince them. Aimee was the first one to take the leather tie and wrap it around her wrist. I think Cindy and Carol just followed because of Aimee. We weren't allowed to explain how the fire was organized but we were allowed to enlighten them as to what Bobbie was planning. We told them the importance of wearing the ties around their wrist so that Bobbie Watson would not be a concern to us.

Once we explained everything, Cindy told us the band members were really getting along really great and that the songs that they were doing sounded excellent. As she spoke about the band we began to feel the excitement in her voice.

"This sounds like its going to be a really cool dance party," said Aimee.

"I know I just can't wait," said Cindy.

"This isn't a casual dance, right?" asked Aimee.

"Oh no, it's formal," said Cindy.

"So we need to go shopping after school," said Carol.

"So, Emma, are you coming shopping with us?" asked Cindy.

"Ah, I'll go hang out with you guys, I was thinking that I'll wear the gown from my dad's wedding and just add some accessories to it," I said.

"Alexis are you coming with us?" asked Cindy.

"Thanks, but I'm not even sure if I'll be going to the dance," said Alexis.

"Ahhhh come on. You can't miss our last dance together," said Cindy.

"Yeah, come on, this isn't fair," said Carol

"Alright, I'll come to the dance. I'll just use the same dress I wore to Emma's dad's wedding," said Alexis.

"Okay, so were all going to have fun, right?" said Cindy.

"Yeah, why not," said Alexis.

"Of course," said Carol.

"I agree," I said.

As we went walking to our English class, I could have sworn that I heard one of the junior girls say something about a beating. I pushed the chatter aside and assumed that the girls were talking about losing their track event or some other sport. It wasn't until we got to our English class that I heard the same chatter. I poked Cindy, who was chatting with a student at the desk in front of her.

"What's going on?" I asked her.

"I'm not quite sure. Word is a girl, a freshman I think, was raped and beaten last night. I guess her mom found her when she got home from work," said Cindy.

"Is she from this school?" I asked.

"Yeah, I guess," said Cindy.

"No way" I said. That's just awful!"

Our regular teacher was out today and we had a substitute for the rest of the week.

"Good Morning! My name is Mr. Styles and I have an important message for you," the substitute said.

Mr. Styles pulled a paper from his folder and started to read:

"Some time last night, before 10 o'clock Kerri Sanders, a freshman at this school, was badly beaten and raped. She is at the Northwest Hospital here in Santa Rosa in a coma. The principal will be allowing students to attend counseling sessions all day today and perhaps the rest of this week. Thank you for you time. Also I'm so sorry to those of you who know Miss Sanders."

We were in total shock. There were a couple of girls up front who were crying because they knew the girl and her family. I had my hand over my mouth the whole time the teacher was speaking. I was remembering the vision I had on the hill, of the girl. I started telling myself that this can't be the same vision. What if this was just a coincidence and maybe the girl in the vision was someone else. Nothing can be definite until we know all the facts. Like was this girl found in her own bedroom? Was her arm or leg broken? Was her bedroom window open? I needed to know what happened to her, and if it matched my vision. If it did, I knew who was responsible.

It was so quiet in the classroom, except for the two girls crying. Our substitute teacher had to have two other students walk the two girls to the office. Once they left the room, we were told to read the next two chapters of the book we were reading for class. If we were having difficulty reading, Mr. Styles said we were allowed to write a short story of how we were feeling at the moment.

I don't think there was one person who was able to read beyond the first sentence, at least without having to repeat it several times before they actually knew what it said. I can't remember ever being in a room so quiet. As I stared at my blank paper, I wondered what exactly I was really feeling.

I took a pencil out from my book bag so that I could erase what ever nonsense I might write down. I thought for a moment and then I start to write.

*Today, actually this morning we received terrible news concerning a fellow student. I believe our teacher said that she was a freshman. This poor young girl was beaten and raped. My body, mind and soul can not understand why one person could violate another person to this extreme. Why? What is this person's reason for doing something so insane? I find it very hard to hold back the tears as I think of this girl and her family. The pounding in my head can not even compare to the pain that she must have gone through. The trembling of my body due to the stress of this situation cannot even begin to match the emotional state and helplessness her family must be feeling right now.*

This was all I could write. When the bell rang and the teacher asked us to hand in our papers, I slowly walked up to the front of the class, to the teacher's desk. For a few moments, I stared at the papers placed neatly on the teacher's desk. Then very slowly, I handed the paper to the teacher without even looking at him.

"Excuse me, are you Emma?" he asked.

"Yes," I said, turning to face the teacher.

"Can you sign your name on the paper, please?" he said.

I went back to the teacher's desk and signed my name on the paper. Out in the hall, Cindy, Carol, Aimee and Alexis waited for me. It was so strange how quiet the halls were.

"It was an eerie feeling not hearing all the yelling and hooting from everyone," I said.

No one said a word; my friends just nodded their heads as we walked to our next class. I don't know when or how long it would take to begin to feel normal again. But for now it seemed like we were a bunch of zombies just going through the motions of our days.

Halfway through our gym class, the principal, announced over the PA system for all students to report to the auditorium immediately.

Mrs. McGee clapped her hands.

"Okay, you heard the man. Get changed and go to the auditorium."

By the time our gym class had gotten to the auditorium, it was jam packed. Every seat was taken and students were starting to stand in the aisles. Our gym class was probably one of the last classes to walk in.

"Is the entire staff in here as well? Can the staff please come and stand on the stage, please?" asked Mr. Baker.

Once all the teachers and other staff were standing up front, Mr. Baker, the principal, raised the microphone to his lips. You could hear him breathing from the back of the room.

"I assume that you are all aware that Kerri Sanders was beaten very badly last night. A few moments ago, we received a phone call from Mrs. Sanders. Kerri passed away a half hour ago from her injuries. She never regained consciousness. The police were unable to get a description of her assailant. You are all free to go home today. Tomorrow, we'll have therapists and counselors here to help you all deal with this terrible tragedy."

The roar of disbelief was like a tsunami as it moved from the front of the auditorium to the back. The crying was unbelievable. I reached for Carol and Alexis, and wrapped my arms around both of their necks. We all started crying.

Cindy and Aimee came over and wrapped their arms around us as well. They were crying inconsolably. It seemed to take us quite a while to compose ourselves enough to feel comfortable leaving the auditorium. We walked together out of the auditorium and continued to hold on to each other as we walked to the parking lot. We made sure Cindy was settled down before we let her drive home, and then we walked Carol to her car and hugged her before she left. Alexis was giving Aimee and me a ride home.

When I got home, I called my mom at work to let her know what had happened. But mom had already heard. She said that one her coworkers was best friends with the family. She said that everyone at work was just shocked.

I told my mom that Alexis and I would be going back to the reservation to sit by the fire. I heard Alexis pull in the driveway.

Mom told me to check on the pot roast she had in the slow cooker.

When Alexis knocked at the door, I let her in and motioned her to the kitchen. Then I hung up the phone and went to the kitchen to check on my mom's pot roast

"Oh that smells delicious," Alexis said.

"I know and it doesn't have any vegetables in it. That's what my mom wanted me to do before we leave," I said.

I opened the fridge and pulled out a large zip lock bag that contained all the chopped vegetables for the pot roast. This was a great idea, having all the vegetable prepared like this. I really need to thank my mom for saving me lots of time chopping, dicing and peeling. As I poured the vegetables into the pot roast, Alexis made sure that everything was well mixed in the broth. I placed the lid on the slow cooker, and I turned and looked at Alexis.

"Alexis," I said.

Alexis didn't raise her head or look in my direction. She just smiled.

"We'll talk about any concerns you have when we get to the fire," she said.

I nodded my head in agreement and asked her if she wanted something to drink before we got ready to leave.

"Sure, what do you have?" she asked.

I looked in the fridge.

"How's iced tea?"

"That sounds good," she said.

I grabbed the iced tea and handed it to Alexis. Then I looked in the meat cooler to see what kind of lunch meat we had.

"Okay we have roasted turkey and olive loaf," I said. "Want a sandwich?"

"Olive loaf sounds good," Alexis said.

She poured the iced tea as I made our sandwiches. As we ate our sandwiches and drank the iced tea, I put a bag of cookies in my book bag. Without saying a word to each other, we rinsed off the glasses and placed them on the rack and made sure that the mustard and lunch meats were put back in the fridge. Then we grabbed our jackets and left for the reservation.

When we got to the fire Alex, Misty and Ms. Hall were already there. Chip was standing with another group of guys near the wooded area. I didn't recognize any of them. Some of them could've been around at the second fire. As soon as Sky, Hunter and the other guys arrived, they went over and spoke with Chip and the guys by the wooded area. Then the guys who were already there wandered into the forest all around us. Sky and his friends came walking toward us. They greeted each of us, and I sat with Sky beside the fire.

Just as Hunter and the others guys took their seats, Sara's old clunker of a car pulled up next to the other cars.

"Just give me a minute and we'll get started," yelled Sara. Sara was carrying a basket. Inside her basket was her famous fried bread.

She placed the basket on the top of the case of water. Then Chip and Sara took tobacco out of their leather pouches and they started praying. They were putting the tobacco into the fire at the end of their prayers.

When they were done, Sara remained standing.

"Ms. Hall and Alex called us earlier and told us about the girl who was attacked and who has since passed away," Sara said. "We can't be sure if this girl is the one we saw in our vision. Does anyone know the details surrounding her attack?"

"The school staff was told that this girl was found by her mother when she returned home from work. We don't know if she was found inside or outside the house," said Ms. Hall.

"One of the freshman girls said that her face was so badly beaten that her mom didn't recognize her. They also said that the only reason her mom knew that it was her daughter was from the clothes she was wearing," said Alexis.

"We heard the same thing at work," said Alex.

"Chip and I are quite positive this girl is not the one that we saw in our vision," said Sara.

"If you guys can, think back about the girl in the vision and try to remember anything so that we can be certain," said Chip.

"I remember the girl in the vision lived in a two-story white house," I said.

"Yeah, I remember that, too," said Alexis.

"So this may not be our girl. We went to see her parents today and they live in a brownish brick apartment building," said Ms. Hall.

"If this is the case, there is nothing we can do to prevent those who he randomly selects as his prey," said Chip.

"When we do not see who his victims are, it's because it's their destiny and there is absolutely nothing that we can do to prevent their death," said Sara.

"Can the vision that we saw a few days ago change?" I asked.

"Yes, they can, but you would have a dream about it first," said Chip.

"So you guys will keep us updated when you get more information concerning this girl?" asked Sara.

Misty, Alex and Ms. Hall all nodded their heads in agreement.

"So we'll take a few minutes to pray for our medicine, so that it maintains its strength," said Chip.

Chip and Sara stood up and then Sky, Hunter and the rest of the guys stood up. When Chip and Sara reached into their leather pouches, the rest of us stood up with them. Chip spoke first.

"We give thanks to our father the Creator. We give thanks to our grandpa the wind. We give thanks to our grandma the moon. We give thanks to our brother the sun and finally we give thanks to all the creatures big and small, friend and foe that were placed here on this planet to protect and help us."

"Great Spirit, we thank you for our brothers the eagles for their sight, for our brothers the wolves for their superior and cooperative hunting skills, and for the bears for their strength in guiding and protecting us through this fire," said Sara.

"Ho he!" yelled the group of guys standing there.

Sara and Chip placed their tobacco into the fire. Sara and Misty walked over to the basket and opened it. Sara then took a piece of fried bread and a small bottle of water and went back to the fire. There, she split the bread into four pieces and placed it in the fire along with the water. As soon as she did this, the fire started crackling. This was something I'd never witnessed before, it really sounded like the fire was chewing the food it was given. I thought the fire would go out when the water was poured over it, but it only made the fire stronger.

When we were done with our fried bread, Alexis and Hunter went toward the car. I got up and pulled Sky's hand and asked him to go for a walk.

"So are you starting to understand what these ceremonies are about?" asked Sky.

"Well, not really. It's all new to me and I'm a little shy to ask about certain things," I said.

"Like what?" asked Sky.

"Well let's see, okay, how does the medicine help someone?" I asked.

"You'll have to wait for one of the visions to happen to really see how the medicine helps someone who is being protected," said Sky.

"Did Alexis tell you about those visions?" I asked.

Sky looked toward Hunter then he looked back at me.

"No, I was patrolling the hill top that night and saw the visions."

"I thought you were sitting by this fire the whole time," I said.

"I was on the hill the whole time you were passing the vision state," he said.

"What's all that stuff about our brother the eagles, bears and wolves?" I asked.

Sky laughed a little and looked toward the fire, and then he looked back at me. Then he led me toward the hill.

"Do you know about skin walkers?" asked Sky.

"No, what are skin walkers?" I asked.

"Well, what about shape shifters?" he asked.

"No, I never heard of that either," I said.

"Okay, don't get scared then. It's people who can phase into a bear, a deer, a hawk or a wolf," he said as he stared into my eyes. I was stunned by what he had just revealed to me. My brain went into a different mode. Sky was just standing there looking at me with a slight grin on his face. I started to think that maybe I didn't hear him right.

"Are you alright? Emma, take a deep breath," said Sky.

"Did I hear you right? Did you say people change into bears, deer, hawks and wolves?" I asked still stunned and unable to blink.

"Yeah, that's exactly what I said," said Sky.

"But how can someone do something like that?" I asked.

"I can't really describe the process to you, but all of the guys who hang out here at the fire are able to become a skin walkers or shape shifters," said Sky.

"So, are you telling me that you are one of those who can shape shift into an animal?" I asked.

"Yeah, don't you remember when you asked us about our tattoos and I told you that I was a wolf clan. Well, that's what I am," said Sky.

"Yeah, I remember," I said as I swallowed hard.

"Are you frightened?" asked Sky.

"Well," I said, stalling.

"Don't be afraid, I'm still the same person whether I'm myself or the wolf," he said.

And with that statement, I knew he meant that as nice of a gentleman that he was, he would be the same when he was in the role of the wolf. Knowing this made me feel safe and it eased the stress I was feeling about not knowing this part of the culture.

"I'm not afraid as long as I know that you and the rest of the guys are protectors," I told him.

"So anyway, the only way I was able to see the visions was to be in my wolf form," said Sky.

Right then, Alexis called out to me.

"Hey Emma we're ready to leave," she said.

"Give me a minute," I yelled back.

I looked toward the path to see if I could see Alexis, but I couldn't see her. Then I looked back at Sky and pulled him close to me, and he gave me one long kiss.

"Emma, let's go," said Alexis.

"I'm coming," I yelled.

We took about four steps before we could see Alexis and Hunter by the car.

"Hey, Sky, what are you doing over there?" yelled one of the guys.

"We're talking," yelled Sky.

"Talking with your lips?" yelled another guy. And everyone laughed.

Sky smiled at me and walked me to the car.

"I'll see you tomorrow," I said.

"Yeah, see you tomorrow," said Sky.

Alexis wanted to know what exactly we were talking about. I told her that Sky said that he was up on the hill that first night we did the ceremony. Alexis and her parents were not surprised at all.

"That's his job," said Alexis.

"Yeah, he told me that," I said.

"You guys were gone awhile, what else did he tell you?" asked Alexis.

"Oh, I just wanted to know different stuff," I said.

"Stuff like what?" Alexis asked.

"You know, stuff that has to do with bears and wolves," I whispered.

"Did he phase in front of you?" she whispered.

"No," I said.

"You know he really likes you," said Alexis.

"Is that what Hunter said?" I asked.

"Yeah, Sky told Hunter he's in love," said Alexis.

I smiled at Alexis and looked out the window and admired the beautiful scenery. I didn't need someone to tell me how Sky felt about me; I could feel it myself. As for the way I felt about him, I'd already spilled my feelings to him by accident. That embarrassing moment will be a part of mine and Sky's memory forever.

*Somber Times*

The following day, there were reporters swarming around trying to interview the students and teachers. I saw a couple of girls, the principal and a couple of teachers talking with a television reporter. It was quite difficult to watch the girls as they wept hysterically every time they spoke of their deceased friend. It wasn't hard to feel the pain they were feeling, for it seemed that the entire community was feeling the same way. For myself, I found it really difficult understanding why someone could take away a young person's life. It just makes no sense.

As Alexis and I walked toward Carol and Cindy, we stood there embracing each other. Today, Aimee was allowed to drive to school. When she parked her car, we waited patiently for her to meet us. As we were embracing Aimee, I noticed Bobbie Watson walking through the parking lot. His dark shoulder length hair was blowing in the wind. He was looking toward the throng of reporters and camera crews as he walked toward us.

"What's going on? Why are the reporters here?" he asked us, when he cleared the group.

Carol being as bold as she usually is, shot him an angry glance.

"Crap, where have you been? Didn't you hear about the

freshman girl who was beaten and raped? You know? The girl who died?"

The look of shock swept across his face and his mouth dropped opened.

"What?" he said in disbelief.

"You didn't hear about it?" said Carol.

"No, I was sick," he said.

"We don't know all the details yet, but we were told that counselors would be provided for all students today," said Carol.

"Did this happen here at school?" asked Bobbie.

"No. The rumors are that she was beaten and raped outside her home," said Carol.

"When did this happen?" asked Bobbie.

"The night before last," said Cindy.

"Wow, this is really disturbing. Well, I'll see you ladies in class," he said.

Bobbie walked swiftly into the school and away from the reporters. It was hard to tell if Bobbie was really unaware of the situation. If he was aware, he put on a really good act. After Bobbie was out of sight, we went into the school and headed to class.

A counselor came into our English class with our substitute teacher. She did a group session with our entire class. We were all encouraged to express our feelings, one after another. There was not one dry eye in our room. This type of counseling session went on from one class to the other; right to the last class of the day. At the end of the day, we were all encouraged to attend the calling hours to meet the Sanders family, or to attend the funeral.

In the parking lot I caught up to Alexis and asked her if she was going to the reserve for the fire.

"Yes, we're leaving in about an hour. Are you going?" she said jokingly.

"Yeah, I'll be ready," I said, as I jumped in her car.

Went I got home I started to tidy up my room. I put my books in order from smallest to tallest. The clothes I had left on my chair were clean so I folded them and put them into the dresser. Then I went to the laundry room and started a load of wash for my mom. I ran downstairs and vacuumed the living room. I was dusting when Alexis rang the doorbell. As I went to answer the door I looked at the clock and noticed that it was almost 5 p.m. I didn't realize that it had taken me that much time to do my chores. I told Alexis to give me a minute so I could put the vacuum and the duster away. As I was putting the vacuum away, my mother, brother and sister walked in. I told my mom that I put a load of clothes in the washer and did some of the chores. My mom was a little late getting home because she had stopped at Side Wok's for Chinese food.

"Emma, I want you and Alexis to have something to eat with the rest of us before you leave," my mom yelled from the kitchen.

"Alright, I'll be right down," I said.

"Sure," said Alexis.

While we were feasting on the egg rolls, fried rice and Chow Mein, my mother told Alexis and me that we should go to the funeral home and pay our respect to the Sanders family. Alexis and I looked at each other and nodded. When we were finished with our meal, I gathered the dishes and rinsed them off and placed them in the dish washer. Then Alexis drove us to the funeral home.

When we got to the funeral home, we had to park a few blocks away - there were so many people there waiting to get in. It took us over an hour just to reach the door at the funeral home.

About 20 minutes after we got in line, Alexis got out her cell phone and called Hunter. She told him we might not make it to the fire because we were at the wake for Kerrie Sanders. She explained to Hunter how long we had been waiting in line and that there were still quite a few people ahead of us. Once we reached the doors to the funeral home, it still took us another 20 minutes or so just to get to the coffin where Kerri Sanders rested. The funeral home did a very good job fixing her face. She looked very beautiful, though maybe she had a little too much makeup to cover the bruises and cuts. Her shoulder length hair looked so silky and smooth. Her lips had a pale pink tint to them and I could have sworn that she was smiling slightly. Kerrie looked very much at peace. She wore a nice black blazer and a white shirt. She had an angel pinned to her blazer. The light pink prayer beads were wrapped loosely around her hands. Inside her coffin were many pictures of Kerrie from her childhood and all the way up to ninth grade. This was a very somber moment for me and for Alexis.

"Wait here for just one minute," Alexis said as she leaned toward me. I looked at Alexis and watched her walk toward Kerrie's parents. She gave them both a hug and whispered something to them and I saw them nod their heads.

Alexis returned to where I stood and reached into her pocket and pulled out a small braid of sweet grass and a small leather pouch. She placed these items under Kerrie's hands.

As we turned to walk away I saw Kerrie's mom and I went over and gave her and Kerrie's father a hug. I was unable to hold back the tears that began to flow. I told Kerrie's parents that we would be thinking of them always. Then I got up and followed Alexis out the door.

When we got outside, there was still a large crowd waiting. Cindy, Carol and Aimee were mingling around with the crowd. We walked over to where they were standing. There wasn't a dry eye anywhere in the crowd.

"How long have you guys been here?" I asked Carol, Cindy and Aimee.

"We got here about two hours ago," said Cindy.

"Yeah, we saw the two of you in the line after we had viewed Kerri and decided to wait out here," said Carol.

"It's unbelievable how sad the atmosphere is here. I just feel so heartbroken," said Aimee.

We stood there embracing each other and our other friends

who were just showing up. There was no way we would be going to the fire tonight. It was already getting too late.

Just before 9 p.m., Ms. Hall came walking out of the funeral home. She was holding a Kleenex to her face. She came over and gave each of us a hug.

Ms. Hall told us that she had been practicing for the past two days with some of her music students. She also told us that while she was playing the piano, Bobbie Watson had walked in and he sat next to her on the bench. She said she finished playing the song, and he asked if she would listen to his version. According to Ms. Hall, Bobbie Watson was an excellent musician. We would get to hear him play at the funeral with Ms. Hall and the other students.

Alexis gave her another hug and they stood there talking for a bit. Then Ms. Hall walked away.

When Alexis came back to our group she asked me if I wanted to leave. The two of us said goodnight to our friends and walked away. Alexis and I were quiet all the way back to my home.

When she parked in my drive way I looked at her and said "Alexis, can I ask you something?"

"Sure," she said with a smile on her face.

"Why did you put sweet grass and that leather pouch under Kerrie's hands?"

"Well, the sweet grass is used to purify, just like the sage. So when someone dies, we always put sweet grass in their hand. In our culture, we believe the body and soul have separated and the soul can still smell. It's just medicine to help her find the spirit world and to keep her safe on her journey," she whispered.

"Oh my God, Alexis, that is so beautiful and it was really thoughtful of you to do that for Kerri. When I die will you do that for me as well?" I asked.

Alexis looked at me and smiled and then she reached over and gave me a hug.

"You will have a long and happy life. But if something should happen, you know I would do the same for you. And I also know that you would do it for me, right?" she whispered again.

I looked her in the eyes and promised to be there if and when that time came.

After our short embrace, we said good night to each other and I went inside.

The next day school was cancelled so everyone could attend the funeral for Kerrie Sanders. The church was so packed that nearly 200 people stood outside and others sat in their cars. Kerrie and her family should be honored and proud to know how much respect everyone had for their family.

Ms. Hall had organized a group of students to sing a couple of songs during the church services. Ms. Hall began playing the church organ and the students began signing their version of Vince Gill's "Go Rest High on That Mountain."

As soon as they started singing my heart started pumping harder and harder. My breathing became even more erratic with each note they sang. I was glad we were standing outside the church. I started walking toward the church parking lot; my need at that moment was to get as far away from this heartbreaking song. By the time Alexis and Aimee caught up to me, I was starting to hyperventilate.

When Alexis and Aimee put their arms around me, I let a huge cry and almost went down on my knees. I would have fallen to the ground if my friends weren't holding on to me. I never knew that anyone's death would touch me in that way. All of this emotional release was so draining on my body and soul. Lucky for me, I wasn't alone in my emotional state. Once I was able to calm down, I told Alexis that I preferred not to attend the graveside service. I've seen people break down at the grave site and didn't wish to go through what I had just gone through again. Alexis agreed with me and so we stayed in the parking lot a bit longer after the funeral procession had left the church. It had taken us almost a half hour after the church service to get back into the car and drive home.

"Do you want to go to the rez?" asked Alexis.

"No, I think that I'll stay home today and try to calm down and relax," I said.

"Do you want some company?" asked Alexis.

"Don't you want to spend some time with Hunter?" I asked.

"I'll give him a call and explain everything to him. He'll understand," said Alexis.

Alexis called Hunter and they talked all the way back to my house. When Alexis parked the car in my driveway, I got out and went into the house. Alexis and Hunter continued talking in her car. About 20 minutes later, she knocked on the door.

"I fixed some sandwiches for us," I yelled from the kitchen.

"Yum, that sound good," said Alexis.

Alexis and I went up to my room and sat on my bed eating our sandwiches. We watched the movie version of "Titanic." Watching a love story right after a funeral wasn't the best idea.

By the end of the movie both Alexis and I were in tears again.

# Indecent Proposal

wo days before the spring dance, everyone was busy decorating the gym and outdoor patio. The hall leading to the gym was decorated with white lights. A long red carpet ran across the hall and went a few feet passed the gymnasium doors. A long deep burgundy rope ran alongside of the carpet and extended just beyond the gym doors. The wall across from the red carpet was a mural that looked like people applauding as they sat on the bleachers. A recorder was attached on the wall with motion detectors on each side of it. These motion detectors activated the sounds of applause. Other students were bringing in boxes of props, such as plastic Oscar statues and large Silver Stars.

Alexis and I saw the excitement these students had on their faces as we went walking past the gym. We were going to the music room to give Ms. Hall some of the sheet music she had requested. When we went into the music room, we saw Ms. Hall standing against the wall and Bobbie Watson was leaning over her within inches of her body and holding both of his hands against the wall behind her. As soon as he heard us, he pulled away from Ms. Hall, walked toward a small table, grabbed his book bag and walked out of the room. Both Alexis and I pretended that we didn't know that something was going on. After Bobbie left the room, we asked Ms. Hall if everything was okay.

"I was playing the piano when Bobbie Watson walked in, so I got up and walked toward my desk. The whole time I was telling him he did a great job at the funeral. When I got to my desk, he was still following me. I was starting to wonder what was going on with him. Before I could pull my chair out, he stood in front of me and the chair. He kept coming closer to me, until I was backed into the wall. When he put his arms over my shoulders, he leaned toward me and said that he wanted to kiss me. I told him that I couldn't allow that to happen because I could lose my job. Then he asked if I would go out to dinner with him. Again I told him that I couldn't and wouldn't date any students, because my teaching certificate means too much to me. That was when you guys walk in," said Ms. Hall, shaking.

"Are you going to report him to the principal?" asked Alexis.

"I'm kind of scared that if I say anything, Bobbie might say that I instigated everything," said Ms. Hall as she fought back tears. "I could lose my job."

"You can tell them we saw what was going on," said Alexis.

"Yeah, I will vouch for you as well," I said.

"Let's just wait and see if he tells anyone first," said Ms. Hall.

"What if we write our statements and that way if you get questioned about it, you will already have the letters of support?" I said.

"Yeah, let's do that," said Alexis. "Is your computer working?"

"Yes," said Ms. Hall.

"Well, let's get it started," I said.

Alexis and I went over to the computer and started writing our statements. Within 20 minutes, we both had our statements printed and signed. Ms. Hall had promised us that she would hand over the statements if and when Bobbie Watson ever spoke to anyone. We stayed in the music room with Ms. Hall. She was rearranging the music room so we decided to help her. Certain instruments had to be packed for the band members to take to the gym.

"Why don't we take the instruments over to the gym, that way the guys don't have to come in here," said Alexis.

"Hey, that is a good idea," said Ms. Hall.

Each of us grabbed one or two of the instruments and went over to the gym. When we got back to the music room, Bobbie Watson was standing by the door.

"I came to pick up my guitar, but the door's locked," he said.

"We just took some of the instruments over to the gym. Some of the guys are already there setting up the stage area," said Ms. Hall very calmly, like nothing had happened between them.

"Oh alright, I'll go help them out," he said.

As he went walking away, Ms. Hall unlocked the music room and we went in to get the rest of the instruments.

When we got back to the gym, half of the band members were there helping out. We set the rest of the instruments off to the side of the stage and asked if they needed any help. Before Bobbie and the guys could answer, the rest of the band members walked in to help them out.

"Hurry you guys, get up there and help them out. Remember to set things up to whichever way will work best for you," said Ms. Hall.

Then Ms. Hall turned to Alexis and me and asked in a low whisper, "Are you two going to the fire this evening?"

"Yeah, we haven't been there in a couple of days," said Alexis.

"Yeah, I'll be going with Alexis," I said.

"Okay, I'll see you two there later," she said.

We all walked out of the gym together. The entire time we were standing in the gym, Bobbie Watson was staring at Ms. Hall. Once we were out in the hallway, we asked Ms. Hall if she noticed Bobbie Watson looking at her. Ms. Hall just shook her head.

"I don't have time to stare at him. That would only give him the idea that I am interested in him and there is no way I can allow that to happen," said Ms. Hall.

"Do you want us to walk you back to the music room?" asked Alexis.

"Sure," said Ms. Hall.

As we were admiring the decorations along the hallway, Bobbie Watson came out of the gym. He stopped for a brief second, but when he noticed that we were still standing there with Ms. Hall, he went walking in the opposite direction, as if he was going to the washroom. Ms. Hall never turned to see who had come out of the gym, so she didn't know that it was Bobbie. She was simply looking over the Walk of Fame and laughing when we walked by the motion detectors. We continued to walk with Ms. Hall back to the music room. While Ms. Hall was unlocking the door, I saw Bobbie peek from around the far corner.

Inside the music room, both Alexis and I commented on how strange Bobbie was behaving.

"Yeah, he was peeking around the corner," I told her.

"Well, the bell will ring soon, so just hang out here and we'll leave together," said Ms. Hall.

We helped Ms. Hall get her stuff together and we talked about the spring dance. Alexis and I were planning on leaving the dance early.

Ms. Hall told us she wished that she could leave the dance early so that she could get back to the fire, as well. As soon as the bell rang, we grabbed our book bags, some of Ms. Hall's file folders and the new brief case she had on her desk. We all walked out to the parking lot together. When we got to Ms. Hall's Jeep, we handed her the file folders and second brief case. She placed everything in the box she had on her back seat.

"Thanks so much," Ms. Hall said.

"No problem," Alexis said.

"Bye, Ms. Hall," I said

I jumped in with Alexis and drove home. When I got home, I went to my room to change into my relaxing clothes, sweats and

T-shirt. When I was changed, I turned on my computer. To my surprise, I had several new emails. There were two emails from Joel and the rest were junk mail. I open Joel's first email and this is what he wrote.

*Hey Emma, I should be in Santa Rosa about 4 o'clock in the afternoon. I was wondering if you want me to pick you up at six thirty or should I just meet you at the dance. Get back to me okay, Joel.*

I opened up his second email and this is what he wrote.

*Hey Emma, sorry I have to change our plans. I'm still coming to the dance. It's just that I won't be arriving until 7:30. I'll just meet you at the dance, okay I'll talk to you later. Joel.*

I began to reply to Joel's email, I wrote that I would meet him at the dance. I also wrote that I wanted to introduce him to my boyfriend. I also told him about Kerri Sanders death and how sad her funeral was. I let him know how crazy the week had been around here and that I was glad it was finally over. Then I opened one of the emails that I thought was junk mail and to my surprise, I found that it was from one of Joel's so-called girlfriends.

*Emma, I've been living with Joel for the past year and just recently I found out that you have been trying to come between us. You shouldn't do stuff like trying to breakup a happy couple like Joel and me. Don't you know how wrong that is? Didn't anyone ever tell you that what goes around comes around? You need to find yourself your own boyfriend and leave me and Joel alone. Joel and I are planning on getting married in a few months time and you're trying to spoil everything. Respectfully yours Liza.*

I hit the reply to Liza's email and wrote the following to her: *Listen, I don't know who the hell you think you are but I've known Joel and his girlfriend Lana for more than two years. They were high school sweethearts. So don't you try to accuse me of trying to break anyone up! Lana had known that Joel and I had been friends and she never tried to accuse me of anything that you yourself might be guilty of.* As soon as I clicked on the "send" button, I got my cell phone and called Joel. He didn't answer his cell so I left him a message.

"Joel, this is Emma. Please give me a call back as soon as you get this message" I said.

Twenty minutes later our home phone down stairs rang.

"Emma, you have a phone call," yelled my mother.

Without thinking, I ran downstairs to answer the phone. I thought that it was one of my friends calling or even Alexis calling to cancel our trip to the rez.

I picked up the phone.

"Hello."

The voice on the other end of the line was not Alexis or any of my other friends. It was Joel calling.

"Emma. It's Joel. Please don't listen to Liza. I was living with her but we broke up several months ago and she continues to stalk me. She is one sick woman," said Joel.

"How did she get my email address then?" I asked him.

"She probably got it from my computer when she was here," he said.

"Look, we all know that we're just friends. Let's just keep it that way. I just want to know something, what happen to you and Lana?" I asked.

"One night, I went out to the bar with a bunch of friends. When I went up to the bar to get a round of drinks, Liza came over to me and we just started talking," Joel said. "When I paid for the drinks, I asked the bartender to bring the drinks over to our table, and I said to Liza, 'I'll see you around.' Later that night, she came to our apartment. For two weeks after that, she followed me around being overly friendly. One day I gave in and I kissed her. Lana saw us in the hall by the cafeteria. That's when Lana and I broke up. The very day that Lana moved out, Liza started moving her stuff into my apartment. It was like she was sitting in the parking lot watching Lana move out. I was with her just over two months and I realized that she was not the woman I wanted to be with. She has mental problems or something. I honestly am not seeing anyone right now."

"What about you and Lana?" I asked.

"She says she's still pretty hurt," he said.

"Well, yeah," I said.

"So do you have a date for the dance?" he asked.

"Yeah, I met this guy a month ago he's studying computer science here in Santa Rosa," I said.

"So I'll see you at the dance even if it's just for five minutes," he said.

"Alright, but we have plans. We may be there for just an hour or so," I said.

"I'll be there before 8 p.m., I promise," he said.

"Well, I really hope you and Lana can work this out," I told him.

"Well, at least we're talking again," he said.

"Do you want me to talk to her?" I asked.

"Gee, Emma, if it's no trouble," Joel said, almost sounding excited.

"Joel, it's no trouble. Listen would you mind having Lana call me on my cell. I'll do my best to convince her to give you another chance, but you have to promise you'll never do something like that again," I said.

"Okay, I'll have her call you in a few minutes," he said.

As I hung up the phone, I noticed my mom was watching me.

"Mom, we'll talk about this later when I get back," I promised her.

Alexis was outside tooting her horn for a few minutes now and I really needed to get out of the house. I gave my mom a hug, grabbed a jacket and went out the door. Half way to her car, I realized I forgot my cell phone in my room. I waved to Alexis for her to wait while I ran back inside for my cell.

"I swear I'd forget my head if it wasn't attached to my shoulders," I told her when I got in the car a few minutes later.

"What's the hold up?" asked Alexis.

"It's Joel. I'll tell you about it later. I'm a little stressed right now and I need to relax," I said to her.

"No problem," said Alexis.

As we drove to the reservation, I put my head back and tried to calm down. Alexis is good in situations like this. She put a calming, classical CD in the car stereo. By the time we were halfway down the road, I was feeling much better. When I opened my eyes, I was able to tell Alexis about the emails and the phone call. I told her that was the reason it took me a while to come out.

"I thought you and Joel were just friends," she asked.

"Yeah, we are friends," I explained. "And I'm also friends with his girlfriend, Lana. But this crazy one thinks that something is going on between me and Joel because we e-mail each other. Anyway, she sent me this email accusing me of trying to break her and Joel up."

"What. Oh my God, no wonder your stressed," Alexis said.

Just as Alexis finished saying that, my cell phone rang. I looked at the caller ID to see who was calling. The number was unknown to me. I flipped open the phone and said "Hello."

"Hi Emma," said the caller.

"Yes," I said still unsure who was calling.

"Hi, it's Lana," the voice on the other end said. "Joel told me you wanted me to call you."

"Yeah, I told him I needed to talk to you. What happened to you guys?" I asked.

"Well, we broke up when I saw him kissing another girl. As soon as I told him that it was over, she moved in the same day," she said.

"Lana don't you want to get back together with Joel?" I asked.

"I haven't decided what I want to do yet. It was so painful when he allowed her to move right in. My entire life was turned upside down. I was so heartbroken and just devastated. So I think I just want to stay friends with him for now," she said.

"I feel so bad for you," I told her.

"Well, you know it only lasted a few months and he realized

that he made a mistake. I really don't want to be the one who breaks his heart next time," Lana said.

"Oh, I understand what you're saying but Joel still cares about you deeply. A good friend of mine once told me that once you find love, it dwells in your heart and stays with you forever," I said.

"Wow, you have a great memory. I'll tell you what, I'll give Joel a call later. Thanks Emma," she said.

"Sure I'll keep in touch. I have your number. I'll save it and give you a call right after the dance," I said.

"Okay. Bye Emma," said Lana

"Bye Lana," I said.

When I closed my phone, Alexis was looking at me with a little smirk on her face.

"What?" I said.

"What's that all about?" asked Alexis

"That was Lana. She was Joel's girlfriend for almost two years," I said.

"Is she the crazy one?" asked Alexis.

"No, the crazy one is the one who broke Lana and Joel up," I said.

"Oh, I get it. So you were trying to get Joel and Lana back together," she said.

"So, do you have a date for the spring dance?" she asked.

"No not yet," I said.

"You little liar," said Alexis. And we both started laughing.

"Well I think I can help you with a date," said Alexis.

"What do you mean?" I asked.

"Well, Hunter is coming with me and we both invited Sky. So if you want to make it look like a date I can ask him for you," said Alexis.

"No I'll ask him," I said.

As Alexis parked her car, we could see that everyone else was already present. We got out of the car and walked over to the fire. There were two empty seats one next to Hunter and one next to Sky. Alexis went and sat next to Hunter and I sat next to Sky.

Sara began with the tobacco burning. When Sara was done, Chip stood up and continued with the praying. For some reason, this time the tobacco burning seemed to last much longer than the last time that we were here. Finally Chip completed his part of the prayers and then Misty, Ms. Hall and Sara stood up and started passing out the drinks and fried bread.

"So have you guys heard any new news about the young girl who died?" asked Chip.

"No," said Alex.

"Nothing yet," said Misty.

"Kerrie's mom told me that the crime scene investigators told her it would take a few weeks to sift through all the evidence," said Ms. Hall.

While everyone was talking about Kerrie, Sky asked me if I wanted to go for a walk. We both got up and we went walking up the hill. On the path leading up the hill, Sky pointed out different types of medicine that lay along the path.

"Do you know a lot of medicine?" I asked him.

"I know all the ones that I need to know," he said as he smiled at me.

Then he pointed at other medicine plants that even animals use for their own well being. About half way up the hill, Sky turned to me.

"Emma did I frighten you when I told you about the shape shifters and the skin walkers? Is that the reason you stayed away for the past few days?" he asked.

"No, you didn't frighten me. That's not the reason that I wasn't here. We went to the wake for Kerrie Sanders and then the following day we went to the funeral. It was just so draining that I just wanted to go home and rest," I told him as I looked deep into his eyes.

"What about the other thing?" he asked still looking at me.

"You know I was a little frightened at first, but then I thought about it and realized that I'm just learning about this stuff and I should just try to understand it," I told him.

127

"Okay, that's a fair answer. I was just worried that you were afraid to come around here," he said as we continued to walk.

"Oh no, I really like coming here. My mother always told me when I was younger that if I want to learn anything about native culture that I should learn it first hand and not from books," I said.

"Sounds like your mother is pretty cool," he said.

"Sky, can I ask you something?" I asked.

"Sure, what do you want to know?"

"Okay. Um…Alexis told me that you and Hunter would be coming to our spring dance tomorrow, and, um well, I was wondering if, um, I don't know what I'm trying to say," I said.

"Just say what's on your mind," said Sky.

"Okay will you be my date?" I said.

"Of course," he said, beaming. "I was about to ask you if you had a date."

"Sky, I really like you and I don't mean just a little," I said.

"I really like you too," he said, his voice low and soft. "I have ever since I first saw you with Alexis in the parking lot of the Redwood Shopping Plaza. I think I really annoy Hunter and Alexis about you. I was always asking Hunter to call Alexis just to find out if you were together. I was really glad when Alexis told us she was going to invite you to the fire. I just want you to know I'm glad your here."

We stood there gazing deep into each others' eyes. As I reached to put my hand on his shoulder Sky put his hands on my waist. Then at the same time we slowly pulled each other closer. We stood within inches from each other and I could feel the warmth of our bodies. Just as we were about to kiss, a growling sound came from deep in the woods. We both looked toward the woods, and then Sky looked and put his hand on my shoulders.

"Don't go any where: Just stay right here."

"Okay, but what is it?" I asked.

"It's just one of the guys," he said.

Sky went running into the woods and I followed his shape

until I couldn't see him anymore. I stared into the woods as long as I could. The various shades of green vegetation and the various brown from the barks of the trees made it difficult to make anything else out. I scanned in all directions that I could see, but I couldn't see Sky or anything else. A few minutes later, I felt like someone was watching me. I slowly turned and looked up the hill, and Sky was sitting there tying his shoe laces. His dark blue shirt was still unbuttoned and his long black hair was all messed up. I began to walk up the hill to meet him. When I reached Sky he was buttoning his shirt.

"So what's going on?" I asked him as I sat beside him.

"It's just a couple of the guys fooling around," he said as he laughed.

"You should see your hair!" I said, giggling.

Sky started running his fingers through his hair trying to get the snarls out. He was pulling dried up leaves from his locks. I couldn't help but laugh.

"I'm sorry, here let me help you," I said and we both started to laugh.

Right at that moment, we heard a car horn honking. The sun was just setting in the western sky. There was still enough light to see down the hill.

"They're probably done with their little meeting, and maybe Alexis is ready to leave," I said.

Then Sky stood up real fast and put his hand out to help me up. I grab a hold of his overly warm hand and pulled myself off the ground. Sky didn't let go of my hand until he knew I was steady on my feet. At the moment, I wasn't sure if I wanted to let his hand go. I held on a little bit tighter and smiled at Sky. We turned to walk down the hill hand in hand and walking fairly close to one another. We walked at a regular pace as we came down the hill. Sky told me a story of the first time he saw his uncle Chip shape shift into a wolf and how it frightened him. He started to laugh.

"I thought he got eaten by the wolf. I was only 10 years old when that happened and I was yelling and screaming for my uncle Chip."

We both started laughing as we reached the base camp fire.

Alexis and Hunter were already standing by her car. Her mom and dad were still sitting by the fire. Ms. Hall was nowhere in sight. I assumed that she must have already left for the night. As we approached the car, Sky walked over and opened the door for me and said "So I'll see you tomorrow."

"Yeah, I'll be dressed in my pale blue gown," I said as I smiled at him.

"Pale blue gown hum, I can't wait." he said as he smiled back.

Sky's dark eyes and gorgeous smile across that tanned skin was enough to make anyone's heart thump louder than normal. When Alexis got into the car, Hunter kissed her on the forehead and closed her door. As Alexis started her car the two guys remained standing in the same spot, just staring. With the car moving in reverse, I waved to Sky and he waved back nodding his head.

"Why did that guy have to be so damn handsome?" I said.

"You know he's so crazy about you," she said.

"I think I already know that," I said.

"Why, did he tell you that." asked Alexis.

"Yeah, I think we said something like that to each other," I said.

"So is there a problem?" asked Alexis.

"I just don't want to make the same mistakes that my parents made," I told her.

"Sky is probably one of the better guys around besides Hunter," said Alexis.

"Yeah, Sky said that all the guys that hang around here are really good guys," I said.

"Yeah, they can't touch alcohol or drugs if they want to be protectors," said Alexis.

"Why? I don't understand," I said.

"The guys that drink and do drugs are lost. When they can't

protect themselves, how can they help out an entire nation?" said Alexis.

"That makes sense," I said.

"These guys who hang around the fire have gone through ceremonies since they were 13 years old. They know the importance of being a man and how to treat a woman. So you can really see the difference between the men who drink and those who don't," said Alexis.

"I can see what you mean," I said.

The rest of the way home, we talked about the dance. There were moments of silence and my mind drifted back to Sky and me sitting on the hill. I remembered Sky running into the woods chasing after one of the guys who had shape shifted into a wolf.

"Alexis have you ever seen Hunter shape shift?" I asked.

"Yea," she said.

"Did you get scared the first time you saw that?" I asked.

"No, cause I knew all about it when I was just a little girl," she said.

"Oh," I said.

"Why?" she asked.

"Well, when Sky and I went walking up the hill, we heard what I thought was a wolf. Sky told me not to move and he went running into the woods. I can't remember how long it was before I saw him sitting on top of the hill putting his sneakers on and his shirt was still unbuttoned. I never actually saw him looking like a wolf," I said.

"Oh, that was Marty. He also likes you and he told Sky that if he didn't make his move that he would," she said.

"Seems like I'm always the last one to know what's going on," I said.

"Well, it's all out in the open now," she said.

"Yeah, I guess it is" I said.

"So did you see Sky turn into a wolf?" asked Alexis.

"No, I watched as he went running into the woods as far as I could see. You know I think I did see when he took his shirt off.

He was quite a ways into the woods though. So I didn't really see him look like a wolf," I said.

"He and the other guys are sworn to protect us until there's no more danger surrounding us or until anyone of us decides we longer need protection," she said.

"Okay so when we know that there is no longer a threat to us, we can just walk away?" I asked.

"No, you don't just walk away. You go to the fire and tell everyone that there is no longer a threat and thank the medicine bundle and the protectors and then put your bundle into the fire. This will release you from having to go the fire daily or every other day and the medicine stops protecting and the guys can go back to doing what they usually do," said Alexis.

"Well, what about Carol, Cindy and Aimee? Do they have to come to the fire with their leather ties?" I asked.

"The leather ties will protect them until the danger is no longer present and then their ties will simply disappear," she said.

"So, is that why they don't have to be at the fire?" I asked.

"Yeah," she said as she pulled into my drive way.

My mom must have just gotten home. Jamie and Ashley were helping her unload the groceries. I waved to Alexis and went over to help them out. Mom and I put all the groceries away then I grabbed an apple and started to go up to my room. There was so much going on inside my head that I needed to meditate to help me unwind. At first it was a little difficult following my breathing knowing I had two guys after my heart. I already knew that if I didn't relax and go through this meditation, I may not be able to fall asleep.

# The Spring Dance

In the morning I awoke to the sounds of the alarm. I hit the snooze button, rolled over onto my back and pulled the blankets over my head. It felt like I had just hit that button when the alarm sounded again. This time, I looked at the clock and hit the snooze button one more time. I tried to convince myself that it was simply too early to be up on a weekend. I turned back over and turned off the alarm and went back to sleep.

I could hear music far out in the distance. Well it sounded like music but it was more like a soft drum beating. I could even hear the sounds of the wind as it past over the tree tops. This sound was so calming and relaxing. I remember how it made me feel like nothing else mattered. As I lay there on the softest mattress in the world, I heard a man whisper my name with the saddest voice... "Emma."

"Hum," was the only sound I could get past my overly relaxed lips.

"Please help me Emma," the lonely man whispered.

Again, the only sound that could escape my lips was "Hum."

"Emma, I know that you can hear me. Please help me." The man whispered again.

I tried to look around for the man with the very sad voice, but all I could see was fog. There was fog in every direction. I looked up at the nicest blue sky and not a cloud could be seen. I began to wonder why the sky was so clear. But the ground was covered with fog. Then as I looked down to my feet, I saw the fog moving away. A few hundred feet ahead of me stood a man in a dark suit. He walked with his head hung down as he walked away from me. I watched him raise his arms up to the sky and he fell to his knees. At the same moment his knees hit the payment he yelled as if I were standing right next to him.

"Emma."

I opened my eyes and heard the sounds that were coming from the bathroom. I turned to look at the alarm clock. To my surprise, I had slept another hour and a half. I quickly jumped out of bed and went downstairs behind Jamie, who had just come out of the bathroom. I grabbed four glasses and put them on the table. Then I reached for silverware from the drawer and placed that on the table. Ashley already had the orange juice on the table and Jamie was buttering the toast.

"Let's have breakfast" said mom.

We took our usual seats and began serving ourselves. Mom said dad called late last night. He told her he had a new job and was moving to New York in a few weeks. He told her he'd be stopping by on Sunday to say goodbye. Jamie and Ashley weren't too happy with the news, but mom told them he would still call once a week to keep in touch with them. As for myself, it didn't really matter where my dad went; I knew I could always count on him if things got hard. Besides, who knows, I might not be that far away from him this fall when I started school. So if my friends got their way and we end up at a university or college in New York, dad and I could drop visit each other. If he's there, it would give me a home to visit when I couldn't make the trip back here.

As soon as we finished breakfast, we all chipped in to help mom out with the chores. Just before 1 p.m., we had the entire house tidied up; the clothes, dried and folded; the trash taken out; and the floors mopped.

With that done, I headed upstairs to take a shower. When I came out of the shower, Alexis was sitting on my bed.

I turned on my stereo and told Alexis to pick a few CDs while I got dressed. I pulled a pair of sweats from the dresser and a light colored T- shirt from the closet and began to change. Alexis was still sorting through the stack of CDs when I finished dressing.

"I just don't know what I want to listen to right now," said Alexis.

"I have a bunch of songs on iTunes on my computer," I told her.

"Let's check that out," she said.

I turned on the computer and clicked on the iTunes icon. A selection of songs popped up.

"I've got pop, country, alternative, rap and some classical. Just click on the top and it will start playing," I told her.

"What if I don't like the song?" she asked.

"Just click on the next one," I told her.

"Ooh, I like this one," she said.

"Yeah, I do too," I said.

Alexis motioned for me to sit in the chair, and she began to wrap small curlers in my hair. When she finished, I made her sit down, and I put the curlers in her hair. We laughed at ourselves as we looked at our heads, all full of curlers, in the mirror.

We had spent almost two hours in my room when my mom called us down for a late lunch. We didn't want to leave the room, our hair still loaded with curlers. Finally, mom came knocking on my door. I unlocked the door and opened it just a little, so I could see what she wanted.

"Emma didn't you hear me calling you two to come down for lunch?" asked mom.

"We have curlers in our hair," I told her.

"Oh, so what? Just come down and have lunch," she said.

Downstairs, you could tell that Alexis was more uncomfortable than I was. As soon as Jamie and Ashley noticed our sudden shyness, they began to tease, but mom put a stop to that immediately. Once we were done and the kitchen was clean, we rushed back to my room. Mom came in with hairspray and some makeup.

"When you two are ready to take the curlers out, give me a shout and I'll come and give you a hand," she said.

"Okay, mom, give us about an hour," I told her.

"That might be cutting it a little too short. Don't forget we need photos," said mom.

As soon as mom closed the door, Alexis and I went online and started chatting with our friends. We were a little curious as to what time everyone planned on arriving at the dance. We didn't want to get there too early. As Alexis was typing, my cell phone rang. The caller ID said it was Carol.

"Hi Carol, what's up?" I said.

"My mom's on her way over to do your hair. She just told me to call you so you're aware," she said.

"Oh my God, my mom said that she was going to help us," I said.

"Is Alexis there with you?" she asked.

"Yeah, she's been here for a few hours," I told her.

"Is she on your computer?" she asked.

"Yeah, she's having a blast chatting with Aimee and Cindy and some others," I told her.

"Someone just rang the doorbell. It must be your mother. I'll call you as soon as we're ready to leave," I said.

"Okay," she said.

"Bye," I said.

I opened my bedroom door and saw my mom and Sue walking up the stairs. Sue carried her little tote with her, just like a doctor making a house call. She began taking the curlers out of my hair. She swept the hair up on the sides and used combs to hold it in place. The long flowing curls draped down my back. She lifted here and there, and sprayed my hair to hold all the curls in place. When she finished with me, she turned to Alexis and did the same type of style on her. Then Sue and my mom put a little bit of makeup on us. When they were done, Alexis and I got dressed.

All of a sudden, this feeling of nervousness took over. But I wasn't the only one feeling it. Alexis was just as bad as I was. We both had to tell each other to breathe.

"What will prom be like if we're this nervous for a dance?" I asked, and we laughed again.

We went downstairs so mom could take pictures of us. Sue was still visiting with my mom, so I went over and gave her a hug and thanked her for her generosity. Alexis, following close behind, also gave Sue a hug.

We all went outside, and mom and Sue took pictures – lots of pictures.

I looked at Alexis.

"Every time we look at these pictures, I'll remember this day and the fun we had," I told her.

As Alexis and I were embracing for one of the pictures, a shiny black Monte Carlo pulled into our driveway. We all turned to see who it was.

Alexis started laughing.

"Oh my god, it's the guys."

It was Hunter and Sky coming to pick us up for the dance. Alex and Misty were in the next car, pulling up right behind them.

The guys got out of the car and walked toward us. Both Hunter and Sky were wearing black pants, off white shirts and shiny black shoes. Their long black hair flowed behind their backs. Sky was wearing a pale blue tie to match my dress, and Hunter was wearing a green tie to match Alexis' dress. We all stood there for more pictures.

First it was pictures of Alexis and Hunter, then pictures of Sky and me. Finally, it was pictures of all four of us. Mom also jumped in on some of the pictures. Alex and Misty also joined in with Alexis and Hunter's shots. Then Sue grabbed the camera and we all got together for a group photo. As Sue snapped our photo, Ms. Hall's dark gray Jeep pulled into our driveway. She stepped out wearing a beautiful gown, with one sleeve covering the tattoos on her arm. Her hair was held back on the sides with floral hair combs. She came over and my mom took pictures of me, Alexis and Ms. Hall. Then we took another group photo with Ms. Hall.

A few minutes later, Ms. Hall looked at her watch and told us that she needed to be at the dance early because she and several of the teachers would be chaperones. Ms. Hall gave us hugs, got into her Jeep and headed to the dance.

I gave my mom a hug while Alexis was hugging her mom and dad. Then we met Hunter and Sky at the car. Hunter opened the front door for Alexis, and Sky opened the back door for me. It wasn't until I got into the back seat with Sky that I started getting nervous. I could feel the warmth on my face as Sky closed the door and smiled at me.

"Oh, by the way, you look amazing," he whispered to me.

I blushed even more, turned to look out the window for a second, then turned back to Sky.

"Thanks. You look pretty hot yourself," I whispered back.

With his reddish-brown skin tone, was really hard to tell if Sky blushed.

"I've never been to a high school dance of any kind," Sky said, laughing nervously. "Do you know how to dance?"

"Well, I think we can get by," I said. "Even if I have two left feet."

"Wow, this is going to be something to see, four left feet on the dance floor," he said, laughing.

"Yeah, at least my feet will be covered with my dress and no one will notice them," I teased.

"Hey, I'm not scared. I'm a fast learner. I'll watch everyone for a minute then I'll rule the dance floor," he joked.

"Are you always this funny?" I asked.

"Yeah, I figure you only live once," he said. "You might as well enjoy it."

I nodded my head in agreement, as Hunter steered the car into the roadway leading to the school. There were already quite a few cars parked in the parking lot. Some of the students were standing around near the front entrance taking pictures with their friends. Sky reached over and touched my hand.

"Hold on. I'll get the door for you."

"That's okay. I'll get out on your side," I said.

Sky opened the door, stepped to the side and held out his hand to help me out. I held his very warm hand and pulled myself out. I stood there in front of him smiling.

"Thanks."

"Your welcome." he whispered.

We walked to the back of the car where we met Alexis and Hunter.

Sky leaned over to me.

"You can have my hand or my arm, if you'd like."

I held on to his arm, only because his hands - maybe his entire body for that matter - were extremely warm, hot really. At the front of the school, we met some of our classmates and introduced them to Hunter and Sky. Then we headed to the gym.

When Hunter and Sky saw the decorations, you could tell that they were impressed.

"This isn't a drinking party, right?" asked Sky as he leaned toward me.

"Oh no, it's definitely not that," I told him.

"Wow. You guys go all out when it's time for a dance," he said almost shocked by everything he was seeing.

"Don't you guys have dances like this on the reservation?" I asked.

"No, not at all," he said.

"Do you at least have a prom?" I asked.

"No, not that either." he said.

"Oh my god," I said.

"This is all so new to me," he said.

Then we went walking down the red carpet leading into the gym area.

"Wow, this is incredible," said Sky.

"Are you blown away?" I asked.

"Yeah, I'm acting like it's my first time off the rez," he said laughing.

Inside the gym, there were tables set up along two walls. These tables were about three to four rows deep in some areas. We walked over to the food and drink table and asked for gingerale. Then we looked for a table. We didn't have to search long. Carol, Cindy, Aimee, Todd, Jimmy John and Dustin, who was Aimee's date, were already putting two tables together for us. Everyone was really friendly with Hunter and Sky.

Carol nudged me.

"Your doll is a cutie."

"Oh my God, what did you say, speak English?" I said, as we laughed.

"Okay, let me start over. Your date is cute and really hot," she said, still laughing.

"Oh, I know that. Thank you," I said.

"Alright girls, listen up. Let's decide right now which college we're going to. We have two guys here who would like to know," Carol said.

We all looked at each other.

Finally, Aimee inhaled deeply.

"My choice is New York," she said.

I looked at Alexis and said, "my choice is New York."

"New York sounds good," Alexis said. "Well, Cindy, are you coming with us to New York?"

Cindy poured her gingerale into her glass, raised it as if preparing to offer a toast, and said "New York, here we come."

We all raised our glasses of gingerale to Cindy's glass. Even our guys were getting in to it.

"So, what's the deal? Are you girls staying on campus or off campus?" Toby asked.

"My uncle is from the area and he found a place with five bedrooms. He said the rent is eight hundred per month, but utilities are not included."

"Tell him we'll take it," Carol said.

Everyone agreed.

The band started playing one of the slow songs Ms. Hall had selected for them to get the dance started. One by one, the couples started heading to the dance floor.

Sky looked at me.

"Shall we go test out our four left feet?"

"Sure, why not?" I said.

Sky stood up and pushed his chair close to the table and reached for my hand. I held his hand and followed him to the dance floor.

Sky put his arm around my waist as he held my other hand. I put my free hand on his shoulder. As we looked into each others' eyes, Sky smiled and pulled me a little closer to him.

My heart was thumping loudly. Feeling his strong hold on me, and that electrifying feeling between us, had made my legs feel a little weak. When Sky pulled me even closer, he started humming the song the band was playing in my ear. At that moment, I wasn't sure if I was still slow dancing or if I was just standing still.

When the song ended, Sky continue to hold me close to him, we were now smiling at each other. The only two left on the dance floor staring into each others eyes.

"Wow, I guess we don't have four left feet after all," said Sky, and we laughed again.

"It appears that you're a pretty good dancer after all," I said.

"Like I said, I'm a fast learner," he joked.

"Yeah, I guess you are," I said.

It didn't matter to me that we were the only two in the middle of the dance floor. I felt so safe and secure in the arms of my protector. Before we could move away from each other, the band started playing another slow song. Sky had this huge smile on his face - his white teeth were impossible to miss.

"Emma, can I have this dance?" he asked.

"Sure, I kind of like this feeling like we're the only ones here," I said.

Sky held me a bit closer and rested his head against mine. This time, he quietly sang the song from start to end. When the song ended, I noticed the gym was nearly packed.

Sky asked me if I wanted to go back to the table. I nodded my head and we held hands as we walked back toward our friends.

On the way back to the table, Mr. Baker began tapping on the microphone.

"Attention, everyone! Welcome to the 2005 High School Spring Dance."

Everyone began applauding and cheering. Some were hooting and whistling.

"I would like to take this moment to thank Ms. Hall for her hard work with this group of very talented students, your Spring Dance Band."

With that announcement came more cheers, whistling and applause.

"Thank you," Mr. Baker continued. "Now, I would like Ms. Hall to come up here and sing a song that she and one of her music students composed. Let's hear it for Ms. Hall."

I could see Ms. Hall walking from the food and beverage table toward the stage. The cheering was nonstop until she reached the stage. Ms. Hall strapped on her guitar and stood a short distance from Bobbie Watson. The entire band was dressed in black dress pants with white shirts and very loose neck ties. I turned on my video camera and started recording. We watched as every one of them put on sunglasses including Ms. Hall. Then one of the band members yelled, "Follow me, ah one, two, three."

And they started playing.

This was a love song written by Ms. Hall, and both she and Bobbie Watson put the words to music. The song was about a madly in love young couple. One is killed in an accident, leaving the other to walk life's path alone with just the voice from the past.

Many of the students had got up to dance, but I told Sky that I wanted to sit this one out just so I could record Ms. Hall.

It was touching when Ms. Hall and Bobbie sang the song, moving away from each and then moving back again.

At one point, their lips were close enough that, from where we sat, it looked like a kiss behind the microphone.

The entire time they were singing, Bobbie stared directly at Ms. Hall. When the song ended, everyone stood up and cheered louder than before. The entire band was also applauding.

Ms. Hall bowed to the student body and then turned to the band, bowed to them and applauded them. Ms. Hall walked away from the stage, stopped, then turned back and shook Bobbie Watson's hand. They embraced each other ever so lightly.

Ms. Hall waved to the screaming students and walked over and hugged every band member, and walked toward the stairs. At the edge of the stairs, she took off her sunglasses placed them on top of her head and stood with the other teachers, who also started embracing her. I turned off my video camera and placed it on the table in front on me.

Then the band started playing "Girls Just Wanna Have Fun," and everyone stood up and started screaming.

Then, the chanting started.

"Cindy, Cindy, Cindy!"

Cindy pushed her chair back and went dancing and clapping, her hands up in the air, all the way up to the stage. When Cindy reached the stage, the band started the song from the start. Cindy went for the microphone and started singing. The entire dance floor was covered with enthusiastic dancers. My friends all stood there beside our table and clapped along to the song. I turned my video camera back on to record Cindy doing her best rendition of "Girls Just Wanna Have Fun."

When the song ended, the band started "She Bob" and once again everyone on the floor stayed right where they were. Even some of the teachers were dancing. To hear all the students singing along with Cindy was a feeling I knew deep inside I would never experience again in my lifetime. I think the entire student body knew this was a moment to remember.

As Cindy ended her songs, the cheering and chanting of her name was like thunder rolling across the sky. Cindy bowed several times and blew kisses to audience.

"Cindy, Cindy, Cindy..." the crowd continued to cheer until Cindy walked back to the microphone and put her finger to her lips.

With that little action, she was able to silence an entire screaming crowd of fans.

"Thank you. Thank you so much," she said and then walked over and shook every band members' hand. With the sounds of clapping hands, Cindy walked off the stage and began shaking the teachers' hands before she came walking back to our table. Each one of us embraced Cindy, including Hunter and Sky.

"Your friend is a very good singer," whispered Sky into my ear.

"Yeah, I know. That's exactly what we listened to for the past four years," I said jokingly back into his ear.

As the band started to play another slow song, Sky looked at me and asked if I wanted to dance.

"Sure," I said.

As we walked away from our table, I noticed someone standing at the doorway. I looked over and saw that it was Joel standing there talking to Ms. Hall.

Sky and I went out on the dance floor and once again lost ourselves in each other's arms. Just before the song was over, I whispered in Sky's ear.

"My friend Joel just walked in. Is it okay if we go over and talk to him?" I asked.

"Hey, I don't mind meeting all of your friends," Sky said.

By the time the song ended and we went walking back to our table, Joel was no longer standing by the door entrance. So Sky and I went back to our seats. JJ and Toby had gone up to the food and beverage table and brought back gingerale for all of us.

Without saying a word Sky reached over and held my hand. The heat from his hands shot excitement through my entire body. I tried desperately to hide my blushing cheeks by resting my head onto his arm. Sky leaned closer to me.

"Do you want to go outside for a walk? It's kind of hot in here."

"Sure," I said.

Still holding hands, we walked out of the gym and headed outside. We walked through the parking lot until we reached Hunter's car. Sky tugged on his tie, loosening it.

"It's really hot in there," said Sky.

"It's only you. You really feel like you're on fire," I said laughing at him.

"It's really your fault," he said. "That's how you make me feel."

All I could do was stare at him with an extra wave of red rushing across my face. Once again I leaned into his warm chest to hide my face. He put his hands first on my shoulders, then slowly across my back, giving me a hug. Automatically, I wrapped my arms around him and we began moving from side to side like we were dancing, only this time it was much closer.

"Are you getting a little chilled out here?" he asked.

"There's no way to get chilled with the amount of heat coming off you," I said as I raised my head to look back at him.

He was already smiling as I met his blazing eyes. His eyes seemed to take in my entire face.

"Emma." he said.

"Yes," I said.

"I'd like very much if I could kiss you," he said.

"I'd like that," was all I could say.

As I closed my eyes, I could feel his warm hand on my cheek. His soft, warm lips were gently moving over mine. I was truly enjoying this sweet moment when I heard someone call my name.

"Emma," said a familiar voice.

Slowly, Sky and I pulled our lips apart, and I turned to see Joel standing not too far from Hunter's car.

"Hi Joel," I said still wrapped in Sky's arms.

"Hi Emma," Joel said. "Wow! You look all grown up. Beautiful, really beautiful."

"Joel, this is Sky, my boyfriend. Sky this is Joel. He's my friend I told you about," I said.

Joel and Sky shook hands and greeted each other. The whole time, I kept my arms wrapped around Sky.

"You guys did a great job getting this dance ready," said Joel.

"Yeah, every senior student had a hand in it," I said.

"Well that was a good idea," Joel said.

"So, have you decided where you're going to college?" he asked.

"Yeah, we just decided before the dance started. We're going to St. Lawrence College in Canton, New York," I said.

"New York!" he said, very surprised.

"Yeah, the girls really want this. It's a university in northern New York. There's also a state university there. They have a great sports program, and one of my friends has family there," I said.

"Wow, New York. Well I hope you guys do really well there," said Joel.

"Yeah, thanks Joel," I said.

Well Emma it was nice to see you again. I wish you the best. You deserve it," said Joel.

"Thanks Joel. It was really nice to see you. I talked to Lana a few days ago," I said.

"Yeah, she told me you two spoke. We had a long talk and we got back together yesterday. I'll probably move my stuff into her place tomorrow."

"Think next time you decide to do something like that again," I told him. "Ask yourself, if I do this, will it hurt someone I love. Don't forget the saying 'what goes around comes around.'"

"Is it Sky?" Joel asked.

"Yes," said Sky.

"Hey congratulations, Sky," Joel said, extending his hand to Sky. "You've got yourself one marvelous woman here, you should consider yourself a lucky man."

"Oh, thanks Joel, I know how lucky I am," said Sky as he shook Joel's hand.

"Well I guess I'll head back inside and chat with some of the teachers."

Then Joel looked back at me.

"Emma, take care. And keep in touch, okay?"

"I will, I promise," I said.

Then he looked back at Sky.

"Take good care of Emma and don't ever make the mistakes I did," he said almost in a sad way.

"You don't have to worry. I'll protect her," said Sky.

I let go of Sky and he let go of me, and I walked over and gave Joel a hug.

"It was really nice to see you. You take care and have a safe trip back to LA," I said.

"Will do," said Joel.

Joel smiled at us then he turned and went walking back into the school. Sky looked at me.

"Do you want to go back inside?"

"Did you cool off?" I asked.

"Sure," he said.

We went back and sat at our empty table. All of our friends were on the dance floor. Sky went up and put some finger food on a plate, grabbed two bottles of water and came back to our table. I took one of the bottles of water and took a drink. It was very refreshing, but it didn't match the warm, fuzzy feeling I still had in my gut.

My body was experiencing some unusual feelings -feelings I had never felt before. And each time Sky got close to me, the feeling seemed to get stronger.

When everyone came back to our table, I leaned over to Alexis and asked her if we were still leaving early. Alexis turned to Hunter and whispered in his ear. Then Hunter leaned toward me.

"This is your last dance at this school. I think that you and Alexis should enjoy it and enjoy the company of your friends."

"It's okay with me, if it's alright with you guys," I said.

"I agree with Hunter," Sky said. "I think you should have fun. So Emma, can I have this dance?"

I took his hand, and we went up to the dance floor and we stayed there for the next three slow songs, just gazing into each other's eyes and holding each other. When we went back to the table, Cindy, Carol, Todd and Jimmy John were getting ready to leave for the night.

"You guys are leaving?" I asked.

"Yeah, our journey begins. Nah, we just want some alone time," whispered Carol, as we hugged each other and laughed.

Then Cindy came over and before she could hug me I said, "Cindy you were so incredible tonight. I recorded the two songs you did. I'll make a copy for you tomorrow."

"I'd like that very much and thanks. Don't ever forget you're just as incredible. You're beautiful, you're intelligent, you're honest and I could go on."

Then she glanced over at Sky then looked back at me.

"Plus you have this over the top male stud standing next to you: who seems to love you more than you know," said Cindy as we embraced each other like never before.

Then she turned to Sky and said "It was a pleasure to meet you."

"Likewise. And by the way, you did an excellent job up there," said Sky.

"Thanks. Take care of my friend here," said Cindy as she winked at me.

"That's my job," said Sky smiling.

Cindy embraced Alexis and whispered something in her ear. They laughed. Then Cindy walked away with Carol, Todd and Jimmy John. About 20 minutes later, Hunter asked Alexis what time she wanted to leave. Alexis looked at me and told me that it was almost 11 o'clock. About half of the students had already left, so we decided to leave, as well.

On the way back to my house, I asked Sky if they were driving back to the reservation tonight. He said he and Hunter needed to check on the guys who were watching the fire, and they would need to take over their role before noon.

"Will you be coming to the fire tomorrow?" he asked.

"Of course, I'll be there. Where else will I get to see you?" I said to him.

"I'm already missing you," he said.

"Don't say that! It's just until tomorrow," I said.

"What? You mean you won't miss me?" he teased.

I thought about it for a minute and then my heart started to ache knowing that once I was home, he wouldn't be near me.

"Yeah, I know what you mean about missing you."

When Hunter pulled into my driveway, I could feel my heart pumping harder. Sky opened the door and I got out and closed the door behind me. Then I grabbed Sky by the shirt and began kissing him. While we were making out, Hunter put his window down and tried to interrupt us.

"Ah hum, hey Emma." he said.

We were too busy to pay attention to him. I was not ready to let this moment end.

"Hey, Emma," said Alexis.

"Yes, what is it?" I asked.

"Do you want to spend the weekend at the fire?" asked Alexis.

"What?" I said.

"We can spend the weekend at the fire if you are up to it," she said again.

"You're going tonight?" I said, excitedly.

"Don't go anywhere, Sky," I said. "I'll be right back."

I hurried into the house and met my mom near the stairs.

"Mom, I was wondering if it would be okay if I went to the

fire with Alexis and the guys for the weekend. Please, Mom," I asked very excitedly.

"Emma, I don't mind if you go there, providing you don't do anything out of the ordinary," she said.

"What do you mean out of the ordinary? Sex?" I asked.

"Yes, that's what I mean," said mom.

"Mom, please, I'm not ready for that, not yet any way," I said.

"Sure you can go. I trust you to do the right thing," she said.

"Thanks mom," I said as I went running up the stairs. Halfway up the stairs, I stopped, turned back and asked my mother to unzip my dress.

Then I went running back upstairs. I grabbed a sweatshirt and a pair of jeans, threw it on the bed and then pulled my dress off. I put my clothes on in a hurry. I grabbed my overnight bag from under the bed and threw a couple of T- shirts, jeans, socks and underwear in. I put a pair of socks and then my hiking boots on. I ran into the bathroom and grabbed my shampoo, conditioner, deodorant, brush, hair-ties, tooth brush and toothpaste, and threw them into the bag. As soon as I had everything, I went running down the stairs. I hugged my mom and told her I would see her Sunday evening.

My mom walked me outside and waved.

"Sky, can you make sure Emma is home before 6 o'clock on Sunday, please?"

"Yeah, I will," said Sky.

Then Sky opened the door for me, and we got back into the car. We drove to Alexis' house so she could change and get some clothes and sleeping bags. Hunter had gone in the house with her while Sky and I waited outside for them.

"So did you have to beg your mom to let you go to the fire?" asked Sky.

"Yes, I did actually. She wants you to behave yourself," I said as I laughed.

"Hey, I can behave myself," he said.

"Good, I'm counting on it."

"You have nothing to worry about. I won't rush you into anything. All I want is for you to be my girl," said Sky as he held me in his arms.

Just then, Hunter came out with the sleeping bags and Alexis came out with her overnight bag. We all jumped back into the car and headed to the reservation. Hunter couldn't find a decent song on the radio; finally he just put a CD into the player. This had to be one of Alexis CDs because Hunter wouldn't play anything Alexis didn't like. As soon as the song started, Sky pulled me toward him. I leaned on Sky and closed my eyes.

"Wake me up when we get there," I said.

"Sure," said Sky.

As we were approaching the Route 101 Redwood Highway and the Luther Burbank Memorial Highway, we noticed the traffic on those two roadways was stopped.

"Hang tight, I need to turn this buggy around. It looks like there might be an accident on the highway. I'll go north on Mendocino Avenue and we'll get on the highway from there," Hunter said.

As Hunter drove, Sky and I looked over toward the highway. We could see all kinds of flashing lights and what looked like dust, steam or smoke.

"Can you see anything over there?" Hunter asked.

"I see a lot of flashing lights; it looks like two fire trucks, four ambulances, no make that five, at least four police cars and steam or smoke. That's it, too many buildings in the way," Sky said.

Hunter knew his way around Santa Rosa and the places to enter or exit the Redwood Highway. There was barely any traffic going north to Hopland. We arrived at the fire a few minutes after one o'clock. There were three guys sitting around the fire.

"Hey, so how was your dance?" asked one of the boys.

"It was pretty good," said Alexis.

"Yeah, it was awesome," said Hunter.

"How was everything here? You guys doing okay?" asked Sky.

"Yeah, everything's cool," said one of the guys by the fire.

"Well, we'll see you guys later, I'm going home to change," said Hunter as we walked to Hunter's car. We all got back in, and Hunter drove us to Sky's parents' home. When we got there, Sky grabbed my stuff.

"Let's go, I'll drive you back in my car."

We went inside and I put my stuff by the front door. Sky turned the TV on for me then he went to his room to change. When he came back to the living room, he was wearing a gray T-shirt and faded blue jeans. He sat beside me on the couch and put his bare feet up on the coffee table. He grabbed the remote and smiled as he looked at me.

"Are you tired?" he asked.

"Yeah, a little bit," I said.

"I have two beds in my room. My brother's away at college, so if you want, you can sleep on his bed," he said.

"You're not going back to the fire?" I asked.

"No, my shift is tomorrow," he said.

"What about Alexis and Hunter? Are they going back tonight?" I asked.

"No, they're going back tomorrow," he said.

"Well, will you parents mind if I spend the night?" I asked.

"No, they won't mind, they've been waiting for me to bring you to meet them," he said.

I was a bit worried about sleeping in a strange house, but I followed Sky to his room. I put my stuff at the end of the bed and removed my shoes. Then I sat on one of the beds and removed my socks. I was a bit warm in Sky's room, so I decided to just lie on top of the blankets. I got myself comfortable and watched Sky remove his shirt. He flopped on his bed. He reached for the light switch.

"Goodnight, Emma."

"Goodnight, Sky," I said, as he turned off the light.

It didn't take very long before I started hearing Sky's breathing drop to a low snore. I turned to face the wall and felt myself fall into a state of sleep. A couple of times, I felt my body twitch but it didn't wake me up. Sometime after that I drifted into a dream. I could hear flutes that sounded like a gentle wind. Then I heard someone beat on one of the huge drums that I had seen at the fire. It sounded like a slow pounding heartbeat. It started beating faster and faster.

It seemed like I had been to this place before. I felt very safe and very much at peace. In the midst of this beautiful sound came the sound of a very sad voice, "Emma," said the man's voice.

I looked as hard as I could but it was too dark to see anything. It was that same sad voice I heard yesterday morning. I slowly started turning in a circle. Once I had completely turned around I was starting to see daylight. I found myself standing in the middle of the Redwood highway near the LBMH off ramp. As it got lighter, I saw a man standing on the opposite side of the highway, about 100 yards ahead of me. He had his back to me, and he was wearing a suit. Again, I got this feeling that I had seen this place before. I even felt that I somehow knew this man in the dark suit. I walked toward him.

"Excuse me," I said as I called out to him. But the man did not turn to look in my direction. He just stood there on the side of the road staring at the pavement below. I was now nearly 50 yards away, when I noticed the man was not wearing shoes. He was barefoot. There was no car or bike around to let me know if he had driven himself there. There was no traffic coming or going, and the overpass ahead was clear.

Suddenly, on the opposite side of the road, I saw four teenagers standing around in a daze. Then the beautiful flute music and drum thumping stopped. Everything went silent and the man I was approaching raised his head toward the sky and yelled, "Emma!"

His screeching sound made me stop in my tracks. The man turned to look at me and the total front of him was burnt beyond recognition. I began screaming and I turned to run in the opposite direction.

"Emma!" The man screamed again.

"Emma, Emma, wake up. You're having a bad dream," said Sky.

I opened my eyes and saw Sky. I reached for him wrapping my arms around him and trying to catch my breath. Tears were running down my face and my entire body was shaking in a cold sweat.

"It's okay. I'm right here," said Sky.

I couldn't say anything; I was just so scared. Sky held me tight in his very warm strong arms. He kissed my forehead and told me to go back to sleep. As I laid back on the bed, I pulled Sky toward me.

"Don't leave me please," I said.

"I'm not going anywhere," he said.

Once I warmed up, I fell back to sleep in Sky's arms. Around 7:30 in the morning, Sky pulled his arm slowly from under my head, and I opened my eyes.

"I'm going to shower. Just rest a bit longer. I'll be right back," he whispered.

I wasn't able to fall back to sleep. I got up and fixed the bed. I grabbed my overnight bag and placed it on the bed. Then I fixed the bed Sky had slept in. Just as I was about to open my overnight bag, Sky walked back into the room. He was wrapped in a huge white towel.

"The shower is the next door on the left. Everyone is already gone to the fire." he said.

"Okay," I said.

I grabbed my bag and went to find the shower. I took a very quick shower and brushed my teeth. I put all my dirty clothes at the bottom of my bag and got dressed real fast. When I came out of the shower, I went back to Sky's room but he wasn't there. I went into the living room and saw Sky in the kitchen.

"Do you like scrambled eggs?" he asked.

"Sure. Can I help you?" I said.

"You can put some bread in the toaster," he said.

"Um, that bacon smells good," I said.

"Do you drink coffee?" he asked.

"No," I said.

"Well, I think we have some orange juice," he said as he looked in the refrigerator. He took the orange juice out and placed it on the table while I buttered the toast. As we enjoyed our breakfast, Sky reminded me of my dream.

"Do you want to talk about it?" he asked.

At first I stared at the kitchen table, and then slowly the details of the horrible dream crawled back into my mind. It gave me chills.

"It was about some guy standing on the side of the road and the entire front of him was burned. He knew my name. He was screaming my name and I remember when he turned to look at me I tried to run away," I said.

"You were yelling no and you were kicking," said Sky.

"I feel like I didn't get much sleep. I don't know if it's possible, but it seems that I had this dream a few days ago," I said.

"Sounds like a premonition." Said Sky in a really low whispered.

"What did you say?" I asked.

"Do you have a lot of dreams like that?"

"To be honest, I don't remember many of my dreams. I probably would have forgotten that horrible dream if you didn't remind me," I said.

"Are you afraid to talk about it?" Sky asked.

"No, I'm not afraid," I lied.

"It's just a powerful dream. There aren't many people who can have a dream like that. It's a gift to be able to dream and see a glimpse of the future," he said.

"Well, I didn't know they were powerful dreams. I just assumed they were nightmares," I said.

"I just want you to know that if you ever want to talk about your dreams, I'll help you figure them out. Sara can help, as well. She does a lot of work with dream therapy."

I shook my head and smiled at Sky. Then I told him that I trusted him and Sara enough to help explain some of my disturbing dreams.

We finished our breakfast and cleaned up the kitchen, and I helped Sky put everything away. Sky grabbed some apples, a few bottles of water and some snack bars and put them in a small plastic bag.

We rushed out the door to return to the fire.

# Revelation

When Sky and I arrived at the fire, he introduced me to his mother, Anna, his father, Dan, and his two younger sisters, Dakota and Cheyenne, who were just getting into their car. They had been here for the past three hours. Alexis and Hunter had not arrived yet. From where we stood, I didn't recognize the two guys who stayed up all night watching the fire. As we waved goodbye to Sky's family, Sky pulled out the abalone shell that rested on a bucket by the entrance and lit the sage. He started to smudge himself with it. Once he was done smudging, he held the shell toward me so that I could smudge myself.

Sky put the shell back on the bucket. He took his tobacco out of his leather pouch and put a small amount of tobacco in my hand.

"You hold the tobacco in your hands and pray to the Creator. You thank him for giving us another day; thank him for everything that you are grateful for. Then put the tobacco into the fire once you are finished thanking him," said Sky.

I held the tobacco in my hand and began to pray the best way that I could. I thanked the Creator for my family, my friends, for being a great student; for the air, the water, the beautiful day we were about to have. Then it hit me. I was grateful too that I met

Sky and that someday we would belong to each other. Then I went over to the fire and placed the tobacco into the fire. After that, I went and sat beside Sky.

"Emma, this is Jason and Montana. Jason, Montana this is Emma, my girlfriend," said Sky.

"Hi, Jason, Hi, Montana" I said as we shook hands.

"Hi, Emma," said Jason.

"Hi, Emma," said Montana.

These two guys were almost as tall as Sky and both wore their long black hair in ponytails. They wore plaid jackets. Jason's plaid jacket was black and white, and Montana's was green and white. Both guys had the same tanned skin as Sky and the rest of the guys, which made them both very handsome.

"You guys can go home and get some sleep," said Sky.

"Cool," said Jason.

"What time do you want us to come back?" asked Montana.

"At midnight," said Sky.

"Let's go before he changes his mind," said Jason as he pulled on Montana.

We listened as the two guys drove away. Then Sky put his arms around me and kissed my forehead. This time I pulled him closer.

"Thanks for coming to the dance with me," I said. "I really had a wonderful time."

"Hey, I had a great time, too. I also learned how to dance," he said. "Besides, I'm your protector, and I'll always be here for you."

Sky got up and said he needed to get wood ready for the next crew. He went over to the large pile of wood and started splitting the large logs into smaller pieces, which would be used during the day. About an hour later he asked me to get the bottles of water he had left in his car. I grabbed the bag from the car and opened a bottle of water for Sky.

"Can I help you?" I asked him.

"No, the guys who watch the fire have to do this," he said.

"Oh, okay," I said.

As I went walking back to the car, Sky put the axe down, snuck up behind me and picked me right off my feet.

"Are you getting bored?" he asked.

"No, I'm not bored. I like watching you," I said.

Sky put me down but continued to hold me close, and then he pulled my sunglasses on top of my head and kissed me again. This time it was a very long kiss.

We could hear a car coming down the road.

"I better get back to work." he said.

"Yeah, you better before someone catches you slacking," I teased, and we both laughed.

Sky went back to splitting wood and the car we heard pulled in next to Sky's. I turned and saw it was Hunter and Alexis. They were carrying a large basket with them.

"What time did you two get here?" asked Alexis.

"Sometime around 8 o'clock," I said.

"Eight," she repeated after me.

"What time is it now?" I asked.

"About eleven thirty," she said.

Then they placed the basket on the little table they had built. Alexis went back to the car and brought a cooler and placed bottles of water in it with the ice. I went over to Alexis to give a hand with the water and asked if I could put Sky's bag of water and snacks in it.

"So how was your night?" asked Alexis.

"I had a nightmare," I said.

"About?" she asked.

"Well, it was kind of weird. I remember flute music and the sound of drums. Then I heard someone calling my name, but it was really dark. When I was able to see, I saw this guy standing on the side of the road. I go walking toward him. Anyway, I never reached him. He turned toward me and the whole front of him was burned and he was screaming my name. It was really scary. I turned to run away then Sky woke me up. He said I was screaming and yelling 'no,'"

"Wow, that is pretty scary," she said.

Then Alexis looked over to Hunter and Sky. They were just standing there talking.

"So why are you guys getting here so late?" I asked.

"We went to Sara's to pick up the fried bread and lunch meat," she said.

When I looked back at Sky and Hunter, they were both stacking the wood in a neat pile. I went and sat in front of the fire and a short while later Alexis came to join me. While I was looking at the fire, I saw the guy from my dream in the fire. This time he was reaching out to me. My breathing was becoming erratic. I felt like I was in a trance. It wasn't like that first time when we came to the first Fire Ceremony. I wasn't able to blink.

"Emma," yelled Alexis.

Within seconds Sky was kneeling in front of me, pulling my face away from the fire.

"Don't stare at the fire," said Sky.

Sky pulled me off the bench and walked me over to his car. At the moment I could've sworn that I heard someone whisper, "I think she knows what's going on."

"What's going on?" I asked Sky.

Sky held me in his arms and whispered.

"Nothing."

"Who said, 'I think she knows what's going on?'" I asked him, almost frantically.

"I didn't hear anyone say anything," he said.

I turned to Alexis and asked her "Did you say that "I think she knows what's going on?".

"Emma, I didn't say anything," she said.

"Hunter, did you hear anything," I asked.

"Emma, calm down. Slow down your breathing," said Hunter.

"Something's going on," I said.

"Emma, listen, you need to breathe slowly. Let's go for a walk," said Sky.

Sky turned me slowly and put his arms around me, and we went walking up the hill. When we got to the top of the hill, we sat on the ground. By then my breathing was back to normal.

"Sky, what happen back there?" I asked.

"The fire is very sacred. When you stare into the fire you see things. It's my fault, I should've told you not to stare into the fire," he said

"You know that dream I had? It's the same man I saw in the fire. He didn't call my name but he was reaching out to me. When I walked away, I heard a voice say, 'I think she knows what's going on.' What does this mean?" I asked him.

"It's a spirit trying to reach out to you," he said.

"I don't understand! Why me?" I asked.

"He probably knows you," he said.

"I don't know anyone who died on the side of the road or was burnt like that," I said.

"You shouldn't be afraid of death or anyone who has crossed into the spirit world," he said.

"I don't know why I panic," I said.

"Just remember, when we are born we begin a journey, and when we die that journey is completed. When life starts, it's suppose to be the happiest time and with death it the saddest time. We're all going to be touched by life and death," said Sky.

"Who gave you all this wisdom?" I asked.

"It's all a part of the teaching that we learn before we are allowed to become protectors," he said.

"I feel like such a fool," I said.

"You're not a fool. You're just learning this stuff. A fool is someone who learned the teaching and does nothing about it." he said.

"Are all the guys who sit by the fire as wise as you?" I asked.

"Yeah, we all have this understanding. Beside our uncles and grandfathers would not allow us to be protectors if we didn't practice what we preach," he said.

"Do you want to go back down the hill? I heard other cars pulling in," said Sky.

"Yeah, I'm ready," I said.

Sky got up and pulled me up by the hand. We held hands as we walked slowly down the hill. When we got to the fire, there was already a crowd. Chip and Sara were doing their tobacco ceremony. We stood back a short distance from the fire and waited for Chip to finish. I kept my eyes focused on the ground in front of me. Not once did I look to see who had gathered around.

As soon as Chip was done, Sara and Misty went over to the food table and started fixing the plate for the fire. Alexis came over to where I was and put her arms around me.

"Are you alright?" she asked.

"Yeah, I'm okay. Sorry about freaking out," I said.

"We should've told you not to stare at the fire," she said.

"Is that Ms. Hall? What happened to her?" I asked.

"I'm not sure. She got here just after Chip and Sara started the tobacco ceremony," said Alexis.

We went walking over to talk to Ms. Hall when my mother pulled up. My mom waved at me as I went walking toward her.

"You forgot your cell phone, Emma. I was worried about you," she said.

"Sometimes there's no service out here," I said. Then I noticed Ms. Hall, Misty, Alex, Chip and Sara had gathered around us.

"What's going on?" I asked as I felt Sky hold my hand.

"Emma, there was a bad accident last night," Ms. Hall said. "A carload of teens drove into my lane, and I swerved out of their way. I rolled my Jeep several times. The car load of teens hit the car behind me and exploded on impact."

"Is that why you have bandages on your forehead and your arm?" I asked. "Are you okay?"

"It's just cuts. I'm not hurt," she said.

"Do you know who the teens are?" I asked.

"No, they're all from San Francisco," she said.

I took a deep breath, because I suddenly knew that there was more that I wasn't being told.

"And do you know who was in the other car?" I asked.

Ms. Hall took a deep breath and started looking at everyone else but me. Then she looked at my mom, as if my mom knew the answer.

"Ms. Hall," I said. She looked back at me and said "I'm sorry, Emma."

"What? Sorry for what?" I asked.

"Honey, the guy in the second car was Joel Turner," said mom.

"What? No. No, that can't be right. It's probably someone else," I said.

"Emma, he didn't suffer. Neither did the other teens," said Ms. Hall.

"Emma, are you okay?" asked my mom as I went falling to the ground. I couldn't feel my legs or my feet and everyone around me seemed to be fading out.

"Emma, are you okay?" asked mom.

"I'm okay," I said as I stood back up.

I felt like someone had kicked the air out of my chest. Mom gave me a hug. The whole time I clung tightly to one of Sky's hand. There were no tears flowing down my face. I was definitely in shock and truly in denial.

The man I saw in my dreams and in the fire was unrecognizable, therefore it could have been someone else driving Joel's car. Maybe someone stole his car or perhaps he loaned his car to a friend. All I knew was that my brain was telling me that it wasn't Joel.

"Emma, do you want to come home with us?" asked mom.

"No, mom, I'd rather stay here," I said.

"Sky, make sure she's home early," said mom.

"I will," said Sky.

My mom turned and went back to her car and waved as she drove away. I stared at her the whole time she was backing out of the parking area. As soon as Mom had driven out of sight, I turned toward Sky.

"I need to sit down."

Sky and I walked toward the edge of the wooded area, where there was a small bench. The rest of that day was a complete blur to me. I can't remember hearing anyone talking to me except for Sky. He would hold my face in his hand and talk to me as he looked deep into my eyes. He wouldn't stop until he knew I understood. If I ate or drank anything that afternoon, I had no memory of that either. I did everything in my power to convince myself the news I heard today was simply not true.

The only place I truly felt safe was in Sky's arms. We sat there on the bench for hours.

That night, when the dream from the night before started again and I started screaming, it was Sky's warm arms that comforted me and let me know I was safe.

"Emma you're having a nightmare. Is it the same dream you had last night." Sky asked.

"Yes," I said.

"Ask the man in your dream what he wants from you," Sky said.

"Okay, I will," I said. Then I held tight on Sky's side and drifted back to sleep. I didn't see the accident scene or the burned guy again. The rest of the night was peaceful.

# Path Of Destruction

On Sunday afternoon, when Sky brought me home, I asked him to stay for a while.

There was a strange car parked in our driveway when we pulled up. I was not in the mood to hear any more disturbing reports about Joel. When we walked into the house, mom called us into the living room. There, on the small, pale green arm chair, sat Lana. She looked up at me with eyes bloodshot from crying and the look of exhaustion.

"Emma," she said as she came rushing to me. I held her in my arms and Sky held onto me. Lana was totally heartbroken. Mom came over to us and handed Lana some Kleenex. With all of this emotional pain I was feeling, not one tear rolled down my face.

Mom went into the kitchen to get us iced tea. I sat with Sky on the love seat across from Lana. Mom sat next to Lana.

"Joel called me last night around 11:15. He said he was still at the dance and he told me that he talked to you and your boyfriend. He said he was really glad that you found someone special. He also said that you told him to call me and apologize to me from the heart."

Lana wept even more than the first time, but I couldn't find it in my heart to go over and comfort her. I knew too well that if I did, I would break down. All I could do was hang my head down and look at the floor. I could hear that voice in my head, telling me over and over not to cry because it still could have been someone other than Joel in that car.

When Lana was finally able to compose herself she continued.

"Joel said you had already left the dance and he was going to call you to thank you for your advice. About 11:30, he called me again and said he was on the highway on his way home to me. He said he was going to stop in San Francisco and he would leave in the morning. We were on the phone when the accident happened."

That was all I could stand to hear. She was confirming that it was really Joel who perished in the accident. I got up and went outside; I didn't want to hear anymore. Sky followed me outside and stood in front on me.

"Please remember that you asked me to help you. I'm here, let me help you," he said.

"Just hold me, please," I said.

"Emma, its okay to cry, it's a natural part of life. That's the only way you're going to heal," said Sky.

I was so fortunate to have someone like Sky in my life. I began to cry until I was gasping for air. Not once did Sky let loose his grip on me.

I didn't even notice Alexis and Hunter were there. Alexis handed me some Kleenex just as mom and Lana came outside. I turned to Lana and gave her another hug, this time I didn't hold back the tears. My head was pounding with pain and my chest felt like it had a huge hole in it. This was grief at its worst. I felt like a huge part of me was also dying. When I was finally able to let go of Lana, Alexis went over to console her.

When Lana was able to speak again, she told us that she was going over to Joel's parent's house.

"They're getting stuff together that will be placed in his coffin, like pictures and letters. The family will be at the funeral home beginning at seven tonight, and the funeral will be on Tuesday at two," I turned and looked at Alexis and without saying a word, Alexis nodded for she knew what my request was.

At that same time, Sky was turning the ring on my finger. I slid the ring off my finger and handed it to Alexis.

"Can you make sure this is put in Joel's pocket, please?" I asked.

Alexis took the ring and she and Hunter pulled out of our driveway and followed Lana to the Turners' home.

"You're doing the right thing Emma," said my mom.

"When will it stop hurting?" I said, as I cried.

"Emma," said my mom as she placed her soft hands on my face and turned my head to face Sky.

"This is your future. He will help you get through this. Right, Sky?" said mom.

"I've already told her that," said Sky.

Then my mom turned and walked back into the house.

Sky and I went and sat on the bench on the side of the door. We waited for Alexis and Hunter to return from Joel's parent's home.

"Did you want to go to the wake tonight?" asked Sky.

"No," I said.

"Emma, he was your friend. It's being respectful," said Sky.

"I know, but I can't do it right now. Maybe we'll go tomorrow or the day of the funeral," I said.

"You don't have to worry, I'll go with you," said Sky.

"We'll go tomorrow," I said.

As soon as Alexis and Hunter returned, they told us that everything was cool with Joel's parents.

"I braided the sweet grass bundle and I put a strand of sage through the ring and I gave it to his mom. They were both very grateful and wanted to know if you'd be going to the wake tonight," said Alexis.

I hung my head down and let the tears flow freely down my face. Deep inside I feared taking that walk to the place where I would have to say goodbye to my friend. My mom came outside

167

and she stood silently by the door. Her eyes were drowning in her own tears. I shook my head, just to let them know I wasn't able to do this just yet.

My mom crouched down in front of me and held my head up to look her in the eyes.

"Honey, how would you feel if that was me who died and my friends couldn't or wouldn't come to see you and the rest of the family?" she asked.

"I would hurt even more," I said as my voice broke apart.

"This is why you need to go and see his family," said mom.

Leave it to my mom to come up with the best ways of explaining things so they make sense. I nodded my head and hugged my mom. Then my friends and I left to go to the wake.

Joel's coffin was closed, of course. A large floral arrangement with red and white roses lay across the top of the casket. On each side of the floral arrangement were two large pictures of Joel. One picture was his high school graduation picture and the other was a more recent picture of him and his parents. At the end of the coffin was a huge board full of pictures of Joel and all his friends. I couldn't even go over to have a look at it. I knew that the picture Joel's mom took of me, Joel and Lana at their graduation would be there.

I squeezed Sky's hand and whispered to him that I wanted to leave. We turned and walked over to give Joel's parents a hug.

"Emma, I'm so glad that you came. It means the world to us to see all of Joel's friends," said Joel's mom.

"I can't even find the right words to tell you how I feel," I said.

"That's okay, dear. Just being here is far greater than all the words in the world," she said.

We cried in each others arms. I was glad that I took my mom and Sky's advise. I finally understood that my grief would have haunted me long into the future if I would have stayed away. There was still much pain in my chest and I knew that Sky would help me heal the ache in my heart.

On the day of the funeral, there was a knock on my bedroom door at 9 o'clock in the morning. I just laid there, not wanting to get out of bed. The door opened slowly and who ever it was came in very quietly.

"Emma, can I come in?" said Sky. I heard his soft footsteps and I felt the warmth of his body as he sat on my bed. I turned on my side, looked at him and touched his face with my right hand.

"Wow, I was having a wonderful dream," I said and Sky closed his eyes and smiled.

"Am I too early?" he asked.

I sat up and put my arms around him, and he wrapped his arms around me.

"No. You could've been here at six and it still wouldn't have been too early. You make me feel better just by being here. When we're apart; I just don't want to do anything," I said.

"I have something to ask you," said Sky.

"Yeah, what is it?" I said.

Sky pulled away from me and knelt by the side of the bed as he reached into his pocket.

"Emma, there's no one in this world that I would rather spend the rest of my life with than you. I love you so much it aches inside me. Will you marry me?" he said as he handed me a small gray velvet box.

The pain I was feeling from my grief seemed to lift off my chest. I suddenly felt overwhelmed with happiness. I climbed out of the bed and knelt on the floor in front of him and put my arms around his neck and looked deep into his eyes.

"Is this what you truly want?" I asked.

"More than anything." he said.

I took a deep breath, wrapped my arms tighter around his neck and said "Sky."

"Yes, Emma?" he said.

I pulled my arms away from him and sat on the heels of my feet. Then I put one hand on his face and looked into his eyes.

"Yes, I'll marry you," I said.

Sky kissed me with more passion than ever.

"So are you going to look at the ring?" he asked.

"Oh, okay," I said.

Then I pulled my arms in front of Sky and sat back on my heels. I opened the box and saw this amazing ring.

"Ah, Sky, it's beautiful. I hope you didn't pay a fortune for it," I said.

"Hey, you're worth a whole lot more than that," said an ecstatic Sky.

Sky took the ring out and put it gently on my ring finger.

"I know we just met a few months ago, but we can wait until we graduate from college, if you want. You set the wedding date. Just make sure I know what date and time so I'll be there," he said jokingly.

Just as we were in another embrace, my mom knocked on my door.

"Emma" she said, as she walked in.

I waved my hand at my mother as Sky and I were locked in his powerful kiss.

"Oh, Emma, it's beautiful," she said.

I pulled away from Sky and looked at my mom.

"Did you know about this?" I asked her.

"Sky asked me if he could have your hand in marriage. I told him it was okay with me, but you had to be the one to say yes, All I want is to know the date so that we can make all the arrangements," she said.

"I really need to think about that, okay? I promise I'll let both of you know," I said.

"As soon as you two come up for air, come downstairs and I'll fix you some breakfast," said mom.

Sky and I finally got ourselves downstairs and we had breakfast with the rest of the family. The rest of the day kind of flew. Before I knew it, it was time to go to Joel's funeral. I didn't want the happiest moment of my life to be soured by saying farewell to my dead friend.

When we came walking out of the funeral home to go to the church for the services, I told Sky that I just wanted to go home.

"I said my goodbyes to Joel that last time I went up to his coffin. There is nothing more I can ever say or do for him," I said.

We waited for all the cars to pull away and Sky drove me back home. We had just gone a couple of blocks from the funeral home when Sky asked if I wanted go to the reserve for a couple of hours.

I didn't mind. I think Sky just wanted to tell all his friends that we were engaged.

A few blocks down, I noticed Bobbie Watson walking along the side of the road. He was no longer walking like the man who could get any woman's attention. His shoulders were hunched forward. Both his hands were in his front pockets. He looked like he hadn't shaven or showered in days.

"Stop the car," I yelled.

Sky pulled to the side and I jumped out and ran toward Bobbie Watson. I stood there in front of him. His eyes were coal black with hatred. His pale looking face resembled that of a dead person, expressionless, and his eyebrows were pulled tight together like he was thinking hard about something. Even his lips were pressed hard together.

I jumped at him and pushed him with both hands. He barely moved from his stance.

"Who do you think you are?" I yelled at him.

I clenched my hand into a fist. I wanted so bad to throw as many punches into his face as I could. But Sky had my fist in his hand.

"Emma. Stop. Don't do this," said Sky.

"Watch yourself little girl," said Bobbie Watson as he tightened his eyes and stared into my eyes.

"Don't you ever talk to her like that again," said Sky as he leaned toward Bobbie and growled. Sky's body seemed to grow inside his shirt, as he stepped closer to Bobbie.

"I'm not afraid of you either, you beast," said Bobbie.

"I could rip your body to shreds, so don't cross me," said Sky with a meaner growl.

"You've got no clue as to who you're messing with," said Bobbie, who got even closer to Sky.

"I know exactly what you are, and if it's a fight you want, you've got it," said Sky.

"I'll show you who's stronger," said Bobbie.

Bobbie went walking around us but kept looking back at us cussing.

Just as he got to the alleyway, he turned again.

"I'm gonna get you in your dreams, little girl."

Then he went running down the alley. Sky and I ran after him, but when we got there he was nowhere in sight. We stopped in our tracks, how could anyone vanish into thin air?

"Let's go," said Sky.

Sky grabbed my arm lightly and hurried me to his car. As soon as the way was clear, Sky made a u turn.

"What are you doing? Where are we going?" I asked.

"You need to go home and get some clothes. I'm not letting you out of my sight." he said.

"I thought the medicine that I'm carrying will protect me from him," I said.

"The medicine and I can protect you from his kind of medicine, but he's right; he can harm you in your sleep," said Sky.

"Should I be afraid of that?" I asked.

There was silence, Sky held tight to the steering wheel as we headed toward my house.

"Sky, should I be afraid of that?" I asked.

"You don't have to be afraid of him hurting you physically, but he's right about getting you in your dreams," said Sky as he looked to see my reaction.

My mouth fell open as I thought about what he had just said. I swallowed hard, a bit in shock as to why I had just put my life in danger. I may have endangered the life of my entire family, as well as the guys at the fire.

"Oh my God, Sky?" I said.

"Yes," he said.

"I'm sorry. I just got so upset when I saw him. I can't explain what came over me. I just knew he had something to do with Joel's death because Ms. Hall was involved in it as well," I told him.

"Hey, it's okay. Anger is a part of the grieving process," he said.

"But I just put so many innocent lives in danger," I said.

"We need to tell your mother everything and hope your family comes to the fire with us," he said.

"Alright, as soon as we get home, I'll give her a call at work," I said.

When we got back to house, I called my mom at work and Sky told her everything that was going on, and how important it was for her and Ashley and Jamie to be at the fire. As soon as Sky hung up the phone, he told me he had to talk to his uncle Chip. I ran upstairs to pack some clothes. When I came downstairs with my overnight bag, I placed it by the door.

That's when I saw Bobbie Watson standing across the street looking at my house. I was hoping that he couldn't see me looking out the door window. Not once did I move or pull back on the sheer curtain over the window. But something was wrong. I couldn't put down the overnight bag: I couldn't call Sky to warn him that Bobbie was outside and I couldn't move any part of my body. It felt like I was in a trance. Finally the overnight bag fell out of my hand and hit the floor hard. Sky was in the kitchen when he heard the noise. He came rushing to my side.

"Emma," said Sky.

But I couldn't turn and I couldn't answer I felt like I was hypnotized. Sky grabbed me by my shoulder and turned me around. I was in a daze, my eyes were wide open and my mouth was shut tight. Sky pulled me to his chest, wrapping his arms around me.

"Come out of it, Emma. Snap out of it. Emma!" yelled Sky.

Finally I was able to gasp for a deep breath. It felt like I was being held under water too long.

"What happened to you?" asked Sky.

I was still trying to catch my breath, so I pointed my finger at the window. Sky looked out and saw Bobbie Watson standing across the street. Sky suddenly got a hard look on his face. He was still holding my shoulders.

"Are you all right?" he asked.

"Yes. What happened to me?" I asked.

"He was trying to control your soul. You only have seconds to look away from him whenever you make eye contact," said Sky.

"But I thought I was protected," I said.

"You are being protected from whatever harm he puts you in front of. This is why we need to get you back to the rez. I'll be right back," said Sky.

"Where are you going?" I asked.

"I need to get him out of here. Your mom will be home shortly," said Sky.

Then Sky opened the front door and he went running toward Bobbie. But Bobbie took off running as soon as he saw Sky walk out the front door. Sky was standing at the end of the driveway. He stood there until my mom pulled in.

Sky went over and started talking to my mom. He told her all about Bobbie Watson and what we had been doing at the fire. I began telling her about our first encounter with him on his first day of school and how Alexis knew that there was something strange about him.

"He's a demon who worships the devil, but we can beat him. But you all need to come to the rez and have Sara give you protection medicine," said Sky.

"You know something, I just remembered my mom telling me

174

stories about stuff like that when I was a little girl, but I always thought they were just scary stories," she said.

"Well, it might sound like a scary story, but it's very much real," said Sky.

"Alright then, let me go and get us some overnight clothes," said mom.

Sky and I stayed outside and waited for my mom and siblings to get ready. After a few minutes, Sky went to the end of our driveway. He looked around and then came back to where I was standing.

"Let's go see if they're almost ready," he said.

When we got to the porch, mom opened the door and handed Sky a big suitcase. Sky took the suitcase and put it in my mom's trunk. Then mom and the kids got into her car, and Sky and I got into his car and we drove away.

When we arrived at the fire, there was a large crowd waiting for us. There were about 20 young men around Sky's age and maybe a year or two younger. Alexis and two other girls were braiding their long black hair back into one long braid.

"Do you know how to braid hair?" asked Sky.

"Yes," I said.

"Okay I need mine braided like theirs," he said as he pointed to his friends.

"Sky what's going on?" I asked.

"We're getting ready to go to battle with you," he said.

"Okay, listen, Sara is making some medicine for us. When you fall asleep we will be in your dreams and when this creep comes looking for you, in your dreams we'll be there to protect you and to stop him," he said. "You have nothing to be afraid of. Do you hear me? Start telling yourself that you're not afraid."

"Okay, I'm not afraid... I'm not afraid..." I repeated over and over while I braided Sky's hair.

When I was done, Sky and his friends stood behind Chip near the fire. I sat on the bench with Alexis and my family in front of him. Then Sara started smudging everyone. As soon as she was done, she took out some tobacco from her leather pouch and started praying. Then Chip did the same with his tobacco. When they were finished, they handed my mom, brother and sister leather ties for them to wear. They explained how the leather ties worked. When Sara finished, she picked up a jug and started giving the guys a cup full of some sort of tea. When she got to me, she knelt down in front of me and said

"Don't be afraid, Emma. You have these warriors who will follow you around in your dream world."

Then she handed me my drink.

"Emma, I need you to sit over here. You must be facing east," said Sara.

I got up from where I was sitting and stood there for a minute then I went and gave my mother, Ashley, Jamie and Alexis a hug and then I moved to where she wanted me to be. Sara had placed a sleeping bag on the ground, and I sat on it facing the east. Sky sat right behind me, the rest of the guys sat in a circle around us.

Every one of the guys, including Sky, wore only shorts. Around their necks were their protection pouches. Some of the guys were holding sage and others were holding sweet grass. The rest, Alex, Misty, Alexis, another girl, Ms. Hall, Sara, Chip, my mom, my brother and sister sat around the fire.

"Emma finish your drink and as soon as you feel tired, lie on the sleeping bag," said Sara.

I took my last sip and handed the empty cup to Sara. I took a deep breath and started repeating to myself "I'm not afraid... I'm not afraid..." After each word I began to get more tired. Finally my head fell forward. Sky grabbed hold of me and laid me down on the sleeping bag. I remembered how hard I tried to keep my eyes open. I tried desperately to watch the hot flames from the fire.

One last blink and that was it, my eyes wouldn't open any more. I felt very warm hands on my legs and arms. At that moment, I didn't know the guys in the circle had to keep one of their hands on me so they could journey with me through my dreams.

Once I felt the last hand touch my ankle, I awoke in an open meadow. The sun was shining but I never looked to see where it was. I was able to recognize the many different shades of green from every tree I looked at. When I started walking toward the center of the meadow, I noticed I wasn't wearing my sneakers. I could have sworn that I had left my sneakers on. I began to feel the softness of the grass between my toes and on the bottoms of my feet. I closed my eyes and took a deep breath of clean fresh air. It felt like I had just walked through heaven's gate. I was very calm and I felt so at peace.

A few yards from the center of the meadow, I heard someone approaching me from behind. I did not turn to see who was behind me, for my senses were telling me that everything was going to be alright. Somehow, I knew it was Sky behind me and that if I turned to look at him I would not be able to see him. So I did not bother to turn around. Up ahead to my left, I saw a bush of dark red roses. As I looked at it, blood started dripping down the rose petals. The blood dripped all the way down the stems and seeped onto the ground. Like acid, it began to burn the ground around it. Then from the corner of my right eye, I saw something move. I turned to my far right and there stood Bobbie Watson all dressed in black. He wore a black hoodie which he had pulled over his head. I could see his wavy hair hanging through his hoodie. The only difference between me and Bobbie Watson was that he wore shoes. My first reaction was that no one that evil could be allowed to walk barefoot on sacred ground. We stared at each other for a second before I remember Sky telling me to never make eye contact with him. I immediately moved my eyes to his chest, so I could watch which direction he was about to move.

"I told you I would get you in your dreams," he yelled.

"This isn't a dream," I yelled back.

"Then where are you?" he asked with a smirk on his face. I began to look around. I looked at the east then to the north, over to the west and then to the south.

"So where are you?" asked Bobbie.

"I don't know but it's not a dream. In my dreams things are not this beautiful, this clear or this quiet," I said very calmly.

"So where do you think you are?" asked Bobbie.

"I'm not afraid of you," I said and I continued to stare at his chest.

I heard Sky whisper, "Don't be afraid, I'm standing right behind you. You can't see me or the other guys, but we're all here. We'll be invisible until he makes his move," whispered Sky.

"You should be frightened to death of me," said Bobbie.

"Well I'm not, so what are you going to do about it?" I said.

Then Bobbie took two steps forward and then he crouched into an attacking position. One of the wolves howled angrily and Bobbie turned toward the direction of the sound.

Bobbie reached into his pocket and pulled something out. He rubbed it between his hands. He stood up slowly keeping his eyes in the direction of the angry wolf and then he clapped his hands twice. Suddenly from the corner of my left eye, I saw something move to the left of me and there where the dark red rose bush once was, stood another Bobbie.

"Which one is the real one?" I whispered to Sky.

"The one standing to the right; the other one is just an illusion. He's just trying to distract you." whispered Sky.

Then the Bobbie to my right put his left hand in his pocket and Sky whispered, "Keep your eyes on his hand."

When Bobbie pulled his hand from his pocket, he put his left hand to his mouth and blew dust into the air. From behind Bobbie I saw tiny sparkling lights move forward. I glanced quickly to my left and noticed the other Bobbie was doing the exact same thing. Now there were more sparkling lights behind both Bobbies. I looked back to the right as the dust was still flying into the air, just as a dark gray wolf, a ferocious black wolf and a white wolf appeared from the sparkling lights. The ferocious black one pounced on Bobbie's back knocking him to the ground. To the left the same thing was happening to the other Bobbie. The black and dark gray wolves bit the back of Bobbie's legs and started pulling back just enough for the dust to fall all over Bobbie's back. As the dust started to dissolve, it turned into a huge black snake. Bobbie struggled to kick himself free of the wolves. The snake slowly started crawling up Bobbie's back and wrapping itself around Bobbie's neck. Bobbie started fighting with the snake. Finally, he got one of his free hands in his pocket and blew more dust and the snake disappeared. With this action, the Bobbie to the left and the snake disappeared together.

As Bobbie sat on the ground trying to catch his breath, several of the wolves and two massive black bears started to approach him. Their mouths were pulled back showing their teeth. They began growling viciously as they got closer to Bobbie. Bobbie bounced to his feet and got himself into a crouching position. The two bears stood up and growled even louder than the wolves.

Bobbie turned to look at me; I saw fire in his eyes and looked quickly to the ground.

Bobbie reached into his pocket and whipped something in my direction. Whatever it was, it suddenly turned into a ball of fire.

Sky's incredible speed moved me out of the way.

Again he threw another fire ball, this time it moved much faster than the last one.

Once again, Sky got me out of its path. Then as the wolves and two bears had Bobbie surrounded within a nine yard radius, he disappeared into thin air.

As I stood there with the wolves and the two bears, we heard Bobbie yell:

"You may have gotten away this time, but there will be a time when your friends will not be around and that's when I will take you to hell with me."

"Don't listen to him, his threats mean nothing. He knows that we have him beat," said Sky.

I turned to look at Sky, but he was still invisible. "Why can't I see you?" I asked.

Before Sky could answer, I heard a whimpering howl and saw one of the smaller wolves held up in the air by the neck. Bobbie had made himself invisible and when the smaller wolf approached the center to investigate, Bobbie got hold of him.

The black wolf threw himself into the air toward the smaller wolf, and both of them went flying to the ground.

A couple of the other wolves pounced on the ground where they heard Bobbie fall. They ripped at his invisible clothes until the ripped pieces of material became visible. It became obvious that the wolf pack had located Bobbie and that they were tearing him to shreds. All of a sudden everything went silent.

The entire wolf pack and the two bears stopped. They began sniffing the ground around them. Then, the big black wolf looked in my direction and howled.

"You need to wake up now. Your dream is over, okay," said Sky.

"What's going on? What happen to Bobbie?" I asked.

"He woke himself up, and I'll bet he's hurt badly," said Sky.

As soon as he was done talking to me, everything went dark and I could see the flames from the fire. Most of the guys who were sitting around me were walking around putting their shirts, socks and sneakers on.

Sky was still sitting behind me, still in just his shorts.

"Welcome, back Emma," said Sara. I pushed myself up to a sitting position. Then I shivered as I was overcome by a cold chill. I turned to look at Sky who smiled and asked "Are you alright?"

"Yeah, I'm going to sit by the fire and warm up a bit," I said.

Sky wrapped his arms around me and said "I can help with that."

"Oh yeah, you sure can. Um, you're toasty warm," I said and we laughed.

After a few minutes, I heard someone's fake cough and everyone started laughing.

Sky helped me up and went to get his clothes. He got dressed quickly and came over to sit with me.

"So what do you guys think? Can he be taken?" asked Chip.

"That guy's disturbed in the head," said Hunter.

"Yeah, he uses snakes and who knows what else," said Doug.

"What time is it?" I asked.

"It's almost 9:30," said Chip.

"That dream was three hours long?" I asked.

"Yeah, you didn't go directly into the dream stage," said Chip.

"So what happened?" asked Sara.

"When he appeared, he was all dressed in black," said Sky.

"Pure evil," said Chip.

"He even tried to distract us by making us see two of him," said Doug.

"Yeah, and then he pulls a disappearing act," said Hunter.

"If Jimmy didn't go and snoop around we never would have known that he was still there," said Sky.

"What do you mean?" asked Chip.

"Well, he grabbed Jimmy by the neck and raised him up in the air, and that's when we attacked him," said Hunter.

"I know that we outnumbered him," said Montana

"Yeah, I brought a piece of his pants back from that dream place," said Jason.

"He has to be pretty sore. We bit and clawed him every where," said Hunter.

"It sounds like you guys did everything right," said Chip.

"Good thing Jimmy got nosey and snooped, otherwise we would have thought that he gave up," said Sky.

"Yeah, good job, Jimmy," said Hunter.

"Hey, Jimmy, did he hurt you?" I asked.

"He tried his hardest to choke the shit… sorry; I mean the crap out of me. My neck hurts a little," said Jimmy.

"Well, I think you guys did well," said Sara.

"Hey, you guys, thanks so much," I said.

"This is our job, were protectors," said Sky.

I looked around at the guys and they were nodding in agreement with Sky.

"Sara, will he try to bother me if I go back to sleep?" I asked.

"Not for a while, he will have to nurse his wounds and besides we have a piece of his pants," said Sara.

"What does that have to do with anything?" I asked.

"His scent is on this fabric and when it's placed in a jar of medicine, we will know whenever he decides to do something," said Sara.

"Don't you think that he will be angrier than ever, because of what happened tonight?" I asked.

"Of course he will, but he will need to heal first," said Chip.

"You should still hang around here just in case he's not that badly wounded. Sky can take you to school and make sure everything goes smoothly. There's no way he can do anything to you during the daylight hours," said Sara.

"You think so?" I asked.

"Will it be okay for us to go home?" asked Mom.

"I think you should really wait until tomorrow so we can go to your home and put medicine on your property," said Chip.

"You and the kids can spend the night at our house," said Sara.

"Sky, I want you to tie this around Emma's wrist and yours. When she falls asleep, you will know if he comes back around," said Chip.

I moved my sleeping bag closer to the fire and sat down on top of it. Sky and several of the guys said that they would watch the fire. At about 11 o'clock, I started getting tired, so I laid down on the sleeping bag. I kind of remember when Sky tied the leather ties on our wrist. I remember my eyes being very heavy and I tried to keep from falling asleep. The crackling of the wood burning was the last sound I remember hearing as I drifted into sleep.

# *Paying Attention*

The next day, Sky drove me to school while Chip and Sara went to my mother's house to place medicine around the property. Some ceremonies, like this one, had to be done at dawn.

As Sky dropped me off at school, he told me he would be in the nearby woods, listening and watching for Bobbie.

"Can't you sit and watch him from the parking lot?" I asked.

"No, I can see and hear better if I'm out there," said Sky.

"You can explain all this to me later. I'll see you after school," I said.

"Yeah, I'll see you later Emma," said Sky.

During my first class, students were talking about Ms. Hall's accident. They said she wouldn't be back teaching until the next year. Another rumor suggested she was so badly hurt that she wouldn't be healed for several months.

Alexis and I knew for a fact that Ms. Hall had only minor cuts and bruises. So Ms. Hall must have had some other motives behind her absence from school until fall. Alexis and I decided we would talk to Ms. Hall about this later at the fire, just so we all had the same story.

As for Bobbie Watson, he was absent from school, and no

one had any idea as to where he was. At our last class of the day, Alexis handed me a note.

*A guy I know was in the office this morning, and he said he heard the secretary take a call from Bobbie's mother. From what my friend said, the secretary made it seem like Bobbie had been attacked by a couple of vicious dogs. His mother said he wouldn't be in school for at least a week, maybe two. The secretary told his mom she'd make sure Bobbie's homework was sent to him.*

When our last class was over, Alexis and I walked together to the parking lot. Sky was waiting for us by his car. Alexis explained to Sky what she had heard about Bobbie Watson.

Before Alexis could go into all the details, Sky smiled and nodded his head.

"I heard the news earlier this morning," said Sky.

"Who told you?" she asked.

"Hunter and I were in the woods and we heard when the call came in. Hunter left right away and went back to the rez to tell Uncle Chip and Sara," he said.

"Are you guys going back to the fire right now?" asked Alexis.

"Yeah, I need to talk to Uncle Chip and Sara," said Sky.

"Alright, I'll see you guys there in about an hour," said Alexis.

"Oh, Emma, is there something you want to tell me?" she asked.

"What do you mean?" I said, as I looked at Alexis.

She looked me in the eye and then looked down at my hand. I looked down at my hand and then back at Alexis and then I put my hands over my mouth.

"Oh shoot, I was going to tell you, but with everything that happened yesterday, I forgot all about it," I told her. "Sky proposed yesterday and well, whenever we're ready, we'll get married."

Alexis hugged me and looked at Sky.

"How many months ago did I tell you that someone would be coming into your life? I'm so happy for you both."

"We'll tell everyone when we get to the fire," said Sky.

"You make sure you wait until everyone's there. Emma, did you tell the girls yet? They're coming out," said Alexis.

"No, I haven't told anyone yet," I said.

We waited for Carol, Cindy and Aimee to approach us and I turned around. I waved my left hand at them showing off my ring. Their eyes widened and their mouths fell open.

"Oh my God, you're engaged," said Carol as she hugged me.

"Uh, Emma, congratulations," said Aimee. "You, too, Sky."

"Yeah, congratulations, Sky," said Carol.

"Let me see," said Cindy, lifting up my hand so she could inspect the ring. "Ah, it's so beautiful. I'm so happy for you both."

"So when's the big day?" asked Carol.

"I really haven't decided yet, but as soon as I do, you guys will be the first to know," I said.

"Are you still going to college?" asked Cindy.

"Yeah, of course, that plan hasn't changed," I said

"We're having a problem with Bobbie Watson," said Alexis.

"What do you mean?" said Cindy.

"I saw him yesterday, just before Joel's funeral and I confronted him," I said.

"No shit," said Carol.

"What were you thinking?" asked Cindy.

"I don't know. I just lost it when I saw him," I said.

"What did he do?" asked Carol.

"I really don't remember everything that happened. I just remember him threatening me," I said.

"You're lucky you have Sky to take care of him. Right?" said Carol as she looked at Sky.

"Emma knows she's safe with me and that I would do anything to stop him from harming her," said Sky.

"That's why I'm not afraid of him," I said.

"Well, we better get going. It was nice to see you ladies again," said Sky.

"I'll see you all tomorrow," I said.

Sky and I got into his car and we headed to the rez. We talked about my friends; he wondered how much they knew about Bobbie Watson. I told him Alexis had told all of us to be wary of him and that they should all keep their distance from him.

When we got to the rez, Sky went straight to his house to take a shower. I sat at the table with his parents and we talked about my grandparents. They told me they remembered them. Sky's parents told me they used to play with my mother when her family went to the rez to visit the relatives. I enjoyed hearing stories about my mother's childhood and my grandparents. When Sky was out of the shower, he walked up behind me and told his parents he had good news for them.

"I asked Emma to marry me," said Sky.

His mother gave me a hug.

"So you're the reason my son has been so happy lately?" she said.

Sky's dad shook his hand and gave him a hug. Then he gave me a hug.

"Welcome to our family."

I've asked all the family and the guys to be at the fire in a half hour, so I can tell everyone at the same time," said Sky.

"We'll be there," said Sky's dad

At the fire, Sky and I did our smudging and went back to stand by his car. A crowd started to gather. A lot of Sky's friends were there. Hunter and Alexis were the only ones who came over to stand with us.

"What's going on?" asked Hunter.

"I want to tell everyone about last night and our news about you-know-who," said Sky.

"Most of the guys already know that," said Hunter.

I couldn't help myself. I started laughing. Alexis started laughing as well.

"What's so funny?" asked Hunter.

I looked at Sky.

"You better tell him."

"Emma and I are engaged," said Sky.

"I knew something was going on. So when were you going to tell me?" said Hunter.

"We were going to tell everyone last night, but this lunatic and his threats became first priority," said Sky.

"I'll let it slide this time," said Hunter.

"Looks like everyone's here," said Alexis.

We walked over to the fire, and Sky put some tobacco into the flames. He told them the guy from my dream – Bobbie - was hurt badly. There was no cheering or hooting.

The guys who watched over the fire and those who wandered into my dream congratulated themselves on a job well done.

Then Sky said that he had something else he wanted to talk about. Sky walked over to where I was sitting and reached out his hand. I took his hand and I stood next to him.

"Yesterday, I proposed to Emma, and she said yes," he said. "We're going to get married whenever Emma sets the date."

The crowd cheered and hooted, and I could feel myself start to blush. I felt the heat creep across my face and up to my ears. Sky pulled me close to him, and I buried my face into his chest.

The women in the group formed one line, and the men formed another. Alexis stood by my side, and Hunter stood next to Sky.

The women came up to us first. They shook Alexis' hand, gave me and Sky hugs, and shook Hunter's hand. The congratulations continued until the last person shook Hunter's hand.

I met members of the Simon side of my family. I met many of my cousins, great aunts and uncles.

Ms. Hall was there, and she was as happy for me and Sky as my mom was.

Alexis and I went over to talk to Ms. Hall after the last cousin shook Hunter's hand.

"Ms. Hall, is it true that you won't be back at school until fall?" I asked.

"Yes, I'm on medical leave. Besides if you-know- who thinks

that I'm hurt that badly, maybe he'll back away from me," said Ms. Hall.

"So, you haven't been back to the school since the accident?" asked Alexis.

"No I haven't. I also moved. I got a small place just a couple of miles from here," said Ms. Hall.

"Wow, were you thinking about moving before the accident?" I asked.

"No," she said. "But when I was in the emergency room in San Francisco, I really thought about what could've happened. I needed a change," said Ms. Hall.

"Well, I'm glad you're closer to the rez," said Alexis.

"Yeah, so am I," I said.

"I'm glad I moved, too," Ms. Hall said. "The guys came over, and within an hour and a half, they had me moved. Chip and Sara came over and blessed my new place, so I really feel safe. Besides, you-know-who will be graduating in a couple of months. Maybe this fall, when all this is over with, I'll move closer to the school."

"Well, I'm happy for you," said Alexis.

"So am I," I said.

"Emma, don't wait too long to marry Sky," Ms. Hall said, in that maternal tone. "You know, you can get married and still go to college. Sky is the type of person who will do anything to make you happy and make your relationship work."

"Yeah, I know that," I said.

As we stood their talking, Misty came over and told us a young girl's body was found by hikers yesterday.

"I saw it on the news this morning," she said. "They interviewed the police chief, and he said they thought it might be that ninth grader that went missing from Montgomery High School about a month ago, Cheryl Starkey."

Cheryl had gone missing a few days after Bobbie Watson moved here.

As Misty told us about Cheryl, I remembered the day my

friends and I helped search for her. Carol, Cindy and Aimee were assigned to a group that put up posters all around Santa Rosa. Alexis and I were a part of search group. We looked through alleys, dumpsters, and abandoned buildings. Other groups searched football fields, wooded areas and side roads. The search was called off after a couple of weeks.

"At least her family will have closure," said Misty.

"Yeah, this will help them to get to where they need to be," said Alexis.

As we talked about Cheryl, Sara, my mom and Sky's mom called everyone together, gesturing toward a table loaded with dishes of food.

"It's tradition for the family of a newly engaged couple to host a feast," Sky said, as we started walking toward the table.

Sky and I led a procession to the food.

"Aren't you going to eat?" I asked Sky.

"Of course," he said. "According to the tradition, we have to share whatever we put on our plate. And make sure to take some of everything."

"That's part of the tradition, too?" I asked.

"Yeah, so fill that plate," said Sky, laughing.

I put a little bit of every dish on the plate and sat down on a bench by the fire. Sky sat next to me.

"Did you grab forks?" I asked.

"No, we have to use our fingers," he said and he laughed again.

I looked around and - like he said - everyone was eating with their fingers.

"Here, take a bit of this," said Sky holding a piece of fried bread close to my mouth.

I took a bite of it.

I took a piece of some kind of meat from my plate and held it to Sky's mouth. Sky quickly took a bite. He took the rest of the meat from my hand and fed it to me.

"Umm, what was that?" I asked.

"Moose," said Sky.

"Wow," I said. "It's pretty good."

"I know," said Sky, grinning. "I was hoping you'd take a lot of it!"

I turned to look toward the makeshift counter that was holding all the food and every dish was empty.

"This is unbelievable," I said,

"Yep, just wait until the wedding," said Sky.

"What do you mean?" I asked.

"My family and your family will bring the food, and the entire reserve will be invited," he said. "If you think this was a lot of food, wait till you see what we serve at the wedding!"

"Are you saying you want to get married here at the fire?" I asked.

"This is who I am," he said, looking in my eyes. "I've never even been in a church. What about you? Where did you want to get married?"

"Can we talk about this later, when there aren't so many people around?" I said.

"Sure," said Sky.

We went back to sharing the food. When I had enough, I handed the plate to Sky, so he could finish what was left.

Sky and I walked over to his car, just to be away from the crowd. Sky lifted me up and sat me on his car. Then he stood between my legs and held me by the waist. I smiled at him as he inched closer and closer.

I'm not sure if it was the heat from his body or his dark brown eyes that did it, but my body trembled inside and my heart almost leapt out of my chest.

"So is it later, yet?" asked Sky. "Do you want to talk about where we'll get married?"

"That's not fair," I said.

"What's not fair?" asked Sky.

"Feeling you close to me like this, my heart is pounding," I said. "If you want to talk, you'll have to put up with me tripping over my words."

"You don't think my heart's pounding?" Sky asked. "You don't think I have this indescribable feeling taking over my body?"

I wrapped my arms around Sky's neck, and he wrapped his arms tighter around my waist. We were lost in each others' gaze. It didn't matter that there were nearly 200 people around. As far as we were concerned, we were the only two people who existed at that moment.

"So, tell me what you're thinking," said Sky. "Are you afraid to marry me?"

"Not at all, I want that more that anything," I said, and this time I was the one who kissed Sky first.

"Are you afraid of the idea of marriage?" he asked.

"Yeah, in a way I am, mostly because my parents' marriage ended in divorce," I said.

"I would never do anything that would make you want to divorce me," he said. "You're like the greatest gift someone could have given me, and I will cherish and take care of that gift until the Creator takes it from me. Our marriage will last until one of us dies, and if you should go before me then I would want the Creator to take me as well."

Tears welled up in my eyes and slowly trickled down my face.

"I don't want to live in a world without you, either," I told him as I looked into his eyes. Sky wiped away the tears on my face.

"Did I upset you?"

"No, I'm just so happy," I said and we hugged each other even tighter than before.

Then one of the guys sitting by the fire yelled, "Hey, Sky, didn't you get enough to eat?"

Everyone started laughing. I pulled back from Sky enough to look into his eyes again, and we started laughing.

"I don't mind getting married here, if that's what you want," I said.

"I promise you won't regret this," said Sky.

"So are you doing anything the second weekend in August?" I asked.

"Second weekend in August, gee, um I don't know. Why, what's going on?" asked Sky.

"The day we say I do," I said.

"Um, oh, yes. No, I mean, no, I'm not doing anything," said Sky.

We burst out laughing.

"What's so funny over there?" yelled one of the guys.

"Can I tell them before they all start leaving?" asked Sky, anxiously.

"Go ahead," I said.

"Hey everyone, Emma set a date," he yelled. "We're getting married the second weekend in August."

The crowd started clapped and cheered.

Later that night, after the crowd had cleared out, I placed my sleeping bag by the fire. Sky tied our wrists together with the leather ties, just in case I dozed off.

I fought hard to keep my eyes open.

It felt like I had just closed my eyes for a second, when I saw myself walking on the street a few blocks from the school. It was a cloudy gloomy day, and I was walking by a white picket fence.

"Well, well, well if it isn't Emma, all by her lonesome," said a male voice.

It sounded just like Bobbie Watson.

I looked all around but didn't see anyone.

"Sky, Sky where are you?" I yelled.

"I'm right here. I'm right behind you," whispered Sky.

I woke up. Sky was sitting behind me on the bench.

"What's wrong?" asked Sky.

"Were you just in my dream?" I asked.

"You were dreaming? What happened?" asked Sky.

"I heard someone tell me I was all alone," I said, my voice shaking. "I looked around, but I didn't see anyone. It sounded like you-know-who. I called out your name. I thought you said you were right behind me."

"You fell asleep?" said Sky.

"You guys get ready," said Chip.

Alexis started braiding Hunter's hair as fast as she could. Only two other guys wanted their hair braided, the rest, including Sky, just pulled their hair back into pony tails. I pulled on Sky and asked him to walk with me over to the car.

"What's wrong?" asked Sky.

"I don't want to fall asleep just yet," I said.

"Don't be afraid," he said, as he reached out for my hand.

"I'm not afraid. I just want to stay awake for as long as I can."

"It's best if we get this over with as soon as possible," said Chip.

"Okay," I said.

We returned to the fire, and I got comfortable on the sleeping bag. Sky sat beside me, still holding my hand. A few minutes later, Sky dropped down beside me. I felt the entire portion of my back warm up from Sky's body. I closed my eyes, feeling very warm and safe, and fell asleep.

I heard several wolves howling, one after another. The sounds seemed far away. I couldn't tell our exact location. It was so dark, it was almost completely black. I couldn't make out any houses, trees, buildings – anything that would help me figure out where I was. All of a sudden, I felt a sharp pain in my abdomen and I heard myself moan.

"Wake up, Emma!" I said to myself.

I turned onto my back and tried to open my eyes. When I opened my eyes, it was dawn. I sat up and saw Alexis and Chip sitting at the fire.

The rest of the guys, Sky included, were still asleep.

"What time is it?" I asked Chip.

"Its 4:50" said Chip.

The guys slowly started moving around.

"Well, that was a wasted night," I said. "I didn't even dream."

Alexis and Chip looked at each other. The rest of the guys looked at Chip and Sky.

"Emma," Chip said. "You were dreaming."

"I don't remember any dream."

Sky lifted his arm to show it to me. There was a four-inch gash. It looked like it was already healing over.

"What happened to your arm?" I asked.

"He tried to attack you with some sort of knife and I kept putting my arm in the way," Sky said. "When he got my arm, he almost got you"

"Why don't I remember any of this?" I said.

"When you're exhausted, you can't remember dreaming," said Chip.

"Look at your shirt," said Sky.

I looked at my shirt, and there was a rip from the middle of my T-shirt to the bottom, with a couple drops of blood on it. I lifted my shirt and saw a one-inch gash.

"Was anyone else hurt?" I asked.

Everyone looked over to my left; I followed their eyes and saw a gray wolf curled up and whimpering.

"Sky, who is that? What happened to him?" I asked.

No one said anything. No one even moved.

"That's Jason," said Sky, breaking the silence. "He'll change back as soon as his body heals. Give him a couple more hours and he'll be alright."

"That lunatic had two razor-sharp knives," added Hunter. "He cut all of us, but only Sky and Jason were really hurt. Mine healed while we were still in the dream."

"Yeah, mine too," said Doug.

"I'm having a hard time grasping this. Was I unconscious in the dream?" I said.

"No, you were walking along the sidewalk when he started

talking to you. You never made a sound until he pierced your skin," said Sky.

"Did this all happen in front of a white picket fence?" I asked.

"No, there was no fence. You were walking on the sidewalk." Hunter said.

"I don't remember any of it," I said. "All I remember is the first time I dozed off. In that dream, there was a white picket fence where I was walking. Could that be where he lives?"

"It could be his home," Chip said. "As hurt as he was from that first attack, he probably made you go to him."

Chip turned his attention to the guys.

"How badly did you guys hurt him this time?" he asked.

"I took a chunk out of his leg when he was going after Sky and Emma," said Hunter.

"His right arm should be pretty hurt," Doug said.

"When he went down, I bit into his abdomen," said Justin.

"I thought we did more damage this time than last time," said Hunter.

"Well, I don't think he would want to take you into his home. If he's smart, he wouldn't want to die in his own bed," said Chip.

I looked over at the lone grayish wolf, still all curled up. He began to stretch his front legs in front of him and he howled as he glanced in our direction.

Sky untied our leather ties, went over to the small bench and poured tea into a flat container. He went over to where the wolf was laying and gave him the tea.

"It shouldn't be much longer, he's almost all healed inside," said Sky.

Hunter grabbed a couple pieces of wood and placed them in the fire. Then he grabbed Jason's shorts and went and stood next to Sky. I looked over at Alexis as I folded up my sleeping bag.

"Alexis, were you up all night?" I asked.

"Yeah, I decided to stay up with Chip and watch over you guys," she said.

A few minutes later, Jason started turning back into his human form. The rest of the guys gathered around him. He put his shorts on and drank more of the tea that Sky had given him. As the guys slowly moved away from him, I could see the scar stretching across his abdomen.

Sky returned to the seat next to me and put his arms around me. His arm was completely healed.

Jason stretched his hands over the fire and Hunter threw a sweatshirt to him.

"Hey, are you okay, Emma?" asked Jason.

"I'm fine. I have no memory of what had happened. I could've sworn I hadn't dreamt at all," I said.

"When you screamed, it echoed around the buildings, and I thought he hit your vital organs. That's when I attacked him," said Jason.

"I'm so sorry you were hurt," I said.

Sky held me tighter than before.

"Hey, you don't have to be sorry for anything," Sky said. "It's our job to protect, and besides, our bodies heal quickly."

"If what happened to me happened to you, you would have died within minutes," said Jason.

Sara's old clunker could be heard coming down the road. We looked at Chip and started laughing.

"The whole rez knows when Sara's on the road," Chip said, smiling. "I keep telling her to trade up for a new war pony, but no, she loves that one too much."

When she parked, the car backfired.

"Alexis, shall we go give her a hand?" I said.

"You shouldn't lift anything heavy until you get a doctor to look at that cut. I'll give her a hand," she said.

Sara brought over some breakfast sandwiches and a thermos of coffee. As soon as she and Alexis had everything ready, the guys went over to help themselves.

Chip called Sara over to look at my abdomen. I turned to my side and lifted my torn T-shirt.

"You should go and see a doctor, Emma, it looks like it might be infected," she said.

"I'll take her to our clinic at 9 o'clock," said Sky.

"When was the last time you had a tetanus shot?" asked Sara.

"I'm not sure; I'll have to call my mom," I said.

Around 8:30, I went over to Sky's car, got my cell phone and called my mom.

"Hi, mom, do you know when I had my last tetanus shot?" I asked.

"Hold on. Let me get your immunization records. What's going on Emma?" asked mom.

"Oh, I got a little cut," I said.

"Well, according to my records you're probably due," mom said.

"Okay, Sky will take me to the clinic here and I'll tell them I need a tetanus shot. I'll call you later," I said.

Sky drove me to the only medical clinic on the reservation. I filled out the information sheet. About 15 minutes later, the nurse called my name, and we followed her into the back portion of the office. The nurse took my temperature and blood pressure, and asked why I was there.

I lifted my shirt and showed her my cut.

"My mom said I was due for a tetanus shot," I said.

"Okay, the doctor will be right in to see you," she said as she walked out of the room.

A few minutes later the doctor walked in and looked over my chart.

"Hi I'm Dr. Cook. So let me have a look at that cut," she said.

I lifted my shirt.

"Do you have any pain inside?" she asked.

"No, there's no pain," I said.

The doctor began pressing on my abdomen. Then she told the nurse to get antibacterial cream and dressing. When the nurse came back into the room, she had the tetanus shot, antibacterial ointment and several large self-adhesive dressing pads.

Dr. Cook gave me the tetanus shot. She said she needed to clean the wound with peroxide.

"This is going to hurt a little," she said.

I reached over and grabbed Sky's hand.

As soon as she put the peroxide on the gash, I took a deep breath and shut my eyes real tight. The nurse reached over and grabbed my other hand.

Not once did I scream, but there were tears running down my face.

"Okay, that looks pretty clean," Dr. Cook said.

The nurse put ointment on the dressing pads and placed it over the gash.

"Make sure you change the dressing twice a day. I'm going to give you a prescription for an antibiotic for the infection. I want to see you in about four days," said Dr. Cook

The nurse handed me a small bag with ointment and several dressing pads. I thanked the doctor and the nurse.

Sky took me to the local pharmacy. My mom had health insurance so I had to call her again for the information. My mom spoke with the pharmacist, and within a few minutes, I had my prescription filled.

Sky and I went to his parents' house to take showers and change.

# No Mercy

When we got back to the fire, Ms. Hall was there with a different group of guys. As soon as she saw me, Ms. Hall stood up and put her hands to her face.

"What happen to you?" she asked.

I looked at the guys sitting around and then at Sky. I didn't want to frighten her or anyone else.

"Well, we had a run in with that lunatic in Emma's dream last night or early this morning," Sky said. "He attacked a few of us and did this to Emma."

"Oh my god," said Ms. Hall as she lifted my shirt.

"We just went to the clinic on the reserve and the doctor said it was infected," I said.

It seemed like Sky's announcement upset some of the guys.

"Emma, you better take your pill. The pharmacist said to make sure to take it with food. The water is in the cooler and I have an apple in that bag," said Sky.

I went over to the water cooler and grabbed a bottle of water. The apple was in the bag, just like he said. I took a bite of the apple and took the pill. I drank half the bottle before I went back over to where Sky was sitting.

"Emma, does it hurt?" asked Ms. Hall.

"No, it doesn't hurt," I said.

Sky raised his head and looked up at the sky.

"What?" I asked.

"Emma, you don't have to be brave," he said.

"Okay, it hurts, it feels like a hot knife is twisted inside of me," I said as I grabbed Sky's hand.

"Sky, can I ask you something?" I said.

"Yea," he said.

"When you guys got cut up last night, did it hurt?" I asked.

"Yeah, but it just hurt for a little while. Once it starts healing, the pain goes away," he said.

"When you guys woke up, you acted like it didn't hurt. I woke up because it hurt so much, and I wasn't even aware I was dreaming," I said. "So are we going to be honest with each other?"

"Yes, and I'm sorry I told the guys not to let you know how much it hurt," said Sky, and we held each other.

"So now that you two have agreed to be more honest with each other, tell us how bad it was last night," said Jimmy.

"It was real bad, but now that we know that much more about what he's really like, Chip's working on a plan," said Sky.

"Emma, did you get scared?" asked Ms. Hall.

"No, I didn't even know I was dreaming," I said.

"Jimmy, you're the youngest we have here, I want you to watch the fire and I want the rest of you guys to go home and get rested," Sky said. "Be back here for 9 o'clock."

Jimmy nodded his head and the rest of the guys got up and left. Sky drove me to his house to take a nap; he can't protect me if he falls asleep in my dreams.

When we got to Sky's house, his father noticed my shirt.

"Sky, we need to talk," his dad said.

I went to the kitchen to see if I could help Sky's mother. She was making fried bread.

She mixed the dough together, cut the dough with a cup and placed it in hot oil.

It took me a while to figure out how long the dough should

fry before it's turned over. I think we made enough fried bread for everyone in the community. While the bread was frying, Anna stirred her favorite stew. When the stew was done, Anna and Dan would take the food to the fire.

Anna told me people in the community were worried about me and wanted something done about this evil man. She told me that there would be a lot more people coming to the fire from now on.

As the stew cooked, I told Anna to have someone knock on Sky's door just to let me know when it was 3 o'clock.

I went into Sky's room and sat on the bed across from him. I did some of my homework and watched Sky as he slept. At 3 o'clock someone knocked on the door. The noise startled me and woke Sky up.

"Okay I'm up," said Sky.

Sky turned around and stretched. He got up, leaned toward me gave me a kiss.

"I'm going to go take a shower," he said.

As soon as I finished my English assignment, I got off the bed and fixed the blankets. When Sky came back into the room wrapped in his towel, I grabbed my overnight bag.

"Is the bathroom free?" I asked, almost whispering.

"Yes," he whispered back.

"You know what?" I whispered.

"What?" he said.

"You're very sexy in your towel. One of these days I just might yank that off you," I whispered.

Sky grabbed me wrapped his arms around me and gave me a long kiss.

"Um, you smell good. I better take my shower, before you lose your towel," I said, and we laughed.

Within 15 minutes, I was showered and brushed my teeth. I tied my T-shirt above my bandage and went back into Sky's room. Sky was lying on his bed reading a book.

201

"Sky, do you have peroxide so I can change my bandage?" I asked.

Sky jumped off his bed and went to ask his mother.

Anna came into the room with him. I had the ointment and the bandage ready.

"Lay back and let me fix this for you," said Anna.

Anna was a retired nurse, so she was a pro at dressing wounds and taking care of people. She pulled off the wet bandage, wrapped Sky's damp towel around me and poured peroxide over the wound. Finally, she put the ointment on the bandage, and re-covered the gash. I untied my T-shirt and thanked her.

"Get something to eat before you go back to the fire," she said.

When we finished eating, Sky and I drove back to the fire. Sky had told his dad about what was going on with Bobbie Watson and what happened to me last night.

Dan offered to help watch the fire so that Sky could get some sleep.

There was a huge group of young men at the fire. From what everyone was saying, they hoped to get a group big enough to take Bobbie Watson down for good.

At 4 p.m., Ms. Hall arrived.

Chip and Sara followed shortly after. They burned the tobacco and asked if there was any news anyone wanted to share.

Ms. Hall stood up.

"I was here this morning and I was told what had happened to the guys and Emma. Later on, about an hour after I got home, I got a call from one of my colleagues. My friend's wife works with the mother of this person that this fire is all about. I was told that Mrs. Watson was hospitalized this morning about 5 o'clock. She's in critical condition in the Intensive Care Unit. Her son told the police that he heard someone being attacked by vicious dogs, and when he looked outside he saw that it was his mother. So I don't know what you want to make of that," said Ms. Hall.

"It sounds like he used his mother's spirit to do his dirty work for him," said Chip.

"So, Uncle, what do we do? We might kill an innocent person," said Sky.

"We could give Emma another medicine so when she dreams, she'll be invisible," said Sara.

Chip stood up, leaned over toward Sara and whispered something in her ear. Then Sara grabbed Sky's arm, and they went walking up the hill with Chip. The rest of us sat around the fire.

Alexis and I went over and sat in her car. At first, we didn't say a word. I put my head back and closed my eyes.

All of a sudden, I could see Sara, Chip and Sky picking what looked like weeds along the path toward the hill. I was standing a short distance behind them.

"You talk with the guys and I'll talk with the women," said Sara.

They turned around and started walking back down the hill. I pulled myself forward and looked at Alexis.

"Alexis, do you believe someone could leave their body and, well, transport themselves to another place they wanted to see?" I asked.

"Yes, I do," she said, a smile spreading across her face. "That's what you just did, didn't you?"

"What do you mean?" I said.

"I was watching you. You closed your eyes. I don't even think you realized you were doing it, but you slowed down your breathing," Alexis said. "Then, it seemed like a part of you wasn't here anymore."

"Do you think we could do that and see what you- know-who is doing?" I asked.

"Of course we can."

"Let's go and talk to Sara and Chip," I said.

We jumped out of the car and went looking for Sara. It didn't take us long to find her.

"Sara, are you familiar with people who can intentionally have out-of-body experiences?" asked Alexis.

"Yes, there're people who are able to do that," said Sara.

"Well, Emma and I can do that," said Alexis.

"One minute, I was sitting in the car," I said. "The next thing I knew, I was walking up the hill. I saw you, Chip and Sky picking medicine, and I heard you tell Sky and Chip to have a meeting with the young men. And I heard you say you would have a meeting with the women," I said.

Sara looked back and forth between us.

"She didn't follow us up the hill?" Sara asked.

"No, we were sitting in the car the whole time," said Alexis.

Sara looked back and forth between us again. She smiled.

"Wait right here," she said. "I'll go and tell our men we're leaving for a few minutes. I think we need to run to my house."

We walked quickly the rest of the way down the hill. I saw Sky standing with the guys. I walked toward them.

Sky saw me and stepped away from the group.

"I'm going with Sara and Alexis," I said. "We'll be back in a little while."

"Okay, I have to meet with the guys anyway," Sky said. "I'll see you in a little while."

Alexis and Sara were still talking to Hunter and Chip. I waited by Sara's car. We decided to take Alexis's car so that no one would hear us coming down the road. We headed over to Sara's house.

When we got there, we all took a seat on her living room sofa.

"Okay, this is the plan," Sara said. "First, we'll go to his house. Then we'll go to the hospital to see his mother."

All three of us sat back on the comfy sofa and closed our eyes. We breathed deeply, and with each breath, we relaxed our bodies a little more. I could feel my body settling into the recliner.

I opened my eyes, and I saw Sara standing in front of me smiling. I stood next to her and smiled. As I grabbed Sara's hand,

I saw Alexis out of the corner of my eye. She, too, was smiling. Sara pointed to her left. Alexis and I turned our heads, following her point. I saw the three of us sitting, relaxed on the sofa.

Within seconds, we were standing in Bobbie Watson's bedroom. I saw him lying in bed. He had one bandage on his forehead, another across the right side of his jaw, a large bandage across his abdomen, and smaller bandages all over both legs.

I pointed to the wall. It was covered in photographs. He had pictures of Ms. Hall, Cindy, Misty Hart, and Kerrie Sanders.

Sara blinked her eyes twice. Just like that we were standing in the hospital. The sign in front of us said, "Intensive Care Unit."

Soon, we were standing in a room with a bed. The woman in the bed looked like she was badly beaten. She had tubes in her nose, a monitor beeping to the rhythm of her heart, blood pressure and oxygen monitors. She had bandages on both legs from the ankles to the thighs, bandages on both arms and around her face and head. She was hooked up to an IV.

As soon as Sara motioned with her eyes, we were back in her living room.

"We did it!" said Sara, as she grabbed our hands.

We were all smiling. I knew that we had just accomplished something exceptional.

"Come with me," said Sara.

We followed her into the kitchen, where Sara took a seat. She motioned for us to do the same.

"Emma, we know for a fact that this guy wants to get you in your dreams," she said. "I think I know how we can get him. I think you should let yourself go to sleep and dream. We know he'll be waiting for you. Alexis and I can get him by projecting ourselves into his home. We'll bring medicine with us."

"Sounds like a plan," said Alexis.

"Are you going to tell Chip about this?" I asked.

"Yes, he needs to know," said Sara.

"Alright, let's go," I said.

When we got back to the fire, we smudged and sat down by the fire. The men were still having their meeting.

Sara had tobacco in her hands. She prayed and gave thanks for our safe journey.

As soon as the men's meeting was over, Sara approached Chip. Sky walked over to me as soon as he saw me. I straddled the bench and motioned for Sky to sit facing me.

"I have something to tell you," I said.

"I'm listening."

"Okay, you know earlier, when you, Chip and Sara went for a walk up the hill," I said.

"Yea," he said

"Alexis and I got into her car, and anyways, before I knew it, I was on the path behind you," I said.

"You followed us," he whispered with a smile.

"No, it wasn't like that," I said. "My body was still in the car with Alexis. I heard the end of your conversation and I saw the plants you picked."

"Do you know what you just did?" he asked.

"Yeah, and there's more," I said.

"What?" he asked.

"We told Sara about it," I said. "Then Sara, Alexis and I went to Sara's house. The three of us projected ourselves to his house and saw his injuries. We also saw pictures of Ms. Hall, Kerrie Sanders and a couple of other girls on his wall. Then we went to the hospital and saw his mother. She's pretty beat up."

"You have a special gift," Sky said. "Were you scared?"

"No, it was exciting. I just wanted you to hear about it from me and not Sara," I said.

"Thanks, I'm glad you told me," he said.

We hugged each other. Before he could kiss me, some of the guys started teasing.

"Ah, come on Sky give her a break," one said.

"Yeah, Sky, she doesn't look like she needs mouth-to-mouth," said another.

"Don't pay attention to them," I said.

Walking arm-in-arm, we heard the sound of an approaching car. Next we heard three car doors slam shut.

"It's your mom, and your brother and sister," said Sky.

I got up from the bench and went over to meet my mother. When I got there I gave my mom a hug and she asked my brother and sister to go sit with Alexis.

"What's going on?" I asked.

"I went to see my doctor today and we talked about you a little," mom said. "Emma, are you planning on going to college?"

"Yeah, that's still the plan," I said.

"Okay, so anyway, I convinced my doctor to prescribe a year's supply of birth control pills," she said.

"Mom, we're not even thinking about..."

Before I could finish Mom cut me off.

"Emma, you don't want to wait to get on the pill," she said. "Sometimes it takes a couple of months to work."

"Oh, I didn't know that. Alright, so when do I start taking this?" I asked.

"The doctor said you could start taking it now or you could start on the first day after your cycle. Make sure to take it at the same time every day," mom said.

"You know I'm not planning on having kids for five or six years, right?" I asked her.

"Well, that's good," she said. "So this should take care of that first year."

"Thanks, mom, I was planning on seeing a doctor before graduation," I said as I took the small bag from my mother.

I took one of the pills out and left the rest in Sky's car. I went and sat with my mom, Misty, Alexis and Ms. Hall.

Alexis leaned over to me and whispered, "Sara and Chip want to wait until most of the crowd leaves before they talk about our adventure."

"Did you tell Hunter?" I asked.

"Yeah, he said that he kind of knew something was going on with us," she said.

A few minutes after the crowd left, Sara spoke to the remaining guys, as well as me and Alexis. She told them of our out-of-body experience and our travels to visit the lunatic and his mother. Alexis told them about their injuries.

None of the guys seem surprised to hear about our abilities. They were, however, surprised by the severity of injuries they had inflicted, especially on Mrs. Watson.

Chip handed me a cupful of medicine and told me it would make me invisible in my dreams. I held the cup but, for some reason, I couldn't bring myself to drink it.

"Emma, you need to drink that and try to sleep," Chip said. "We don't want a repeat of last night."

"Yeah, I know that," I said. "Sara, will you and Alexis be going back to his house tonight?"

"Yes," said Sara. "We're going to leave medicine that will weaken his medicines."

"Hear me out for a minute," I said. "If he can't see me in my dreams, he'll be on guard. If he sees me in the dream, it will keep him distracted. That would give you and Alexis time to do what you have to do."

"You're absolutely right," said Chip.

"I agree," said Sara.

Sky, sitting behind me, lowered his head on my shoulder. I reached around and pulled his arms around me.

"It'll be alright," I said.

"Sky, is there a problem?" asked Chip.

"Yeah, I don't like seeing Emma get hurt," said Sky. "I'll never forget the sound of her scream when he cut her."

I turned around and faced Sky. I looked him in the eyes.

"Sky, I know how much you care, but it's just one last night. We need to help Alexis and Sara to get in and out of that house safely. Every night after that, I can be invisible. Do we have a deal?" I said as I held out my hand.

"Deal," said Sky.

I turned and handed Chip the cup of tea.

"Can this be saved for tomorrow?" I asked.

"Sure," said Chip, as he took the cup.

Sara and Alexis put a large sleeping bag on the ground and lay down next to each other.

Sky kissed me.

"You stay real close and I'll see you in a little bit," I said, as Sky tied the leather bands around our wrists.

As soon as Sky finished, he touched my neck and whispered, "I love you."

"I love you more," I said.

I leaned back onto the sleeping bag and started relaxing my body. With each deep breath, my body felt heavier. I felt this warm sensation on my back and smiled - I knew it was Sky letting me know how close he was.

It seemed like someone put an extra log in the fire. The flickering light was so bright I had to open my eyes and look at the fire.

Except the bright light wasn't the glowing fire, it was the sun. It looked like it was the middle of the day.

I quickly sat up and began to stretch. The guys were still lying around, and Alexis and Sara were snoring on their sleeping bags.

As I turned, I saw Chip resting his head and arms across his lap. I rested back on my sleeping bag and closed my eyes.

After a few moments I whispered, "Sky can you hear me."

"Yes, Emma, I hear you," Sky whispered in my ear.

Then I took a deep breath and tried to fall a sleep.

"Hey, Emma, is that you," asked a male voice I didn't recognize.

At first I didn't answer. I wanted him to speak again. I wanted to hear his voice. But he didn't speak again, so I opened my eyes.

I found myself standing on the side of the Redwood highway

heading to San Francisco. I turned in a complete circle and found that I was all alone. It was completely quiet.

Out of the corner of my eye, I saw something move. I turned my head and saw him – it was Joel Turner standing on the side of the road about a hundred feet ahead. He was wearing his dark suit. There were no signs of fire. In fact, he looked more handsome than he had in all the years I'd known him.

Finally, he looked up at me. When he noticed I was looking at him, he smiled and waved. I couldn't help but smile back. We walked toward each other.

When we were directly across the road from each other, I saw four teenagers standing a short distance behind him. They looked like they were maybe 18 to 20 years old.

Joel and the teenagers looked confused. Every time Joel smiled at me, he would look to his right or his left. He never waited long enough to see me smile back.

I tried to cross the road to get to him, but something held me back. As much as we wanted to comfort each other, we couldn't. I could see the pain on Joel's face every time he looked down at the road.

"Emma, do you know what's going on?" Joel whispered.

"What do you mean, Joel?" I whispered back.

"Something's not right," he said. "I can hear them but they can't hear me."

"Who can you hear?" I asked.

"My mom, my dad, Lana," he said. "I can hear them."

"Joel, do you remember the Spring Dance?" I asked.

"Yeah," he said. "Why?"

"What else do you remember?" I asked.

"I remember talking to Lana," he said, excited. "She forgave me."

"Yes, she told me she forgave you," I said.

"So why can't I go home?"

"Joel, there was an accident, a very bad accident," I said.

"Is that why I can't go home?" Joel asked.

"Sky, please help me," I whispered.

"You're doing alright," Sky whispered.

"Oh God, it doesn't feel like it," I whispered

"What is it Emma?" Joel asked.

"You were hurt badly in that accident," I said.

"No, I remember getting out of the car," he said. "And I remember helping Ms. Hall out of her Jeep. I don't understand. I got in the ambulance with Ms. Hall."

"Joel, it was your spirit helping Ms. Hall," I said. "And it was your spirit getting in the ambulance with her."

"That's not true," he said. "I have too much to live for. Please help me."

I began crying like I did when Lana confirmed it was Joel in the car accident. My knees went limp and I crashed onto the roadway. I put one hand on my head and the other over my heart and just cried.

Across the road, Joel was on his knees, and he was weeping. My whole body hurt. My throat felt like it was being stabbed with a knife. I couldn't take the pain anymore, so I rested my body on the side of the road. With tears in my eyes, I could still see Joel on his knees across the road. I closed my eyes tightly and prayed to the Creator to help me. I kept repeating the words, "please God, help me."

I stayed there for what felt like forever, until I heard what sounded like birds chirping.

Finally I was able to turn onto my side and see the campfire burning brightly. Most of the guys were starting to sit up. I didn't want to get up. I knew every person here witnessed the saddest part of my dream. I closed my eyes and pretended I was still sleeping. Sky reached over and touched my shoulder.

"Emma you're cold, do you want to cover up?"

"Um, okay," I whispered.

Sky covered my body with a wool blanket and he moved closer to me. He kissed my neck with his warm lips. I did my best to pretend that I was still sleeping.

Then my stomach growled loudly, and everyone started laughing.

I sat up slightly.

"What's going on?"

"Your stomach is letting you know you had a busy night," Sara said.

"Oh my God, Sara, you're still here?"

"Oh yeah, we had a very busy night," Sara said.

"Well, fill me in," I said. "Is anyone hurt?"

"Well, Alexis and I took medicine to his house," Sara said. "I don't think he'll try to do anything for a while."

"I wish I could believe that," I whispered.

"When you threw the stone at his window, he got out of his bed, stepped all over the medicine, and went to look out the window," Sara said excitedly. "When he did that, we put medicine all over his bed."

Now I was more confused than ever.

I had no memory of being in that dream. I didn't remember seeing Bobbie Watson's house or standing outside of it, and I definitely didn't remember throwing a stone at his window. Just at the moment, Sky put his warm arm around me. I closed my eyes and leaned into his body.

"Emma is something wrong?" Sara asked.

"Is it normal not to remember every detail in one's dream?" I asked.

"What part don't you remember?" Sara asked.

"All of it. Everything you just talked about," I said.

Everyone seemed confused. They began looking around at each other.

"Tell us about your dream," Sara said.

I felt Sky tighten his arm around me. I looked up at him.

"Well, don't you remember? It seemed like someone put extra logs in the fire. It got really bright, so I opened my eyes and saw everyone scattered all over the place. Alexis and Sara were on the sleeping bag."

"Where was I?" Chip asked.

"You were sitting in that same chair. You were resting your arms on your legs and your head was resting on your arms," I said.

"What time of the day was it?" Chip asked.

"It seemed later than it is now - say sometime between ten and eleven," I said.

Everyone looked around at each other and then to Chip. Chip poked the fire a couple of times and looked back at me.

"Emma, how far were you in your dream when you came back here?" Chip asked.

"That was the first thing I noticed," I explained to him. "I assume it was the very start of my dream."

"Okay, did any of you guys see that part of her dream?" Chip asked.

The guys shook their heads from side to side.

"Yes," said Sky. "I remember catching a glimpse of that part of the dream. It was really quick. That's when you asked me if I was there."

"Okay, I want everyone to listen to me. I want you to raise your hand if you saw Emma in her dream," Chip said.

Everyone raised their hands, including Sara and Alexis.

"Okay, Now I want you to raise your hand if you saw Emma outside this guy's house," Chip said, and once again every hand went up.

"I think I know what happened," he said. "As far as I can tell, you left your body outside this guy's house and went off to another dream."

I couldn't understand how they all saw me in front of Bobbie's house, when I was standing on the side of a highway having a conversation with Joel Turner.

"So, Emma, are you ready to tell us about your dream?" Sara asked.

The description of my dream, as well as the tears, poured out of me.

"I was standing on the side of a highway, and Joel Turner was there with four teenagers. I only talked with Joel. He didn't understand why he could hear his parents and Lana but they couldn't hear him. I told him about the accident. He told me he remembered the accident. He said he helped Ms. Hall out of her Jeep and rode in the ambulance with her. The only thing that I can't remember is if I told Joel he died."

"We heard you crying uncontrollably, and we saw you drop to you knees on the sidewalk, but we never heard your conversation with Joel," Sara said. "Even the lunatic seemed moved by how much pain you were in. He walked away from the window saying he was sorry."

"I need to know something," I said, still wiping tears from my eyes. "Why is Joel having a hard time crossing over and understanding what happened to him? I thought the sweet grass was supposed to help him to have a safe journey."

"When someone close to us dies, their spirit leaves their body," Sara said. "The sweet grass helps the body on its journey, but we usually do a special ceremony for the spirit. It helps the spirit cross from where it died into the spirit world."

"Would you be able to do a ceremony for Joel? It would make me feel much better if he was not left on the side of the road," I said.

Sara and Chip sat close together and they began speaking in their own language. Their conversation appeared to start off very serious, almost stern, but soon their demeanors changed. Chip and Sara smiled.

"Because Joel was a good friend of yours, we'll do a ceremony for him in a few days," Chip said. "In the meantime, you'll need to get permission from his parents."

I nodded.

"Thank you so much. I'll go over to Joel's parents later."

The guys were eating breakfast, provided by Sky's mom. Sky told them to go home as soon as Jason and Montana showed up.

# *Exchanging Deeds*

Sky and Hunter drove Alexis and me over to visit Joel's parents. We were there a few hours talking to them.

Alexis could explain everything better than I could. Joel's parents said they had heard of Native American spirit ceremonies, and they wanted their son to journey safely to the spirit world. Alexis told them we would let them know when we had a date for the ceremony, and she called Hunter and told him we were ready to leave.

As we waited for Hunter, Joel's mom asked us if we saw the crosses and flowers Joel's cousins placed at the crash site.

"Yeah, we saw them on the way here," I said.

Just a few minutes later, Hunter picked us up, and we headed back to the reservation.

"I'm glad you didn't tell Joel's parents about your dream," Alexis said.

"I think it would have crushed them if they found out their son could hear them, but they couldn't hear him," I said. "I just couldn't do that to them. I'm just glad they agreed to have Chip and Sara do the ceremony for Joel."

As we approached the site of Joel's accident, I was sure I saw a small patch of fog near the crosses. The more I look at the crosses, the more I thought that it was probably just my mind playing tricks on me.

I rested my head on Sky's shoulder and closed my eyes.

As we got back to the reservation, Sky asked Hunter to drop us off at his house so that he could get a couple hours of sleep before heading back to the fire. I thanked Hunter and Alexis and told them I would see them later.

Sky went to his room to take a nap, and I went to help his mom in the kitchen. Anna was sewing a traditional outfit for her daughter, Cheyenne. I helped her cut out the pattern and placed the cut pieces in neat piles. Anna just wanted the pieces cut.

"I'll have the sewing to keep me busy while Dan's at the fire," she said.

When we finished cutting the pattern, we cleaned the table and Anna started preparing dinner.

"Emma, do you like spaghetti?" Anna asked.

"Definitely," I said.

"Good, my sauce has been slow cooking all day and my apple pie should be just about ready," Anna said.

When she opened the oven, the aroma from the apple pie filled the kitchen. I could smell the cinnamon and apples. She took the pie out and placed it on a rack. Just after she had put the spaghetti in the boiling water, I went to see if Sky was awake.

I opened his door slowly and crossed over to his bed. I knelt down beside him. Sky must have felt me watching him. As soon as I leaned closer to his face, he opened his eyes. He actually kind of startled me.

"Sorry," he said.

"Oh, I didn't mean to wake you up," I said.

Sky lifted his blanket, reached out and grabbed my hand. He pulled me into his bed.

I stared into his beautiful dark eyes, and he pulled me closer to his bare chest. The warmth of his body caused my heart to race faster than ever. My body began to ache and we started to lose control of our breathing. As soon as Sky stopped kissing me, I started kissing the side of his neck.

"Emma, that feels so good, but we need to stop. I need to take a shower and get to the fire," Sky said as he kissed my forehead.

"Sky, I love you so much it hurts," I said.

"I know," Sky said, kissing me again.

He got out of bed slowly, covered me with the blanket and walked out of the room. I decided to wait for him in the kitchen.

I knew what would happen if he walked back in the bedroom wrapped only in his towel, and I was the one who told him to behave himself.

I helped Anna set the table and she called her family to dinner. We all enjoyed the spaghetti and meatballs, and when we were finished, Anna cut a piece of apple pie for each of us. This was the first home-cooked meal I'd eaten in almost a week. I was enjoying every bite.

I asked Anna if she wanted help cleaning, but she told us we needed to hurry back to the fire. It was almost 8 o'clock. Sky grabbed his book bag and put several bottles of water and a few apples into the bag. He gave his mom a hug and a kiss, and we left.

As soon as we pulled out of the driveway, Sky started laughing and shaking his head.

"Do I want to know what's so funny?" I asked.

He smiled at me.

"I'm anticipating the teasing I'll get when we show up an hour later than usual."

"Well you know them better than I do, so I'll stay out of it," I said jokingly.

"Feed me to the wolves," Sky said.

"You took the words right out of my mouth," I said, and we both laughed.

As soon as we found a place to park, I began searching for

Alexis. Sky was right - as soon as he walked around the car, the hooting and teasing started.

"Hey Sky, were you at CPR training?" Chip asked.

"Sky, you getting dementia?" Hunter asked.

"Here, Sky, we drew you a map," Doug said

"Hey, Sky, were you taking care of your own fire?" Jason added.

"Alright you guys, give Sky a break," Sara yelled, but they kept laughing.

As I stood with Alexis and Ms. Hall, I couldn't help but laugh.

"Sky warned me they would be in a teasing mood," I said.

Ms. Hall laughed.

"This reminds me of home. It's probably like this on every reserve."

"Yeah, it's like this with my other family in New York," Alexis said.

Shortly thereafter, the crowd started to leave. Chip asked the young men to set up a 20-by-30-foot tarp on each side of the fire. He didn't want anyone getting wet if it rained while we were in my dream world. Around 9:30, Alexis and I took our places under the tarp. A short while later, Sky came and sat on my left side and tied the leather bands around our wrists. Sara took her place next to Alexis.

"Pleasant dreams, Emma," Sara whispered.

"Thanks Sara, I'll do my best," I said.

I leaned back on my sleeping bag and turned toward Sky. He was already staring at me with love in his eyes.

"I'll see you in a little bit," he whispered.

I nodded my head. Without speaking a word, I moved my lips, mouthing "I love you." Sky nodded back and smiled.

As I closed my eyes I clung to that smile and those sparkling eyes for as long as I could.

Chirp, Chirp, Chirp, tweet, tweet - I heard the sounds of birds in the forest. I lifted my head. I was sitting in the middle of a huge meadow. It looked like that meadow where we had our first encounter with Bobbie Watson. I scanned the area, but didn't notice any rose bushes - just a bunch of wildflowers. In the distance, I could see a couple of squirrels chasing each other up a tree trunk and a white rabbit at the far end of the meadow.

I decided to get up and do a little exploring. The meadow was bordered by forest on two sides. As I turned around, I saw the valley below. It was beautiful.

From where I stood, I could see several huge brown brick buildings. They were no more than three stories tall. I immediately assumed it was a hospital. There were no large office buildings, and no huge apartment buildings to indicate that it was a city. In seemed like a small town, far out in the country. As I turned to look in the opposite direction, I was no longer standing in the meadow. I was standing in front of my house. Alexis, Hunter and Aimee had just pulled up in Alexis' car. Sky had his car's trunk opened. As I came out the door with two suitcases, Sky came over to help me. Mom came out right behind me with an overnight bag and my book bag. I watched her and Sky pack my stuff into his trunk. My mom gave me and Sky hugs. Sky and I were wearing matching wedding rings.

"Make sure you guys stop before dark and get a room," mom said. "Remember, it takes three days to get to New York. There's no need to rush."

"Give Ashley and Jamie a hug, and tell them I'll call once we get settled," I said.

"I'll tell them," mom said.

She went over to Sky and whispered in his ear.

"Make sure you and Hunter take care of these girls."

I woke up. The first person I saw was Chip.

"Hey, Chip what time is it," I asked.

"It's almost five," he said.

I poked at Sky and asked him to untie the leather straps so he could go back to sleep. I got up and went over and sat with Chip and Sara.

"So how did everything go?" Chip asked Sara in a very low whisper.

"Good. Alexis and I went over to our friend's house and watched him for awhile. He was just sitting up on his bed watching movies. Every 20 minutes or so, he would check his clock. He looked out his window twice – once when it was almost midnight and once at just before two," Sara whispered back to Chip.

"Well that's good," Chip said.

"Shortly after that, he turned the television off and went to sleep," Sara said. "We waited nearly an hour before we went looking for Emma."

Montana got up and got some wood for the fire. As soon as he placed the wood in the fire, Chip told him to go home, get some sleep and be back at 8 p.m. Montana nodded and gathered up his sleeping bag and pillow.

Sara told Chip she was going home to make coffee and breakfast sandwiches. Alexis offered Sara and me a ride. She didn't want everyone's sleep disturbed by Sara's deafening car.

We brought Montana home and went over to Sara's house.

Sara sent Alexis and me out to collect eggs from her chicken coop. We were lucky it wasn't dark anymore. Most of the chickens were starting to wander out of the coop. Alexis and I moved along collecting eggs, at least until I stuck my hand in something wet.

"Oh my God, what is that?" I asked.

"Ah, its chicken doodles," Alexis said.

I ran into Sara's house, turned the sink on and started washing my hands. Alexis handed Sara the basket of eggs and started laughing.

"What's going on Alexis?" Sara asked.

"Emma put her hand in chicken doodle," Alexis said, and we all started laughing.

Around 6:30, we had all the breakfast sandwiches done and two big containers of coffee. We cleaned Sara's kitchen so she could relax when she got home later.

"Oh, Alexis were you able to get a hold of Joel's parents?"

Sara asked. "We were planning to have that ceremony for him at 3 o'clock. I almost forgot."

"Yeah, they'll meet us there before three," Alexis said.

"Did you also tell them to bring an apple, a sandwich and a drink?" Sara asked.

"I'll call and remind them," Alexis said.

"Oh, good and make sure you tell them to bring an umbrella, just in case it rains," Sara said.

When Alexis parked the car, the guys were still sleeping under the tarp. Chip and Justin were the only two sitting by the fire.

We got out of the car and closed the doors slowly. Justin ran over to give us a hand. He took the two large thermoses of coffee and placed them on the table. Since Justin was the first one there, he fixed a cup of coffee, put a breakfast sandwich on a napkin and went walking back to the fire.

Sara placed a sandwich on a napkin, and I gave her a cup of coffee. She walked over and gave it to Chip. Chip started making noises, just to get the rest of the guys to wake up.

"Rise and shine guys," he said. "We have coffee and breakfast here."

Sky got up, rolled up the sleeping bags and placed our pillows on top of them. He took the bags and pillows to his car. After he grabbed a coffee, he came and sat next to me.

"Good morning," Sky said as he kissed my forehead.

"Good morning to you. Don't you want a breakfast sandwich?" I asked and smiled back at him.

"Not right now, maybe after this coffee wakes me up," Sky said.

I pulled on Sky's arm and asked him to go for a walk.

We went on top of the hill to the sacred ground. Sky started a small fire and we thank the Creator for blessing us. When we were done, I asked Sky to sit with me and talk about our future.

I reminded him about how close we came to giving in to each other the night before. We knew we wanted to spend the rest of our lives together, but there were other things we needed to discuss.

"So what about children? Will they be apart of our future?" I asked Sky, as I got on my knees and faced him.

"I would like to have a kid of my own some day," Sky said.

"So, one child would make you happy and complete?" I asked.

"I would be happy with just one, but if you say you want more, I'll be happy with more," Sky said.

"I would like to have three or four children. I just don't want you to think that we need to start making them right now," I said.

"Okay, I'll do my best to control myself. I just want you to know it's not always that easy when I'm around you," Sky said.

"Okay, I'll do my best not to tempt you when we're alone," I said. "The next important issue is our home. Where will we raise our children?"

"Well, I have land here, and there will be enough room for us and our three or four children," Sky said.

I wrapped my arms around Sky and thanked him for helping me plan out our future.

"Is there anything else you'd like to talk about?" Sky asked.

"Yes, what are we going to wear to our wedding? I mean do we wear jeans?" I asked.

"Hey, you're the one getting married. It's your choice. You can wear a wedding dress, a plain dress or a traditional buck skin dress," Sky said.

"Has anyone ever gotten married at the fire before?" I asked.

"Yeah, many people have," Sky said.

"Okay, I think I'll ask your mom to help me decide what to wear," I said.

"She'd be more than happy to help," Sky said.

We looked into each others' eyes until Sky couldn't stand it anymore. He pulled me close and kissed me softly. I pulled away from him when his stomach started growling.

"Let's go get some breakfast," I said.

Sky and I walked hand-in-hand down the hill to the campfire. We both ate a breakfast sandwich and, for the first time, I tried coffee. It made the sandwich go down easier but it also made me feel jittery.

After breakfast, Sky and I went back to his house to take showers. While Sky was in the shower, I talked to his mom, Anna, about my dress. Since Anna was also an excellent seamstress, she offered to design it. She asked me all kinds of questions as to what I like and didn't like in a dress. Then she started sketching out a dress.

I told Anna to take her time, but she was so excited she wanted to get started immediately. As soon as I finished my shower, Sky and I went back to the fire to prepare for the ceremony for Joel.

Just as we were pulling out of Sky's driveway, Anna came running after us. Sky pulled back into the driveway and asked his mother what was going on.

"Alexis' called and said you need to take these ribbons to the fire," Anna said.

Sky handed me the small bag of ribbons.

When we got to the fire, Alexis came over to greet us. We went over to Sara to give her the bag of ribbons.

"When the guys are done painting the boards, I'll attach the ribbons," she said, gesturing to five separate one-by-one-inch boards, each four feet long.

"You look confused Emma," Sara said.

"Well, yeah, I am," I said.

"Okay, I have four colors of ribbon. When we put the four colors together, they are sacred. Once we place them on top of each board, they represent each person who has past on. When we get to the accident site and we place these boards into the ground, the ribbons will move when Joel and the four teens are present. It could be a very calm day with no breeze, and the ribbons will still fly around when they are present," Sara said.

"Okay, I understand," I said. "But what about days like today?

Won't the wind make the ribbons fly whether a spirit is present or not?"

Alexis, Sky and the rest of the guys looked at the ground and smiled.

"Okay, see that ribbon tied to that branch over there? Can you see how the wind is blowing it around?" Sara asked.

"Yes," I said.

"Okay, the ribbons we put on these boards will blow around just like that until Chip smokes his pipe and blesses the boards. You'll see when we get there. It can be very breezy and if the spirits are in someone's dreams or mind, the ribbons will not fly," Sara said.

"Okay I understand. How long will the ribbons stay on the boards?" I asked.

"Usually they fly away before the first anniversary of the death. Sometimes, the ribbons fly away within two weeks. Others drag on until the first anniversary. It all depends on us, the survivors. We're the ones who hold them back from crossing over because we're selfish," Sara said.

Sara touched the boards to make sure the paint was dry. She cut five strips of white, red, yellow and black ribbon. The ribbons were attached in a specific order onto each board. When Sara finished, she handed the boards to Chip.

Chip took the boards and put them in his trunk and he and Sara got into the car. Sky and I decided to ride with Hunter and Alexis.

We pulled up to the accident site right at 3 o'clock. There were several cars parked on the side of the road. Alexis told us that Joel's family had contacted the families of the teens, and they all wanted to attend, so Chip told them they could come. They were told to write letters to their loved ones. In their letters, they were to express any words that were left unsaid when their loved ones died.

We parked behind Chip and Sara, and Hunter opened his trunk and took out his hammer. Chip and Sky got the white boards out of the car, and we walked over to where the group had gathered.

Chip explained the boards and the purpose of the colors. When he was done explaining everything to them, he told Sky and Hunter to place the boards in a small circle next to the crosses placed by the families. These boards had to be close enough to each other to support a plate of food on top. Sara began explaining to them what the ribbons represent and how the wind will affect them. The ribbons were blowing around in the wind, as Hunter and Sky finished putting the last board in the ground. Sara took a paper plate and asked each mother of the deceased to place an apple, sandwich and cup full of water on the plate. Chip explained to everyone that when we did ceremonies for the dead, food always had to be left for the spirits. Sara took the plate and placed it on top of the boards.

Chip took out his pipe and started smoking it. Every time he puffed on his pipe, he raised his hands to the sky and spoke in his own language. As Chip did this pipe ceremony, the ribbons stopped blowing in the wind.

As soon as Chip started calling out to the dearly departed, the ribbons began moving in unison. I looked over at Alexis and she leaned toward me and whispered.

"They're all here, I can see them."

Chip finished his pipe ceremony and asked Alexis to join him. He explained to the family that Alexis was able to see and speak to those who are no longer living. Chip looked over to me and asked if I would start. Sky walked me over to face the boards. He stood behind me and kept both hands on my shoulders. I took a deep breath.

*"Joel, I want to thank you for being a great friend, for watching my back in school, for being honest and for making me laugh the whole time we knew each other. I feel this amount of pain because I know I will never see you again, that I will never hear you speak again and that I will never see that smile on your face. I want you to*

*know that I miss you every day, but as much as it hurts, I want you to journey safely to the spirit world. Goodbye Joel."*

I felt the pain swelling in my throat and the tears clouding my vision. Sky walked me over to where Hunter had a portable fire pit and I placed my letter in the fire. I walked as far away from that site as I could. I couldn't bear to hear what the others had to say.

Just before the ramp where Sky and I stood, I could see everyone, including Lana, weeping. We couldn't hear what was being said. Sky told me we should go back because Joel might feel offended that I walked away. We got back just in time to watch Lana put her letter into the fire pit. She came walking over to me and we hugged each other.

Sky gave her a hug and some Kleenex

Joel's parents were next; they wanted to read the letter together.

*"Joel, this is so difficult to try to talk to you and not see you."* His mom said.

*Son, we, your mom and I both want you to know that we love you very much. You know there were times in the past when I said things I'm not proud of. I'm sorry for not taking the time to truly understand you. Can you please forgive me?"* His dad said.

*Joel, you brought so much joy to us in every thing you did. You left us with a lifetime of memories, but the hardest memory was having you taken from us way to soon."* His mom said.

*Joel, your mom is right about the memories. I will always remember the time we spent together, like when we went fishing, or when we played baseball or - better yet - the time we went to see the Giants beat the Yankees. When we were heading back to Santa Rosa you said...”*

Mr. Turner was overcome with emotion and couldn't finish his sentence.

"Mr. Turner, Joel wants you to know he remembers that day and he told you it was the best day of his life," Alexis said.

He also wants me to tell you he didn't think your words were harsh but if you feel that you need to be forgiven, he forgives you," Alexis said.

Mr. and Mrs. Turner walked over to Hunter and placed their letter in the fire pit. They hugged Hunter, Lana, me and Sky.

"May I say one final thing?" Mr. Turner asked.

"Yes you may," Chip said.

"I've done many things in my life but this was the hardest one of them all," he said. We all shook our heads in agreement.

A young couple in their mid-thirties, walked up to the center.

"Our daughter Jane was a passenger in the second car that was involved in the accident. Our little girl just turned 17 two weeks ago.

*Jane, since the accident happened, your mom and I have been blaming each other for allowing you to go out with your friends. I want you to know that I will stop blaming your mom and you. I understand that we can't change the past, and we have no control over how or when we are to die. I want you to know that I forgive you for leaving us way too soon. Please remember how much we love you,"* Jane's dad said.

*Jane, its true what your dad said about us blaming each other. I promise you, I will stop blaming you, your dad and anyone else. I want us to heal and be back to how we were before the accident. I will never forget you and I will love you always,"* Jane's mom said.

Jane's parents walked over and placed their letter into the fire pit.

*Our daughter Julie was 18. She was best friends with Jane. Julie and Jane went to San Francisco to see a baseball game with their boyfriends and they were on their way home when the accident happened.*

*Julie, it hasn't been easy for your mom and me since you haven't come home. We're still hoping that you will come walking up the driveway or call us and tell us you're okay. We're both in a state of denial since we never got to see your body, but I guess no one here got to see their loved ones. Julie we want you to remember that we loved you dearly,"* Julie's dad said.

"Julie, I'm sorry I can't do this," Julie's mom said as she broke down. Her husband consoled her but it was just as difficult for him.

"Excuse me," Alexis said. "I have a message from Julie for her parents. She said, 'Mom I know this is hard for you, but it's hard for me as well. I can hear you cry and I can hear you call my name. If we could turn back time, believe me we would have done things differently, but we can't change what happened. Mom and dad, I want you both to know that all the love you ever gave me is still felt in my heart. Death can not take that away.'"

"Julie, I miss you so much and I want you to know that I will stop blaming others for the accident. Please know that I'll love you until I die," Julie's mom said.

Julie's parents walked over to the fire pit and placed their letters into it. Hunter gave Julie's mom a hug, and then he hugged her dad.

Hi, my name is Tammy; my son Tyler was driving the car. Tyler and his best friend Thomas invited their girlfriends, Julie and Jane, out to a baseball game.

*Ty, I always told you that I would warn you if I ever saw any type of danger in our paths. Usually I can feel or sense danger within a few days before it happens, but on that particular night, I dozed off while I was watching a movie. The last time I looked at the clock, it was eleven fifteen. Ty, it was eleven thirty three when I woke up from the dream. I saw you guys on your way home and I saw you swerve to avoid hitting the guy in the middle of the road. I tried to tell the police this but they look at me like I was crazy. Ty, I'm hurting deeply because I feel like I let you down. I wish I knew how to reach the woman who was driving the Jeep. It would make me feel better if she could tell us if she saw a man in the middle of the road. Ty, I drew a picture of the man in the middle of the road. All I want to know is if this is the man that caused you to crash. I'm sorry son but I can't let you go until I clear your name."*

Tammy walked over and put her letter into the fire pit. She asked Chip if she could show Tyler the picture she drew. Chip told Tammy to give the picture to Alexis. Alexis took the picture and unfolded the paper but did not look at it.

Alexis turned to look at the spot where all the white boards stood and then she looked down at the drawing. I could tell by the look on her face that it was a picture of Bobbie Watson.

Alexis looked at Tammy.

"Tyler and everyone else standing here saw this same guy, and he is the reason your son swerved out of the way." The rest of the parents wanted to have a look at the picture but Chip told them to wait until after the last two parents have said their peace.

"Hi, my name is Marsha and this is my husband, Mark we are here today for our son, Thomas. As you already know, Thomas was with his best friend, Tyler and their girlfriends. Mark and I were watching TV that night, and we both heard screaming. This screaming wasn't coming from the TV show we were watching," Marsha said.

"When I heard the screaming, I looked at Marsha and asked her if she heard it," Mark said. "She said 'yes.' We looked at the time, and it was eleven thirty three. We called Thomas' cell phone and it didn't even ring; it went directly to voice mail. We called it again, and again it went straight to voice mail. We knew something terrible had happened to our son."

*"We couldn't sit here and wait for someone to come and inform us that something happened to our son. We both jumped in our car and headed to San Francisco. About a mile that way, we notice all the flashing lights. I believe we stopped at a marker and we started walking toward the lights. We knew it was Tyler's car, but not because we recognized the car, we recognized his license plate. So we called Tammy and told her where we were. She knew right away that our boys were gone. Tammy showed us a picture of the guy she saw in her dream. I've seen him around our office building several times in the past. His mother is in charge of some health or wellness program that just started up in January or February. I know that she hasn't been*

*at work for a few days or more because she was attacked by vicious dogs,"* Mark said.

Marsha and Mark went over and put their letters into the fire pit and exchanged hugs with everyone. The rest of the families asked to have a look at the drawing of the guy who may have been responsible for the accident.

Mark took the photo and raised it over his head for everyone to see.

"This guy is responsible for our loss," he said. "And the police have said that there was nothing they could do because the woman who rolled her Jeep couldn't remember what happened. I mean, the woman claimed she tried to avoid hitting some guy on the road, but when they went back to talk to her in the morning, she couldn't remember anything. If our sons and daughters are here right now and they can hear us, they need to find this man and give him a taste of his own medicine."

"Oh, my God, I don't believe it," Sky whispered in my ear.

"What? You don't believe what?" I whispered back.

"I'll tell you later," Sky whispered

Chip and Sara thanked everyone for coming and told them not to turn their child's room into a shrine. Dust, spider and cob webs are not things you want your memories buried under.

"These ribbons will let us know how long it takes your sons or daughters to cross into spirit world," Sara said.

Chip lit his pipe and spoke in his language. As soon as he was done, he and Sara shook everyone's hands.

# Restless Souls

Our ride back to the reservation was a bit quiet. Hunter, Sky and Alexis were disturbed by some of the parents, the ones that wanted their dearly departed to seek revenge on Bobbie Watson and maybe even his mother. I, on the other hand, didn't understand at first what they were upset about. But when we got back to the fire, it was very clear that Chip and Sara were also upset with some of the parents.

"Chip, I'm sorry for asking you guy's to help Joel's parents. I didn't know it would cause this much trouble," I said.

"Emma, you don't have to be sorry about anything." Chip said.

"Can you explain what's wrong?" I asked.

"It's Mark, he's so angry for not being a better dad," Chip said. "Now he's lost that chance to do the right thing for his son. He wants his son to be hateful and seek revenge on the one who caused his death. He was the only one who didn't even speak to his son. He didn't tell him that he loved him or that he'll miss him. Not once did he even mention any memories."

"Yeah, I noticed that. Do you believe Joel and the rest of them can harm or disturb you know who or his mother?" I asked.

Everyone around the fire nodded their heads.

"Yes, when you call the spirits to gather, there is nothing but peace and happiness around them," Chip said. "Then you have Mark putting out that negative energy. They'll listen and may even follow his commands."

I rested my arms on my legs and placed my head on my arms. I knew that some have blamed me for Chip and Sara's silence. Maybe I'm wrong. Maybe Chip and Sara were hoping something good could come out of this.

Sky returned from taking his shower and sat beside me. He put his arms around me and kissed the back of my neck.

"Hey, are you already tired?" Sky asked.

'No, I'm stressed out," I replied.

"Well, let's go for a walk. Exercise relieves stress," he said.

I sat up and turned to face Sky. Some of the guys looked away from me.

"Okay, let's go for that walk," I said.

Sky took my hand and led me up the hill.

"No, let's go down the road," I said.

Once we were on the dirt road, Sky let go of my hand and put his arm across my shoulder.

"Emma, what's wrong?" Sky asked.

"I don't know, maybe I'm just being silly. The tension at the fire is more than I can handle. I think I'm being blamed because I don't know the culture."

Sky stood in front of me with one hand on my shoulder and the other holding my face.

"Hey, no one is blaming you. Chip and Sara are just upset with that one guy. They're not upset with you. Trust me," Sky said.

"Maybe I should've gone home with you instead of staying at the fire. I just wanted to tell Chip and Sara that I was sorry," I said as the tears rolled down my cheeks.

Sky took me down a path that led to a small creek.

"This is the place our medicine people tell us to go when we are not thinking straight or when we feel like we've done wrong,"

Sky said, as he sat down on a huge rock and pulled me on his lap.

He told me to relax and close my eyes.

"Can you hear the sound of the creek as it passes by?" Sky asked.

"No, I can't hear anything," I said.

"Okay, reach into the water with both hands and ask the water spirit to make you feel better," Sky said.

I did as I was told, splashing the water with my hands. After a couple of minutes, I asked the water spirit to help me calm down and take my anxiety away. I shook off the excess water and wiped my hands on my jeans. I leaned back on Sky and closed my eyes.

A few minutes later Sky asked again, "Can you hear the sound of the creek now?"

To my surprise, I heard the slow-moving current. I didn't feel stress.

"Sky, don't get upset with me, but I almost went home," I said.

I turned to look at Sky and saw the saddest eyes looking back at me. I wrapped my arm around his neck.

"Hold me please."

"Emma, I don't know what I'd do if you left me for something I had nothing to do with," Sky said.

"Hey, I wasn't going to leave you. I just felt like I wasn't wanted at the fire. That's why I wanted to go home, not because of you. I love you more than you can imagine," I said.

Sky kissed me passionately. I wanted to marry him right at that moment. Lucky for the both of us, one of the guys yelled out for Sky.

"Hey. We're by the creek," Sky yelled back. We jumped off the ground, straightened our clothes and walked up the path hand in hand. We met Justin a short distance down the path.

"Hey, what's up?" Sky asked.

"Oh, Chip just told me to look for you. I guess someone saw you two walking up this way," Justin said.

"Emma, you look tired." Justin said.

"I know," I said. "I could fall asleep as soon as I hit that sleeping bag."

"You're that tired?" Sky asked.

"Yes," I said.

All three of us walked a bit faster than normal. Right at the entrance to the fire, we met Alexis. She looked a little worried.

Sky told me that he was going to see what Chip wanted.

"I'll be right back," he said.

I could tell by the look on Alexis face that she knew I wanted to be away from this place.

"Hey, is every thing alright?" Alexis asked.

I nodded my head as I stood in front of her.

"I got worried when I didn't find you here. I had a vision of you leaving," Alexis said.

"I wanted to leave," I said. "I stayed behind because I felt I needed to apologize to Sara and Chip. It was my idea to have them help Joel and his parents. When Sky got back, he asked me to go for a walk. We went to the creek and that's when he realized how stressed I was, so he told me to put my hands in the water and ask for help. Now I'm just tired."

"Emma, please tell me you're not leaving," Alexis said.

"I'm not leaving," I said. "You know I'm not a quitter, I've never left anything unfinished."

We took our sleeping bags out of the car and went under the tarp to set up for another adventure.

Everyone gathered around the fire, and Chip and Sara told everyone to listen.

"Chip and I have been thinking about how we can better protect everyone here at the fire," Sara said.

"So, with the help of Alex, we've decided to have everyone's head point toward the fire, forming a circle," Chip said. "We don't want Sky and Emma to be the only ones with leather ties. Here are longer ties. We want everyone here to connect to the person next to them. Alex told us that on the reservation in New York, everything is in a circle, so this is what we're going to try."

"Another reason we want everyone connected is that we're not sure how many forces we're dealing with. Up until yesterday, it was just one disturbed guy, and it was okay to just place your hand on Sky or Emma. It took us a few hours to come up with this solution. We don't want to lose anyone. By tying everyone together, everyone comes home together," Sara said

"Are there any question?" Chip asked.

"I have a question," I said.

"Yes, Emma what is it?" Chip asked.

"What do you mean when you say you're not sure how many forces we're dealing with?" I asked.

"Good question, Emma," Chip said. "We all know Mark's behavior at the ceremony could have stirred those dearly departed souls to take some form of action. What we don't know is, if these souls will act - as individuals, as partners or as a group. What I can say is that we'll know the answer by morning," Chip said.

"I have another question," I said. "I'm a little confused about the reason we all need to be tied together. How can someone get lost?"

"As far as I know, there is only one person here who has seen spirits or ghost. Seeing a spirit can be startling. Anyone of you may accidently push the person next to them, resulting in a disconnection within our group," Chip said.

Chip's explanation made a lot of sense. Everyone in our circle seemed to be in agreement. We all started tying the leather bands and getting comfortable with our new positions. We had to lie on our backs and try to remember that if we decide to turn either way, we'd be pulling on the person next to us.

"This is awkward," said Justin. "I need to scratch."

Everyone started laughing.

"Not with my hand." Hunter said

"I just need to rub my eye you pervert," Justin said.

"Well, why didn't you say that?" Hunter asked.

"Scratch and rub mean the same thing. I wasn't trying to be funny," Justin said as he was still trying to pull a hand to his eye. I couldn't recall ever hearing this much laughter around the camp fire before.

"Alright, everyone, listen up," Sara said. "Do your best not to scream or yell. If at anytime you are overcome with fear, just close your eyes and repeat to yourself. I'm not afraid."

"If there are no more questions, you can start drinking your tea," Chip said.

When we realized no one had any questions, Chip gave us the word to drink our tea. I looked over at Sky and waited for him to look over at me. He smiled and leaned over for a quick kiss.

"Hum, yum. I'll see you in a little bit," I said as I leaned back on the sleeping bag. Sky smiled and shook his head

"Yeah, I'll be waiting." Sky said.

Sky leaned back on his sleeping bag, turned slightly to face me and reached for my hand. It didn't take much time before I began struggling to keep my eyes open. Then I heard a guy's startled scream and I looked at the direction of the noise. I saw nothing but complete darkness. I heard footsteps approaching from the left. It sounded like women's shoes.

Right behind that woman was someone with very light footsteps. As they approached, their footsteps got louder and ran by me. Not even a minute later, I heard the sounds of a man wearing fine shoes. He went running in the same direction as the two girls. I still couldn't see anything but darkness.

Then I heard heavy thumping footsteps.

"Oh my God, don't scream," I thought to myself, this guy was standing right in front of me.

I couldn't see him, but I could feel a cold sensation from my head to my toes. Then another heavy thumping set of footsteps approached, stopping next to the one in front of me.

My heart beat seemed to be thumping louder than the footsteps.

"Oh my God, calm down," I told myself.

I was completely frightened, especially when the thumping moved up to my head. I decided to close my eyes and slow my breathing. It was working; the thumping was easing.

In the distance, I could hear the five sets of footsteps gathering together as a group. Then, everything went completely silent, including my heart. I opened my eyes very slowly and I noticed it was still very dark, not a ray of light anywhere.

Straight ahead, I could hear the creaking sound of a door opening very slowly. Then, without warning it slammed shut. The sound echoed. I nearly jumped out of my skin. The slamming door sound startled someone.

"Ah," the voice, a male voice, said.

Once again, there was nothing but silence. Next, I heard the sound of five sets of footsteps running heavily above my head. They opened and closed doors as they moved. They began to knock books off the shelves, as well. Silverware could be heard falling to the floor. I heard what sounded like a dish shattering.

"Stop it. Leave me alone," a guy yelled.

Then, for the first time in nearly five minutes, everything was silent. It didn't stay quiet for long.

It seemed those behind the noise took pleasure in being disruptive. This time, the unruly ones stomped their feet harder. They slammed every door louder and they slammed silverware and dishes.

"I said stop it! Get out of my house. Leave me alone!" the male voice yelled again.

But the noise did not subside. If fact in got louder and scarier.

I could see light in front of my eyes, but I didn't want to open them. I was afraid that I would see Joel looking creepier than one of the characters from Michael Jackson's "Thriller." I wanted to remember Joel just the way he was the last time I saw him.

A loud shrieking sound sent me to my knees. I heard a voice, a male voice.

"Why, Bobbie? Why, did you do this to us? We had lives to live. Why did you do this to us?"

I clasped my hands over my ears. The shrieking sound was hurting me.

"Oh God, make it stop. Please make it stop," I said.

I started to smell a sweet aroma. I figured Bobbie was burning incense. After a few whiffs, I started to feel peaceful. I also felt like I was being protected.

All of the banging, thumping, slamming and shrieking stopped. There were no more footsteps moving about.

I took a few deep breaths.

"I know that smell," I said to myself. "It's ylang ylang, rose, geranium and sandalwood. But there's something else mixed with it."

The fragrance started to burn my nostrils. As I tossed my head around, searching for fresh air, I woke up. I took in two deep breaths of fresh air. I turned to my side and saw Sky smiling at me.

"How long have you been awake?" I asked.

"I heard you taking deep breaths and I woke up," Sky said.

"Did you smell that stuff he was burning?" I asked.

"Yeah, it worked on everyone, including the spirits," Sky said.

"It smelled like a combination of herbs called white angelica," Sara said.

"So, are the spirits after what's his name?" Chip asked.

"Yes, they are. It took them a while before they got into a group. They're very angry with him," Sara said.

"Emma, did you get scared?" Sky asked in a whisper.

"Yeah, I did," I whispered in Sky ear.

"So, Sara, do you think that he'll leave Emma alone for a while?" Chip asked.

"I really don't think that he'll be much of a problem for a while. He'll be too busy trying to keep the five spirits at bay. I mean, they asked him why he did this to them, so he should know who they are," Sara said.

"Okay, Sky I think we can give the guys a schedule. I think everyone needs some time off," Chip said.

"I'll get that together later," Sky said.

"Are you driving me to school?" I asked Sky.

"Yes. Do you want to go back to my house to get ready?" he asked.

I nodded. We got up, rolled up our sleeping bags, gathered our pillows and went over to his car. Then I told Alexis that I would see her later at school.

# Calm Before The Storm

**T**oward the end of April, Sky and Hunter were preparing for their final exams in English 101. The first part of their test involved word definitions. The second part was true or false questions, and the final part was a two-page composition on a selected topic. They both couldn't wait to get this exam over and done with.

As for my own studies, I had five weeks before finals. It seemed like forever. Every Monday and Thursday, Sky would take me to spend the evening with my family. We had fun baking cookies with Ashley, Jamie and mom. Mom always enjoyed our visits, and she would let Sky know how much she appreciated our mother and daughter time, especially when he would take Ashley and Jamie out to run errands.

My mom wasn't too happy when I told her Sky and I decided to move the wedding date from the second week in August to the end of June.

"Why so soon, are you pregnant?" Mom asked.

"No, I'm not pregnant. It's just that I'm already living at Sky's house and I don't want people thinking badly of me. I just feel that if were going to sleep in the same house, we should do it right. You know, if I had my way, I would marry him tonight," I said.

As soon as Ashley, Jamie and Sky came back from the store, I told mom that we needed to get back to the fire before nightfall. Mom, Ashley and Jamie gave me hugs, and mom told Sky to get us home safely.

Every time Sky brought me to visit my family, he passed the accident site before we would head north.

Alexis and her parents checked on the ribbons often, as well, since they lived just south of that spot. When we went back to Hopland, we always took the same route. On this particular afternoon, we noticed the ribbons were moving as we drove by the accident site. For the past three weeks, the ribbons draped straight down, even in the wind.

"They're back, I wonder if this means that they've given up on spooking you know who," I said.

"I guess we'll find out later," Sky said.

"Do you think you might have to call some of the other guys back?" I asked.

"It looks like we might have to," Sky said.

As soon as we got to Sky's house, Hunter and Alexis were waiting for us. They noticed the ribbons as well, and Hunter had already called Chip, Sara and several of the guy's and told them to be at the fire

We all headed to the fire. We left our sleeping bags in the car and went over to talk to Chip and Sara first.

They both believed that something would happen that night. Sara told us that she was brewing the special tea I had refused before.

"It's time we make everyone invisible," Sara said as she looked directly at me.

"Is there a plan?" Sky asked.

"Yes, I want everyone in a circle, tied together, with their heads close to the fire," Chip said. "Do your best not to scream or yell. Sara and Alexis, I want you two to sit this one out."

"Why? I don't understand," Sara said.

"Dear, you and Alexis can not heal like these guys can," Chip said.

"We're just going to watch what he's doing." Sara said, almost pleading.

"What if he's invisible when you get there and you don't know that, and he attacks one or both of you?" Chip asked.

"Chip, Alexis and I will be invisible as well," Sara said. "We'll be drinking the same tea as everyone else."

"Okay, just keep safe," Chip said.

We went after our sleeping bags and pillows and set them around the fire. Many of the guys who had been given the day off were there to help. Some were there to sit with Chip, while the rest wanted us to be strong in numbers.

As we sat on our sleeping bags, Sara, Chip and some of the other guys handed us our cups of special tea. Before I took a drink, I whispered into my tea, "Please guide us and bring us back safely."

We all tied our leather straps together. I reached for Sky's hand as I stared up at the stars.

By my third breath, I was standing on the road by the accident site. I could see the crosses and the boards with the colored ribbons. The ribbons were moving in unison. There stood Joel, Jane, Julie, Tyler and Thomas.

Joel stood between the two girls. Tyler and Thomas stood right behind them. Tyler's face was not calm like the rest. His eyes were dull and full of hate.

He looked up at the sky and yelled.

"Bobbie Watson, show yourself!"

But Bobbie did not appear.

Once again, Tyler looked up at the sky and yelled, this time louder than before.

"Bobbie Watson, show yourself, you coward!"

There, right across the road, appeared Bobbie Watson dressed all in black. He flexed his head from side to side.

"Who are you calling a coward?" he asked.

"You. Didn't you hear me?" Tyler said.

"What do you want from me? I've already told you it was just an accident," Bobbie said.

"You are the reason we no longer live in your world. You are the one who decided to play with people's lives. We want you to pay for what you've done. You know what we want," Tyler said.

Just like that Bobbie was gone. Joel and the four teens were gone, too. The ribbons hung motionless by each board.

I began wondered if Bobbie was playing the disappearing act like he did that time in the meadow. If he had gone home, we would be outside his home. Just then the ribbons started moving in unison again. Just like that, Joel, Jane, Julie, Tyler and Thomas were back.

"Hey, Bobbie, we know you're still here. Your mommy doesn't look too well," Tyler yelled.

Bobbie appeared in the same spot as before.

"Stay away from my mother. She's hurt because of people like you." Bobbie said.

"There you go again blaming others for you're wrongs," Tyler said.

The next thing I knew, we were standing in the Intensive Care Unit by Bobbie's mother's bed. Tyler, who seemed to be the leader of the group, looked at Bobbie with a smirk on his face. He reached out his hand and pulled the plug for the oxygen machine. Bobbie's mother's eyes opened and she gasped for air. Bobbie took the plug from Tyler's hand and reconnected it.

Tyler started turning off the controls for the blood pressure monitor, the echocardiogram machine and the oxygen. As fast as he was turning off the equipment, Bobbie was turning them back on.

It was at this point that I realized, and perhaps Bobbie realized, Tyler was working alone in his quest for revenge.

Sure Joel, Thomas, Julie and Jane were in the room with him, but they seemed to want nothing to do with murdering an innocent woman.

Tyler tried to reach for Bobbie's mother but each time, his

hand passed right through her. When Bobbie realized Tyler couldn't touch her, he disappeared from the room.

Just like that we were all standing behind Bobbie's home. He had a fire going and he was adding an assortment of herbs to the flames. It was the same smell as before. We were overpowered with a feeling of tranquility and joy.

"I brought you here to make a deal with you," Bobbie said. "I thought you should know that it was really Ms. Summer Hall and Emma Niles that caused the accident."

I was ready to scream out and call him a liar, but Alexis and Sky had their hands over my mouth.

"They're into taking innocent lives and trading them for a power so evil you can't imagine. They work with the devil in a craft that involves shape shifting bears, wolves and who knows what else. My mother is in the hospital because of them. Look at my scars; this is what they did to me."

Tyler looked over Bobbie's scars then he turned his back on Bobbie and looked at Joel, Jane, Julie and Thomas. He winked at them.

Slowly, Alexis and Sky removed their hands from my mouth. They knew from Tyler's action that I wouldn't scream. I was shocked that Bobbie would blame Ms. Hall and me for being that wicked, but Tyler was right when he called him a coward. Tyler turned slowly toward Bobbie and shook his head.

"Okay, where can we find Ms. Summer Hall and Emma Niles?" Tyler asked.

"Ms. Hall is a teacher and Emma is a student at Santa Rosa High School," Bobbie said.

"Okay, Bobbie, we're going to look for them. If we find out you were being deceptive, we'll be back," Tyler said.

Joel, Tyler, Thomas, Julie and Jane vanished into thin air. Bobbie looked all around. He continued to burn different herbs and he started chanting in a language unknown to us all. I wanted to go over and push Bobbie into his burning pit, but I didn't want to be as pathetic as he was, so I decided to end the dream.

As soon as I woke up, I began to untie the leather ties.

"Emma, what are you doing?" Sky asked.

"We need to go to the accident site and talk to Joel, Tyler and the rest of them. We have to explain to them that Ms. Hall and I had nothing to do with that accident," I said very anxiously.

"Emma, we can go there, but it'll be better if we go just before sunrise. It's the most powerful time of the day," Chip said.

"Chip, I think you better tell Emma what you did," Sara said.

"Oh my God, Chip what did you do?" I asked.

"Emma, I didn't do anything bad. When Thomas' dad deliberately upset the spirits, I took advantage of the situation. I was upset by his lack of respect and by what he did, so when I smoked my pipe to close the ceremony, I left them with some of my own feelings," Chip said.

"I'm sorry, but I don't understand," I said.

"He told Joel and the rest of the spirits that the guy in the drawing was responsible for the accident," Sara said. "He also told them that you confronted him after the funeral and since then, he has been terrorizing you in your dreams."

"Is that why Tyler winked at Joel and the rest of them?" I asked.

"Yes," Sara said.

We hung around the fire, keeping each other awake. A few hours went by and Chip spoke up.

"Well, we better get going. By the time we get there it'll be sunrise."

We got into two cars and drove over to the accident site. From where we parked, we could see the ribbons flowing in harmony.

Chip led the way, followed by Sara, Alexis and Hunter. Sky and I walked slowly toward the circle they had formed. Chip smoked his pipe and began speaking in his language. When I looked up, I was shocked to see Joel staring at me with a smile on his face. I tightened my grip on Sky's hand, for I could also see Tyler, Thomas, Julie and Jane. They were also smiling. Tears rolled down my face as Chip explained to them how Bobbie was trying to hurt me because I confronted him for taking their lives. Alexis came over to me and told me that they wanted to see where Bobbie had stabbed me. Sky lifted up my shirt, and Joel and the rest of the group leaned forward to get a better look. The wound had healed, but the scar remained.

I could see their lips move but I couldn't hear what they were saying. Chip and Alexis would nod their heads every now and then just to let them know they agreed with what they were saying.

"Emma, they want you to know they didn't leave Bobbie's house last evening to go and look for you or Ms. Hall," Alexis said. "They left because the smell of the herbs made them feel sick. They also said Bobbie Watson had his mother taken out of the hospital a few hours ago. Joel said that from now on, your dreams will be pleasant. He said it's his way of repaying you for your help with his situation with Lana. He said they'll make sure Bobbie doesn't come near you or the rest of us ever again."

Sky wrapped his arms around me, and I cried because I couldn't go over and give my friend a hug. I cried harder when Joel put his hand to his lips and blew me a kiss.

## About The Author

Linda is member of the Five Nation Iroquois Confederacy. Her father was a wolf clan from the Mohawk Nation. Her mother's side of the family is snipe clan who were sent from the Onondaga Nation in the 1800's when the State of New York was trying to eliminate the Iroquois Confederacy.

Linda was born in Toronto, Ontario, Canada. She graduated from Trent University in 1982 with a diploma in Native Studies and took a couple of years off before returning to SUNY Potsdam New York campus. Her intended major upon entering was Political Science but at the beginning of her second semester, An English professors ask her what her major was. She told Dr. Taylor that her major was Political Science and he told me, I was in the wrong field of study. Two weeks later she changed her major to English Writing.

Linda loves sports and is a great fan of the Toronto Maple Leafs, Toronto Blue Jays, Toronto Raptors, Tom Brady and the New England Patriots, And Dale Earnhardt Jr. Nascar driver number 88.